WITCH WAY DID SHE GO

SILVER SISTERS BOOK 2

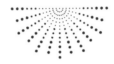

JENNIFER L. HART

WITCH WAY DID SHE GO

SILVER SISTERS BOOK 2

Witch Way Did She Go
Hart/ Jennifer L.

1. Women's—Fiction 2. Multiple Sclerosis—Fiction 3. North
Carolina—Fiction 4. Witches—Fiction 5. Sisters—Fiction 6.
Amazon River—Fiction 7. Fae—Fiction 8. Married Life—
Fiction 9. Motherhood—Fiction 10. Chronic Illness—Fiction
11. Magic—Fiction. I. Title

ISBN 978-1-951215-88-0

This one is for the spoonies.

WITCH WAY DID SHE GO

PROLOGUE

Maeve -20 Years Ago

"*A*nd will you be having dessert?" The pretty waitress that my date had been eye-humping all night asked with a professional smile. "The new pastry chef is a genius. I think there's one piece of chocolate turtle cheesecake left."

I opened my mouth to refuse when Henry—aka smelly Henry as I'd mentally dubbed him since he stank as though he'd never heard of this newfangled thing called deodorant—piped up.

"No thanks, sweetness. We're on a diet." And then he winked at her.

I reached for my water glass. My hand shook and a little water spilled onto the burgundy tablecloth. Last time. The absolute last effing time I was doing one of those online dating profiles. Henry had seemed normal enough over the computer screen. Then again, there was no way a computer could project scent.

He'd been disappointed since the moment I'd walked in wearing the black and red floral wrap dress I'd been proud to put on after my shift at the hospital. I'd felt very feminine and flirty, two things I didn't get to be very often. Seeing my date's disappointment had killed my pleasure.

I was a healthy size twelve. I'd gotten down to an eight once, but that was before working twelve-hour shifts in the hospital maternity ward and caring for my Aunt Jess, who had cancer. Fitness had taken a backseat to life.

And now "we" were on a diet. Who the hell was this smelly bastard talking about? Him and the mouse in his pocket?

"Just the check, please." I forced a smile at the waitress, set the water glass down, and picked up my purse. "I need to freshen up."

Get a breath of fresh air was more like it.

"Hurry back." Smelly Henry smiled as though he hadn't been mentally judging every bite I'd taken all damn night. As if I would gladly follow the jackass upstairs to his hotel room, take off my pretty dress, and have sex with him. Idiot. Were all men so utterly ridiculous?

I should unleash my big sister on him. It would serve him right. Alys would have his guts for garters.

I walked toward the hostess who had been a classmate in high school.

"How's it going?" Cara whispered.

"You know that scene in *Saving Private Ryan* when they're all getting blown to bits on the beach? It's the emotional equivalent of that."

Cara cringed. "Sorry, Maeve."

"Where's the nearest restroom?" I asked. "I need a few to regroup."

"Over there." She pointed to the far side of the grand staircase that led to the top floor of the resort. "Though if it's as bad as you say, maybe you should just head out. I can make an excuse for you."

"Thanks for the offer, but I need to see this through to the bitter end." After he paid for the pleasure of my company, of course. Alys always insisted on going Dutch on the rare occasion she actually went on a date. She said it was fairer that way. Personally, I didn't see a problem with having a man pay for a meal he had so thoroughly spoiled.

I stalked into the ladies' room and braced my hands on either side of the sink and then raised my gaze to the mirror. I was pale, but that could be chalked up to the mountain winter and the fact that the only time I went outside lately was the trek from the cottage to the car to the hospital parking lot and back.

And okay yes, I was plush. No denying reality. I was built like my mother. Soft and round, though healthy. Trying to get down to a weight that society deemed acceptable was more work than I had time for. Did I wish I was slender like Alys who ran on the regular, or Sibby, my younger sister who I hadn't seen in years? Why did I have to lose the genetic crapshoot?

"Self-pity isn't a good look for you," I told the woman in the mirror. "Don't let that smelly fool in your head. He paid for dinner, not mental real estate."

No, he didn't. But the bad date only highlighted how incredibly lonely I was. Aunt Jess was dying. Alys was busy with her life in the low country. God knew where Sibby was this week. She was a rolling stone, gathering no moss and taking no crap.

I wanted someone who would stay. Someone I could count on.

Someone to love who loved me the way I was. Was that too much to ask?

After using the facilities, I squared my shoulders and took

a deep breath—for air as much as reassurance—and headed out into the hall.

That was when the skier burst into the lobby, still carrying his poles. "Help! He's hurt. Call an ambulance."

My training kicked in and I rushed forward, past the people who had stopped in their tracks to talk. "Where? What happened?"

The guy blinked at me.

"It's all right," Cara ran up. "She's a nurse."

"We were on the east slope. A deer ran in his path and he swerved into a tree."

"Is he unconscious?" I asked. "Did he hit his head?"

The panicked skier shook his head. "No, but his leg is busted up real bad."

"Do you have an emergency kit?" I asked the shocked woman who stood mutely behind the concierge desk.

She nodded and then scurried off to get it.

I turned back to Cara. "Call an ambulance. I'll go out and do triage until they arrive."

Mountain roads in the winter were no joke. It might take them half the night.

"What's going on?"

I caught a whiff of my date which, sadly, was more recognizable than his voice. "There's been an accident on one of the slopes. I'm going out to help."

"Now?" He sounded put-out. "You can't go dressed like that."

He was right. I was dressed for indoors, though my coat and gloves were warm enough, I would be kneeling in the snow. The concierge was hustling back with the first-aid kit.

"I need a maintenance suit. And skis."

"Check the clubhouse," she said. "There are always a few extra in the locker room."

"You can't just leave," Henry whined as if that would change my mind.

I turned to glare at him. "Look, I'd say it was nice meeting you, but I'd be lying. So why don't you go on up to your room and take a nice, cold shower? It'll improve your chances with the next one."

He said something unflattering but I was already out the door and heading to the staff clubhouse.

Fifteen minutes later and dressed in an ugly gray jump-suit, I had the medical kit secured in a borrowed backpack and skis on my feet. I followed the skier to the eastern slope. He had reflective tape on the back of his coat, which the light on my beanie illuminated in the darkness. The hat came in handy when I had to walk Aunt Jess's old beagle at night.

I wasn't a big fan of downhill skiing but could manage okay cross country as long as the hills weren't too treacher-ous. Luckily, the injured man had had his accident close to the bottom of the slope.

"What were you two doing out here so late?" I asked as we trekked on through the chill January night.

"The staff can use the slopes after hours," Skier guy said. "Kal's an experienced skier. We've been out here loads of times and nothing went wrong."

We came to a trailhead and he turned to the right. I followed.

About a hundred yards ahead we came to a clearing in the pines. The moon peeped through the evergreen branches enough to highlight the body in the snow.

The skier swore. "I shouldn't have left him."

I didn't bother to reassure the man that he'd done the right thing in going for help. Instead, I moved to the injured man and did my best to assess him.

He wasn't dead, but he wasn't conscious either. And even

my tiny light could see the bone jutting out of his shin and the blood on the snow.

"What did you say his name was?"

"Kal. Short for Kallik."

"Kal," I said. No response.

Had he cut an artery? There was no way to tell, but I had to proceed as if he had. I kicked out of the skis and then unslung the medical pack and fished for a bigger flashlight. "Hold this," I said to Kal's buddy. "Right at his leg. I need to see what I'm doing."

In theory, I knew how to apply a tourniquet. There wasn't too much need for them in maternity, but I had learned. I had to cut off blood flow to the wounded limb so the man didn't bleed out.

There were some gauze rolls in the first aid kit. After putting on some blue plastic gloves, I unwound it and then reached down to a spot just above the knee that appeared undamaged.

Doing my level best not to jostle him any more than necessary, I wrapped the gauze strips around the leg. I don't know what prompted me to look up at his face at that moment but I did. His eyes were open.

"This is going to hurt," I told Kal. "But it's necessary."

He dipped his head in acknowledgment or permission, I couldn't tell.

I tied the gauze loosely and then pulled tight. He hissed out a breath but didn't try to move as I finished securing the tourniquet.

That done, I reached for the flashlight. Kal's buddy looked like he was going to puke.

That was the last thing the situation needed.

"Go back to the trailhead and wait for the ambulance," I ordered him.

He shot me a relieved glance as he skied away.

"Am I going to lose my leg?" The voice was like the rumble of distant thunder over the mountaintops.

I turned back and looked down at Kal. "Do you want the truth?"

"Always," he said.

"I don't know," I told him honestly. "If they get here soon enough, they can take you into surgery."

He let out a ragged breath and his eyes slid shut. "Sorry I ruined your night, doc."

I laughed. "First of all, I'm not a doctor, I'm a nurse. Maternity, though you don't look pregnant to me."

"Pretty sure that's true." His lips were bloodless in the pale moonlight but at least he smiled, was conscious, and responding. All good signs.

"And secondly, my night couldn't really get much worse."

His lids lifted and those dark brown eyes fixed on me. "What happened?"

He was probably just trying to distract himself from the pain and the fear of losing his leg. I decided I'd entertain him. Smelly Henry ought to be good for a story. "I was on a first date. And the guy wouldn't let me order dessert. He told the waitress that he had been mentally undressing all evening that we were on a diet. And he smelled like a bin full of used jockstraps."

"What an idiot." Kal's lids drifted closed. "I hope you threw a drink in his face."

I heard the sounds of sirens and spotted the reflection of red and blue lights on the distant white hills. "I thought about it. But no, I didn't. I said to myself, Maeve, it might be momentarily satisfying to drench the stinky creep but there's no need to lower yourself to his repugnant level."

"Maeve," he murmured and then his lips turned up again as he murmured, "Evie."

I got a chill that had nothing to do with the gusts blowing from the North. "That's what my mom used to call me."

His eyes were open once more. "I'm sorry that your date sucked but I'm really glad you're here, Evie."

I took his gloved hand in mine and squeezed lightly. "Yeah, me too, Kal. Me too."

CHAPTER ONE

MAEVE

I always knew when something bad was about to happen. Long before my sisters and I drank the empowerment brew and became witches, I got this sense of uneasiness right before a major shift in my world. The phone would ring and I would know instantly that Kal had an accident at work and was being taken to the ER for stitches. Or that Sibby was in tears because her latest lover hadn't worked out. Or that it would be Alys calling to tell me that the house we had just closed on and planned to restore had mold and was going to cost a boatload more than our projected budget.

Some people might call it intuition, others instinct. I called it *the knowing*.

I *knew*, for example, as I waited for my doctor to arrive that I had multiple sclerosis. Or, as I was coming to think of the incurable autoimmune disease, Ms. Priss.

Whenever I thought about Ms. Priss, I pictured a pinch-faced tight-lipped woman. Steel gray hair twisted up in a no-nonsense bun. High-necked long-sleeved purple dress with silver buttons down the front. Crow's feet winging out from her narrowed eyes. She carried a cane and I could never predict when she would give me a whack that would make part of me go numb.

MS was often a diagnosis of last resort, which translated to a monkey butt-ton of expensive and invasive tests to rule out other causes for the weird hodgepodge of symptoms. Fatigue, diminished eye sight, numbness. I'd been dealing with them all. The bevy of tests were as bad as the symptoms. MRIs, CT scans, lumbar punctures. I'd had them all, ruling out one diagnosis after another, narrowing the field. I'd seen more doctors in the last year than I had my entire life, including when I was having trouble conceiving.

I'd spent more of my life in a backless gown than any one person should.

Too bad no one else believed in *the knowing*. I could have saved time, discomfort, and money. Well, Kal did. But Kal didn't know about Ms. Priss.

I still hadn't figured out how to tell him his wife had an incurable disease. After a while, it seemed safer to just wait to get the diagnosis. Hit him up with facts instead of hysterics.

I'd played the conversation over and over in my mind. Kal would ask, "Are you sure?"

I would respond with, "I *know*."

And then he would have to digest it in his own, quiet way. And that's where my imagination hit a brick wall.

No gown required for my latest visit. I sat in the doctor's office wearing jeans and a white button-down shirt and waited for *the knowing* to be confirmed. Ms. Priss was with me, the way she always was. Expressionless and severe, her cane at the ready. I tried very hard not to panic.

Bad things happened to the people around me when fear took hold.

The door opened and Dr. Steinberg strode in. Her black

hair was cut in a short bob and beneath her white lab coat, she wore a gray pencil skirt and a cream shell with black heels. The woman exuded a sort of confidence that I envied.

She sat down behind the desk and asked, "How are you feeling, Maeve?"

Not how are you. How are you feeling. It was a subtle difference in word choice that stripped away my personhood and stuffed me into a mental hospital gown. "I have good days and bad. My energy levels are all over the place and I can't seem to concentrate."

"That's to be expected." She exhaled and took off her glasses, pinched the bridge of her nose.

I waited for her to look up. "I have it, don't I?"

To her credit, she didn't back down. "I'm afraid so. I've spoken with other neurologists and we all agree. I'm sorry. You have Multiple Sclerosis."

Whack.

The blow wasn't physical this time. But the words had an impact. I had *known* but foolish me, I'd held out hope that maybe I was wrong. Even though I never had been before.

Hope was such a damn dirty tease. Ms. Priss knocked her right off her stripper pole with her cane.

Because while what I was dealing with was scary, the full list of symptoms that Ms. Priss could bring about….

Dr. Steinberg was still talking. "Have you thought about treatment? In your case, we believe you have the relapsing-remitting form of the disease. Our goal should be to…." She droned on and on and on, about things like monitoring brain atrophy and cortical lesions and recombinant interferons. I barely heard because I had only one thought.

I *knew* how Kal was going to respond. He was going to be hurt. Because he wasn't here, taking part in this conversation with me. I had waited too long to tell him.

I was going to be sick for the rest of my life. The rest of

our marriage. What would that look like? A walking aide? A wheelchair? Sexual disfunction? Incontinence? There was no way to tell how the disease would progress. What systems it would affect.

Kal was either going to leave me. Or he was going to stay for all the wrong reasons.

Whack.

"I'm sorry," I stood, unable to sit still any longer. "I just… need some time."

The doctor studied me for a long moment then she rose. "I have some literature for you to look over. I'd like to get you on a treatment plan as soon as possible."

I followed her down the hall to reception. The receptionist handed me a few pamphlets, which I stowed in my oversized shoulder bag.

"The doctor wants to see you back next week. Should I book you an appointment now?"

I gave her a tight smile. "Let me check my husband's schedule. I'll call to set it up."

It was a lie and we both knew it. She would have to track me down through multiple phone calls. A distant part of me felt bad for making her job more difficult.

Then again, she wasn't the one with the incurable disease.

"Is there anything else?" I asked but then froze when the blank expression on her face registered. *Shit.*

The receptionist moved toward me, but the plexiglass separated us. Behind her, a nurse had taken on the same unfocused countenance.

Fear had triggered my magic. The only thing I could do now was run and hope they returned to normal.

I beat feet out of there.

Sibby was sitting behind the wheel of my minivan, typing something on her phone. This week my youngest sister's hair was peacock blue, though she was growing out the shaved part. Her fingers flew over the screen as she texted someone.

Her head jerked up when I opened the passenger side door. "Well?"

My eyes filled and I squeezed them shut. "Get me out of here."

"Oh honey," Sibby reached across the center console so she could give me a hug. "I'm so sorry, Maeve."

I pulled back. "I mean it, Sibby. I freaked and now—"

The lobby door opened and medical professionals poured out. They wore scrubs and lab coats and the same empty expression that all my mindless enchanted wore.

Sibby swore and then threw the minivan into reverse. She cut the wheel sharply and then pounded on the gas. I was tossed back against my seat, my hands clenched in white-knuckled fists.

"You okay?" Sibby glanced my way.

"Relatively speaking." I sucked in air in a shaky breath.

"I should have gone in with you." Sibby sounded pained.

"I told you to wait out here. I thought I had a handle on it." I'd never been so wrong.

She reached out and covered my tightly-clenched fist with one hand and gave it a squeeze. "I'm sorry."

"Me too." Sorrier than she would ever know. Sorry that I hadn't given Kal the option to have hope for a little while. Even if she proved to be a faithless skank in the end. Sorry that I couldn't seem to get a grip on the fear enslaving countless people.

I turned around and checked the road behind us.

"No one's following," Sibby murmured. "We put enough distance between us and them."

I nodded and then asked, "What about Alys?"

"Alys got stuck in traffic," Sibby said. "The closing on the

13

cabin was delayed for some paperwork BS and she got stuck in traffic. She's fit to be tied because she wanted to be here."

I knew she had. My big sister always wanted to be there for me. But one of us had to sign the paperwork and since Sibby wasn't a full partner in *Silver Demo and Design*, and it was my appointment, it made sense for Alys to drive down from the high country after the job was done.

"She said she would meet us at the hotel." Sibby withdrew and studied me. "Unless you want to go home?"

I considered for a long moment. We had originally planned a night in the city. Dinner at a nice restaurant to help get our minds off of everything.

But after what had just happened, I didn't dare risk it.

"Let's go back to the cottage." Alys lived in our Aunt Jess's cottage. It was remote and situated on a lake just outside the town limits of Eckhart.

There was nowhere else on earth where I wanted to be at the moment. Nowhere else felt safe.

*A*lys's Suburban was parked in front of the cottage. I shivered as a gust of cool mountain air blew off the lake just as I opened my door. Winter had set in hardcore.

"Do you think that's her?" Sibby asked.

Alys's magic came from the mother nature caste of witches. She had control over the weather and when she spiraled emotionally storms would gather and weather patterns would shift. If she was really pissed, sinkholes would open and the ground would shake or lightning would rain down from the sky.

I shook my head and hustled to the steps. "It's winter in the mountains in case you forgot."

Sibby had spent most of her life being anywhere but in

Eckhart. She was in for a rough winter if she thought this was bad.

Sibby wrinkled her nose. "Well, I've tried to forget. Watch your step. The moss is slippery."

I wanted to snap at her that I wasn't an invalid, but stifled the impulse. I didn't like the person Ms. Priss and magic was turning me into. A big old ungracious witch.

"Enchantress, my Aunt Fanny," I mumbled.

Sibby shot me a look. "You've been watching too much *Bridgerton*."

"Not possible." I adored romance stories, especially period dramas. I was still trying to figure out how to convince Kal to roleplay the Duke to my Duchess. He'd been resistant but he owed me for the surprise corgis.

Ms. Priss had to go and screw up my fantasy life as well.

Alys greeted us at the door in her cut-to-the-chase style. She gave me a fierce hug and then asked, "Coffee, tea, or liquor?"

It was a little after three in the afternoon. As tempting as it would be to lose myself in an alcoholic haze, I sighed and said, "Tea, please."

While Alys moved off to the kitchen, Sibby and I hung our coats on the same pegboard that had been hanging behind the front door for as long as I could remember. As a restoration and renovation expert, Alys had the skills and the ability to upgrade the cottage and make it into whatever she wanted it to be. For some reason though, she hadn't done much other than dumping her stuff in the primary bedroom.

Of course, she'd been busy what with her new werewolf lover and all.

That and worrying herself sick over me and Sibby.

Sibby moved toward the couch, intentionally shifting the old rocking chair out of the path toward the sofa. Clearing a space wide enough for an elephant to traverse. I blew out a frustrated breath but didn't comment.

Alys didn't bother to ask what sort of tea we wanted. Our orders were always the same. Mine was green tea straight up. Sibby drank herbal with milk and honey and Alys was black tea with exactly one level teaspoon of sugar.

Alys appeared carrying two earthenware mugs, which she set down on the battered old coffee table that was little more than a log with some sanding and lacquering perched on four squat legs. I reached for mine as my big sister returned to the kitchen.

I shot a glance at Sibby, feeling like I ought to say something. But she was on her phone once more, thumbs flying over the keys.

"Is that your mystery guy?" I asked.

She nodded absently.

Sibby had been having some sort of virtual relationship for a few weeks now. Texting mostly. I had no idea who the guy was or where she'd met him and was hesitant to ask too much. Sibby would confide when she was ready.

She stowed the phone when Alys returned, probably to keep from the interrogation that was sure to follow if our big sister knew what was up.

"Tell me exactly what happened," Alys demanded once she was settled in the squat chair opposite the couch.

"How about you ask instead of ordering?" Sibby raised both her brows and took a sip from her mug.

Alys shot her a withering glance and then refocused her attention on me. "Maeve?"

"I lost it." My hands wrapped around the mug and the warmth seeped into my palms. I breathed through the emotion the way my yoga guru instructed. Not that it helped.

"When you heard the diagnosis?" Alys asked.

"No. It was afterward. All these thoughts popped up of all

the things that would need to change. I thought I was ready to hear it but it overwhelmed me." By imagining Kal's reaction, but I kept that bit to myself.

My hands were shaking. I set the mug down, afraid I would spill it.

Both Sibby and Alys had been haranguing me for weeks to tell him about my diagnosis. And while my sisters wouldn't rub my nose in it, they had been right.

"You've got to get better control of your emotions." In typical Alys fashion, my oldest sister decided to focus on the part of the story that didn't terrify her. Not that I blamed her. None of us were truly prepared to process my diagnosis. "Maeve, you're the only one still having slip-ups with your magic."

"Do you really think I don't know that?" I snapped. "It's not like I'm doing it on purpose!"

The two exchanged a glance.

"I'm sorry," I put my head in my hands and exhaled wearily.

Why did some lucky people manage to waltz through life only having to deal with one challenge at a time? Meanwhile, I was in it hip deep with magic and Ms. Priss.

A hand landed on mine. Sibby. Alys moved too and my sisters settled on either side of me, like when we had been little. It was an old sofa, small and sturdy and barely fit the backsides of three grown women, one of whom was plus-sized.

"We know you're trying," Sibby said quietly. "And it makes sense that you're struggling with everything going on."

She didn't go into the source of the danger. That there were magic hunters out in the world looking for bursts of unregistered magic. Supernatural bounty hunters who would strip us of magic and our souls if I didn't rein in my fear.

I was more afraid than I'd been in my life. At a time when I couldn't afford to be.

"What can we do?" Alys sounded uncharacteristically helpless.

I picked at a loose thread on my jeans. "I keep thinking that I have these two problems that manifested together. Like there should be some way to get them to cancel each other out."

"Like having two enemies fight one another while you slip off to safety." Sibby nodded thoughtfully.

That wasn't exactly what I meant, but the idea had merit. "Wait. You're saying that there could be some sort of magical cure for MS?"

Sibby's lips parted.

"I hadn't thought of that," Alys murmured. "But it's worth a look."

I didn't point out that she had just been giving me grief for unintentionally enchanting people at my doctor's office and now she wanted to deliberately use magic. Hope, that dirty skank, was back on stage and doing a striptease while Ms. Priss looked on with patented resting bitch face.

Sibby clapped her hands on her thighs and rose. "To the Bat-cave!"

CHAPTER TWO

*T*he "Bat-cave" was the greenhouse attached to the side of Aunt Jess's house where all the magical herbs and spell books, talismans, and amulets were kept. Oddly, the greenhouse retained enough moisture for the plants at the same time as the magical tombs stayed perfectly dry.

We didn't know what most of the items in the room did, though I did recognize many of the plants. Aunt Jess was a horticulturalist and she had spent a good chunk of her life devoted to uncovering the secrets in all things green. Any medicinal uses she monetized by selling to various pharmaceutical companies. Any magical assists she must have kept to herself.

After three hours of searching, Hope was once again knocked off stride by Ms. Priss. I pictured the disease pointing her cane at the free spirit sprawled in the dirt and commanding her, "*Now this time stay down.*"

I stared out the window at the lake. My thoughts were on Aunt Jess while Alys and Sibby continued to comb through volume after volume of family lore. She had been our aunt only in the honorary sense, as in my mother's best friend. After our mother died, Aunt Jess had finished raising us. I had been her caretaker, the only one of us who had been content to remain in the high country.

Why had she never told me about the magic? The question plagued me. I had been right here, in this house. Cooking and cleaning and doing all the little caretaker-type tasks that I never got a chance to do for my own mother. I had thought the two of us were close. That we shared a special bond. Aunt Jess had understood about *the knowing*. Had encouraged me to trust my instincts.

There had to be a reason she had kept the truth hidden.

"Hmm, this is interesting," Sibby's voice broke me from my reverie.

"It says here that witches who bleed at the dark of the moon have one foot beyond the veil. They can see things others can't, in the dreamscape and have a deeper understanding of all things mystical."

"Fascinating," Alys said dryly. "I suppose you're in tune with the lunar cycle?"

"Not as much as your werewolf." Sibby quipped and then turned to me. "Anything?"

I shook my head. "Not that I can see about curing autoimmune diseases."

"Our ignorance here is only going to get us into trouble," Alys snapped a book shut. "I think we need expert help."

"What do you mean? We're the only witches we know." Sibby propped a hip on the worktable.

"I can ask the pack." Alys was referring to the werewolf pack that her boyfriend, Brock, belonged to. He was their *de facto* leader, a reluctant Alpha in much the same way we were reluctant witches. "I was supposed to go over there for dinner tomorrow night but I could call now."

I held up a hand to stop her. "Tomorrow is good." My

energy levels had bottomed out and I was ready to get off the emotional roller coaster for a spell.

"You okay?" Sibby asked.

I nodded. "Just exhausted. I think I'll head to bed."

My sisters exchanged a speaking glance.

"What?" I asked.

"We thought that you would want to go home," Alys ventured tentatively.

"To be with Kal and the kids," Sibby clarified.

I did want to be with my family. I wanted to snuggle with them all on the sectional and watch feel-good movies with happily ever afters. Like *The Princess Bride*, my all-time favorite. We would make popcorn, the real kind coated with actual butter, and cheer for Westley and Buttercup, Inigo and Fezzik. The mental picture even included those ridiculous corgis, Gimli and Grogu, aka the G&G wrecking crew. The small, fluffy dogs bounced more than walked and would claim any spot they wanted for a cuddle, no matter whose sensitive bits got stepped on in the process.

But I couldn't have that comfort. Not until I had a talk with Kal.

And deep down I feared that the conversation would take that comfort away forever.

"Tomorrow," I murmured and then headed up to the soothing darkness of the house.

There were two bedrooms on the second floor. One had been ours when we had first come to live with Aunt Jess. The large bed and crib had been replaced with three single beds and separated by curtains for privacy. It was where Sibby and I still stayed. My feet naturally took me there but I hesitated at the threshold.

Instead, I moved to the closed door of the other room. Mom's room. It was where I'd gone for comfort after having a nightmare. Part of me expected to see her sitting on the bed, her readers perched on her nose as she devoured whatever book she'd picked up at the library that day.

The candlewick bedspread was the same as I recalled. But the light was off and the bed made. No one was there.

My eyes filled with tears. I'd never been angry with our mom for dying the way Alys had. But I missed her almost every day. The hurt had never faded. My phone buzzed. After extracting the device from my sweater pocket, I stared down at the message from my husband.

KALLIK: HOPE YOU LADIES ARE HAVING FUN

I curled up on the bed and let the tears fall. I wanted to tell him that no, we weren't having fun. That I was worried I had forgotten what fun felt like.

That I had been lying to him for months and it was all about to blow up in my face.

"I'm scared." I didn't address anyone in particular, but still, I could swear I heard my mother ask.

Of what, my Evie?

The familiar soft voice echoed in my head almost as though she had whispered it right in my ear.

What was I really afraid of? Ms. Priss? I'd been living with her for months. That was nothing new.

"Of losing my family," I whispered the answer. "Of losing Kal."

"You won't."

I looked up and spied Sibby standing in the door.

"How do you know?"

"Are you kidding?" she rolled her eyes. "That man is stupid for you."

"He's going to be so upset."

"Alys and I are upset, too." Sibby moved into the room and lowered herself onto the bed. "We're still here. Waiting for you to tell us what we should do. Where's Mistress Maeve, the one who barks orders like a drill sergeant? Alys is going to go mad with power if you don't start pushing back."

I rolled onto my back and stared up at the frosted glass overhead light. It should have been covered with dust, but much like the greenhouse, my mother's room seemed to be on hold. "I don't know what to say to anybody. I don't know what to do."

"Well, what do you want to do?"

She made it sound so simple. As though there was a solution waiting for me to unearth it.

I blew out a breath and sat up. "I want to find out if there's a magical cure. Something that will heal me."

"And if there isn't?" Sibby asked. "What then?"

"I have to believe there is," I told Sibby. "I'll do whatever it takes to make sure we find it."

For Kal. For our family. I would do it.

SIOBHAN

I lay in the dark and listened to Maeve's steady breaths. She'd finally fallen asleep after hours of carefully muffled sobs. I was emotionally exhausted from not going to her but knew my sister. She wouldn't welcome the intrusion.

Maeve was a giver. She sucked at accepting help. I had to cram it down her throat.

My phone lit up with an incoming text. A smile stole over my face as I read the name there.

Sebastian.

I reached for the small folding table that acted as a night-stand and snagged the device.

SEBASTIAN: HOW ARE YOU HOLDING UP?

I let out a shaky breath and typed.

SIOBHAN: DRAINED.
SEBASTIAN: I'M SORRY ABOUT MAEVE.

He'd said as much earlier but I appreciated his sympathy.

I had the feeling offering it was a foreign concept for him. Sebastian was a high-priced divorce attorney. We had met when he'd come to town to represent my former brother-in-law. Because of that, Alys and Maeve weren't his biggest fans. Which is why we were taking things slow. I hadn't told either of my sisters that I was still in contact with him.

Sebastian had surprised all of us by accepting our magic and even helping us when we searched for a missing child. He was a good guy, if a little odd.

I couldn't recall the last time I had been so utterly enchanted by someone.

And that scared me to death.

SIOBHAN: THANKS. I APPRECIATE IT. HOW WAS THE REST OF YOUR DAY? DO ANYTHING FUN?

SEBASTIAN: DEPENDS ON YOUR DEFINITION OF FUN. I HAD TO STASH ONE OF MY CLIENTS IN A SAFE HOUSE BECAUSE HER ABUSIVE EX SHOWED UP AT HER DOOR DRUNK AND THREATENED HER AND THEIR CHILD. A CHILD WHO HE IS FIGHTING FOR CUSTODY OF, BY THE WAY.

SIOBHAN: DON'T TAKE THIS PERSONALLY BUT YOUR JOB SUCKS CANAL WATER BACKWARD.

SEBASTIAN: DO YOU WANT TO TALK FOR A FEW?

Did I? My gaze veered over to where Maeve was sleeping. I'd have to go downstairs so I didn't disturb her. Risk Alys finding out. The woman had ears like a bat.

Then again, Alys's McNibblet werewolf boyfriend had come over after Maeve had retreated. I'd spied his headlights just before I made my excuses and headed upstairs. She might be otherwise...occupied.

My teeth sank into my lower lip. Of course, there was another way for us to talk.

SIOBHAN: HOW ABOUT IN PERSON?

There was a pause. And then three dots bounced across the screen along with the words, *Sebastian is typing.*

Way too much typing for a one-word answer.

Finally, the reply came.

Sebastian: I'm in bed. Give me a minute to get dressed.

"Siobhan, you're playing with fire," I muttered and shifted onto my back. The image of him, naked and sprawled in dark sheets gave my traveler witchy mojo the jump-start it needed.

Before I had committed to the decision, my body moved. Not by muscles. No, this movement was deeper, it came from my mind, my will. I ceased occupying space in my bed at the cottage and instead, I lay in a much larger bed.

Luxury sheets slid against my skin. The room was dark save for the male face illuminated by the glow of a phone screen as he texted. For a moment I thought his eyes were glowing with eerie amethyst color, but that might have been a reflection from the screen. There was an odd mark on his shoulder. It looked almost like a pitchfork. Not a tattoo, I didn't think. A scar perhaps.

"Hi," I said to Sebastian.

He set the phone down and snapped on a low-wattage lamp so he was backlit. "I guess you didn't get my last message."

"Oh, I got it all right. Why do you think I traveled here so fast?"

"You will do wonders for my ego, Siobhan."

I loved the way he said my full name. It rolled off his tongue in that sexy, lilting kind of way. With the lamp behind him, I couldn't see his features clearly but something about the bed, the room, felt familiar.

It hit me in an instant.

It was wrong to tease him, but I couldn't seem to help myself. "This isn't the first time I've been in your bed."

"Think I would have remembered." His voice was a low purr.

"You were asleep. It was the very first time I traveled. The morning after my sisters and I became witches."

Sebastian shifted and I saw that his eyes were closed. "I didn't even know you then."

"Yeah." It meant something that I had come to him on my first magical trip. I just had no idea what.

We sat there for a moment, the sexual chemistry that was always present between us building and building like a fire contained in a closet. If either of us dared to open the door the backdraft would be all-consuming.

"Siobhan," he whispered and I could tell he was reaching for the doorknob.

I couldn't do it. It was one thing to tease us both, to kiss and imagine all sorts of wickedness, another to play fast and loose with his life. "I'll just go wait for you in the other room. Want some coffee? I make bitchin' coffee."

I bounded off the bed and for the door before he could say anything else. That was too close.

Little witches that play with fire will be burned at the stake.

The troubling thought echoed through Sebastian's head as he retreated into his bathroom and reached for the contacts that would conceal the otherworldly glow of his dark fae irises.

Siobhan Silver was a problem for him. One he had no

idea how to solve. Initially, she and her sister witches were his targets. As a dark fae and a magic hunter, Sebastian stalked the unregistered magic users and stripped them of their powers. His bounty was a portion of the magic he reacquired for the council of elders.

Siobhan knew magic hunters existed and that they would suck out her soul. She didn't realize that *he* was one of them. He had been close to succeeding in his mission too. But something had stopped him.

Sebastian felt... altered. He couldn't figure out when the shift had occurred. When Siobhan had gone from target to obsession. He thought about her *constantly*. Not her magic, though her powers were impressive. Her, smile, her wit. Her luscious little body. All of it drove him to distraction and like an addict, he kept coming back for more.

He had retreated back to his persona of a hot-shot divorce attorney and returned to the city, hoping to put some distance between them and regain his perspective. How many weeks had he spent trying to puzzle it out?

He should be hunting. His magic was finite and he needed a new target to replenish his stores. But then she would text him and he would lose his focus, ensnared by thoughts of her once more.

And now she was here, within striking distance. Within kissing distance.

Sebastian pulled on a pair of pajama bottoms and a t-shirt before heading out into the common room. The air was scented with strong coffee and the softer, hotter smell of a witch's arousal.

The sight of her in his kitchen made him still.

Siobhan stood in front of his refrigerator bent at the waist, unashamedly studying its contents. She wore a short skirt that cupped her rounded backside enticingly and bright pink leggings with some sort of animal print. Her sweater was loose at the waist but slid off one shoulder, revealing the delicate curve that he had the sudden urge to kiss.

Kiss a woman's shoulder? Where were these bizarre thoughts coming from?

"This is pathetic." She straightened and shut the fridge with a dramatic sigh. "One of the most gorgeous kitchens I have ever seen in my life." She waved a hand at the Corinthian marble countertop, the stainless-steel appliances, the white shaker cabinets. "And you have no food here. Not so much as a single egg or ketchup packet."

His focus was still on her body when he murmured, "I prefer to eat out."

There. He saw the moment Siobhan responded to his tone, the insinuation. Her gaze dropped to his pants and her blue eyes went wide as she took in his arousal. Because Sebastian was watching for it, he saw the stiffening of her spine and her almost audible retreat back into herself.

It had happened earlier, in the bedroom. She flirted and cajoled and needled him shamelessly, but when he responded in kind, she shut down hard.

What sort of game was the little witch playing? Was she onto him? He hadn't believed she thought him anything more than a mortal, albeit a rich one. But perhaps she had discovered something. If so, she should be running in fear, not popping over for a midnight visit.

"Well, it's a waste of a great kitchen." Siobhan turned her back on him to retrieve two plain white mugs from a glass-fronted cabinet. "You wouldn't believe some of the places I have had to prepare food in the past. There was this Irish pub in Boston and I swear, the level of scunge and disorganization there actually made me have sympathy for Alys and her OCD."

"Alys has Obsessive-Compulsive Disorder?" He lowered

himself onto one of the barstools, putting the counter between the two of them.

She set the mugs down on the counter and then reached for the coffee pot. "Not really. I just like to tease her because she's so anal-retentive. So anyway, that kitchen? I seriously doubt anyone ever cleaned the grease traps or scraped the stove. I spent a week just scrubbing it down."

Sebastian didn't know why she was telling him all this. He only knew he never wanted her to stop.

Not ever.

CHAPTER THREE

MAEVE

"Shit," I grumbled as I spied Kal's car in the driveway.

"What?" Alys sat behind the wheel of my mini-van. Her gaze was trained on the ice-encrusted walkway that led up to the front door. "Here, wait a second and let me help you."

"It's not—" My words were cut off when she parked the vehicle and hopped out wearing boots with heels that should have put her own stride at risk. She deftly picked her way around the front end of the car.

"I'm going to kill Sibby," Alys muttered when I opened the door. "Just as soon as I find out where she went."

I'd awoken at first light to find our youngest sister was missing again. She hadn't left a note but there was a text waiting on my phone telling me she was okay and would be back soon. I'd begun to think of these disappearances as her nocturnal prowls for a little some-some. What had once brought on cold terror—Sibby vanishing mysteriously—had become run-of-the-mill.

"I could have driven myself home. Or stayed at the cottage." I protested. "Really, Alys. I'm fine."

Her lips compressed into a tight line and I knew she had bit off a pithy retort. Because of Ms. Priss. She treated me differently now. It wasn't as bad as I had imagined though. I'd worried she insist I give up my role in the company altogether. That she would put me in a hermetically sealed bubble and never let me do anything for myself or anyone else. But even her carefully worded comments served as a reminder that I was the sick sister.

"Just let me fuss a little," she said instead. "It's my right as your older sister."

"What's going on?" Kal stood in the doorway, two straining corgis tugging on neon blue leashes. He ought to have looked ridiculous, standing there in his pajama bottoms and snow boots with the dynamic dippy duo on full morning alert.

Instead, the sight of him brought tears to my eyes.

"Evie, are you hurt?" Kal's dark gaze was intent on me.

"No," I managed and squeezed Alys's arm in silent communication. I couldn't outright lie to Kal. The lies of omission were bad enough.

"She slipped at the cottage. I'm just being a mother hen," Alys chirped.

That was the thing about my big sister. She was a very flawed human being and she knew it. But she owned her dysfunction like nobody's business.

I cast her a grateful glance. I wanted to be like her when I grew up.

Kal nodded, accepting her words. Even that made me wince, as I hated the misdirection. I focused on the dogs, which always proved an excellent distraction. "Taking them for a walk?"

"They need the exercise." He said grimly. "Want to come with?"

I did. But I didn't dare. I never knew when Ms. Priss

would give me another whack. Ice and snow made walking doubly treacherous. I offered the first excuse that came to mind. "I'm not wearing the right shoes."

Kal stared at me for a beat. My stomach twisted. Neither of us suggested I change my footwear. It was an excuse. He knew it and I knew it.

I'm sorry, I thought. Hating the disease for what it was doing to us.

Kal simply nodded and then hastened down the steps being yanked by two enthusiastic dogs that were all fluff and no sense.

Alys didn't say anything as we entered the house. Being in this space used to fill me with so much joy. The place was the first home Alys and I had ever restored together. Years after the project had been completed, she had gifted it to me and Kal as a wedding present. All the best parts of my adult life had happened within its walls.

I should have known it was too good to last.

Alys's SUV pulled up behind my minivan, Brock behind the wheel.

"Will you be okay?" My sister put a hand on my arm.

"Of course." I sighed.

She stared at me for a long moment. "You need to tell Kal. Keeping this secret is hurting you both."

I lifted my chin. "Not until I find out if there's a cure."

"Maeve—"

"Listen to me. There's nothing he can do. There is absolutely nothing worse than worrying about someone you love being sick and being unable to do anything about it." Tears sprang to my eyes.

"You mean Aunt Jess," she said softly.

I nodded and sniffled.

Alys pulled me into a hug. She wasn't overly affectionate,

at least not with anyone but Brock, but on the rare occasion she trotted them out, Alys gave the best hugs.

"Thanks for driving me home, you big worrywart," I sniffled. "But you better go. Your boy toy is aging out there."

She laughed. "Okay, wiseass. But just think about telling Kal. If not the diagnosis at least tell him the witchy stuff."

I blinked at her. "But we agreed not to tell anyone."

"We did. And then I told Brock and Sibby told that asshole lawyer she was all hot for. After all that it doesn't seem right to keep Kal in the dark. Especially not when it's affecting his wife. He's a smart guy. I'm sure he knows something is up. And you can practice your confession skills. I hear it's good for the soul."

I nodded, not committing to anything, and watched her pick her way down the icy walkway to the Suburban.

Because I'm nosy, I studied the way Brock's gaze followed her progress. Even from yards away I could sense his anticipation. When Alys drew close he scrambled out of the vehicle to open her door for her.

If it had been anybody else, Alys would have given him a sharp put down, snatched the keys, then taken her rightful place behind the wheel. With Brock, she gave him a long, slow kiss, and allowed him to help her up into the passenger's seat.

I smiled, happy for my sister. She deserved all the joy life had to offer.

After shucking my coat and boots, I carried my shoulder bag into the kitchen. My cellphone charger sat beside Kal's. His phone was gone.

Odd that he had bothered to take it when he was just walking the dogs.

Then again, Bella and Philip were in school. I usually kept my phone on me in case they needed anything during the day.

The coffee pot was full. After plugging my phone in, I snagged my favorite mug, the sixteen-ounce blue one I had imprinted with the *Silver Demo and Design*.

Even though it was barely nine AM, I felt drained. Coffee didn't do it anymore. My body craved nothing more than a long, hot shower and several more hours of sleep.

I paused with the cup partway to my lips. Maybe I could convince Kal to come back to bed with me. We used to lounge beneath the covers together all the time before the twins were born. Even on a weekday. He was a chef so his hours fluctuated. So did mine, first as a nurse and then when I became self-employed. We never had a normal schedule. I missed our stolen interludes. The sort when the world shrank down and time lost all sense of urgency. Minutes or hours no longer held their shape as we immersed ourselves in each other.

Though I didn't have enough oomph for a proper seduction, it usually didn't take much more than a hint that I was interested to get Kal in the mood. He could crate the corgis and then we could go upstairs and….

And maybe I would follow Alys's advice and open up about the witchy stuff. Kal was Inuit. He might accept the magic better than I had.

It was a start.

I wandered into my office and studied the bookshelves crammed full of romance novels. It seemed a long time since I felt the urge to get lost in one. Maybe because my own happily ever after wasn't working out so great at the moment. Is there a limit for how much a person is allotted in a lifetime? Had I reached my quota?

A red light on the answering machine pulled my focus out of my dark thoughts. It was unusual because the only calls that ever came in on the landline were trying to sell us extended car warranties.

What if it was the doctor's office? They only had my cell, but our number was listed in the directory. Had they left a message about scheduling a follow-up?

I hit the button. And then froze at the sound of a woman's sultry voice saying my husband's name.

"Kal, it's Harper. Call me as soon as you get this. I need to talk to you."

Then a click.

"Who the fuck is Harper?" I snarled at the empty room.

The front door opened and Kal came in, face red and corgis crusted with snow.

I ducked into the laundry room and grabbed two old towels and then hurried forward to help clean up the critters.

He didn't speak. That was his way. Kal wasn't a big talker. Usually, I babbled to him about whatever random thoughts popped into my head. But after hearing that message if my lips parted accusations would come spilling out. So, we dried the dogs in total silence.

All the while my mind whirred over possibilities. And numbers. When was the last time we had sex? I couldn't remember. That was a first because up until a few months ago, the answer would have been, *last night* or even, *in the shower five minutes earlier.*

But it had been weeks. And that was not like Kal. Or me and Kal.

It bothered me that I hadn't noticed so much time had passed. It upset me more that in a way, it had been a relief. One less thing to think about, to angst over.

What concerned me the most though, was that he hadn't said anything. Hadn't even hinted at the fact that it had been so long.

Alys's ex claimed he had strayed because she wouldn't have sex with him. Of course, Kal wasn't a bastard-coated-bastard with bastard filling like Kyle.

Men had needs. So did women. It was just that with women, we usually put our needs behind everyone else's.

Had Kal begun to outsource his?

My throat had gone dry. *Just ask him who she is.*

But I couldn't. Kal knew me too well. I was absolute shit at hiding my true feelings. The question would come tearing out of me like a crossbow bolt. And it would hit him center-mass, causing irreparable damage.

If this was just my wild imagination running away with me, I couldn't take that risk.

"Did you have fun?" Kal asked.

I blinked, startled to realize that I was still crouched down on the floor, towel in hand. The corgis were nowhere in sight, something I would normally fret about because the wee beasties got into all kinds of mischief.

"Not really," I muttered.

He tilted his head, inviting me to talk.

But the urge to open up had withered on the vine. Instead, I asked, "Why aren't you at work?"

"I switched days off with the new pastry chef. Remember, I told you last weekend?" He held out a hand but instead of taking it, I handed him the damp towel and then got up without his assistance.

I had no memory of that. Damn Swiss cheese brain. Damn Ms. Priss. Had he told me about Harper too?

"Sorry, I forgot. What was his name again?"

"Albert Sorensen."

Damn. There went the easy explanation.

I studied his features. I couldn't see any guilt in his brown eyes. What I did see on his face made me sick. Unhappiness. Regret. Longing.

There was an easy way to tell if he was cheating. It took a sheer force of will for me to reach out a hand and slip it into his. I made my tone lower, into a husky approximation of the sultry-sounding Harper. "So, you're home and I'm home. Maybe we could go upstairs and...hang out?"

I knew my husband. There was no way he could touch me if he had been with someone else. *Please say yes. Please, dear sweet dark chocolate, let him agree to this.*

He didn't. He stepped back, withdrawing his hand from mine. We stared at each other for a moment. I could swear I heard it. The crack. The break that sundered our marriage.

He studied me for a long moment before heading toward the stairs. "I was gonna go to the gym. Maybe later."

No. Not the gym. *Anywhere* but the gym. I might have been happier if he said he was heading to a motel that rented by the hour.

Relationship 101. Men who went to the gym were hunting for new mates. Contented men didn't worry about ab workouts. Especially not pastry chef dads. Kal hated the gym. We both did. Our idea of exercise was a leisurely nature walk followed by hours of sweaty sex.

I reached for my phone and texted my sister.

Maeve: Changed my mind. Heading into the office.

There was no way I could stay in this house and wonder who Kal was getting in shape for. I might as well go to work and pretend I was doing something useful.

ALYS

"Crap," I said.

Brock put a hand on my thigh as we drove up to the construction site. "What is it, possum?"

"Maeve is going into work. *Not* doing what I suggested. *Not* resting. *Not* talking to Kal." I looked over at him. "Why can't I just tell everyone what to do and have them do it? It would make life so much simpler."

He flashed me that too freaking cute for words dimple and then squeezed my hand. "Maeve and Kal will get through this."

"Not if she keeps running away. Besides, that's Sibby's M.O." I glanced up as we rounded the bend to the Mid-Century Modern, the house that was *waaayyyy* behind schedule, thanks to my vindictive ex. After causing a boat-load of trouble, Kyle had fallen off the face of the Earth. At least he'd had the decency to sign the divorce papers first. They'd showed up in my mailbox about a month ago. All official.

Damn, I liked being a divorcee.

The replacement windows had finally come in and

gleamed in the winter sunshine. The new paint, a slate gray with white trim stood out boldly against the fresh dusting of snow that had fallen overnight.

All the mischief Kyle had caused was finally erased. The house would be ready for the spring market. A fresh start for it and for me.

We were the first to arrive on the job site, which wasn't unusual. What was unusual was the wolf standing by the front door.

"Is that Nate?" I asked, referring to the young pack member.

Brock put the Suburban in park. "Yeah."

I hadn't seen the teenager since he helped me rescue a missing child. "How is he?"

Brock reached for his travel mug of coffee. "Not great. I thought maybe having him stand guard over your project house would help him alleviate some guilt."

I blinked. "What does Nate have to feel guilty about?"

"Nothing and I keep trying to tell the dumbass that. But he's been sulking in wolf form for several weeks."

That explained why he hadn't been to the pack's Thanksgiving diner the week before.

"Do you want me to talk to him?"

Brock shot me a grateful look. "Anything you could do, Lys. I would appreciate it."

"I have a set of your sweats and boots in the back." Since discovering my contractor was a werewolf, I'd taken to keeping a few extra items of clothing in the car. Just in case anyone showed up in wolf form but needed to deliver a message.

Golden eyes glowed with appreciative warmth. "Have I ever told you how sexy you are when you plan ahead?"

He was the only man who ever thought so. My efficiency scared many people off, except narcissists like my ex who saw it as a way to have their needs taken care of so they didn't have to do anything.

I adored the way Brock looked at me. The way he made me feel. As though I was strong and sexy and every damn thing I had ever wanted to be in his eyes.

We got out of the Suburban and I marched over to where Nate stood guard. The wolf looked scrawnier than he had the last time I'd seen him. He ducked his head at my approach.

I tapped in the code for the house and then held the door open. "Go in and change. Brock's getting you something to wear."

Nate's lip curled back in a snarl. I couldn't tell if that was the defiant teenager or temperamental werewolf and didn't much care.

I crouched down low. "Listen to me. I don't know what's eating at you and I already have two difficult pains in my ass named Siobhan and Maeve to deal with. So either you go in there and change or I will skin you and toss your pelt down as a decorative accent in front of the fireplace. Got it?"

Nate's ears went back. He lifted his gaze to mine then dipped his head. Stalked into the house.

I straightened as Brock approached with the clothes. "You just need to have a firm hand with them is all."

"I'll try to remember that," the Alpha werewolf said.

CHAPTER FOUR

MAEVE

"*T*his budget is killing me," I grumbled as I deleted all the items from my wish list for the Mid-Century Modern.

Lora, our gal Friday and interior designer apprentice came to stand over my shoulder.

Her husky voice was soothing as she reminded me. "It couldn't be helped. Not after all those windows had to be replaced."

She was right. But it was easier to grumble over the budgetary restrictions that were flushing my design down the toilet than all the things that were truly bothering me.

"Okay." I leaned back in my desk chair to face Lora. She wore a cream-colored sweater and dark wool skirt that emphasized her curvaceous form and chunky gold jewelry that was perfectly accented against her café au lait skin tone. Our office didn't have a dress code but Lora always presented herself professionally. She always looked so well put together. So did Alys. I knew next to nothing about fashion and typically dressed for comfort. I was known to sport yoga pants with fraying hems and shirts with holes from corgi teeth. We had no client meetings so I hadn't bothered with make-up. I looked like what I was, a run-down middle-aged mother of two.

I wondered if Harper was well dressed.

"Okay," I said again, forcing my mind back to the task at hand. "So, we have little money and the only thing we have for the main living space is that accent rug you picked out. It's time for creative solutions."

"Fresh flowers," Lora said immediately. "Or maybe green plants. They'll fill any space in the main area and add the pop of color and life."

"Yup. And there's always the fallback clear bowl of lemons." I clicked my pen a few times, a habit that had driven my classmates nuts when I'd been in school. "We're going minimalistic on the furniture. Just enough to make it look intentional. Couch and side tables with clean lines. What about the bookshelves?"

Alys had wanted built-ins flanking the fireplace. Initially, I had agreed, envisioning custom shelving that would match the design. But custom equaled money which we didn't have.

"What about floating shelving?" Lora suggested. "You could use some geometric wallpaper that matches the rug behind them to add a continuity."

I tossed the pen aside and pivoted back to the computer. My fingers flew over the keyboard and I opened another tab to Pinterest. Clicked on my hodge-podge and neat stuff idea board. Scanned down the listings until I found the one I wanted. "Like this?"

She studied the image. "Yup, just with something that will offset the rugs instead of the blue. We might even have a few rolls in stock that would match. I can check the inventory."

I blew out a breath. "Okay, so the last thing is the artwork. I wanted a big landscape for the wall opposite the fireplace. Maybe something that mirrors the view out of the windows, but maybe captures a moment in time."

"Your usual sources are pretty steep," Lora murmured.

It was true. I had spent a pretty penny over the years on local artists, trying to support the community in Eckhart as best I could. But many of them charged way more than I was able to pay for our current project. Especially for a large piece.

I drummed my nails on my desk. "What about if we had a talent contest at the high school?"

Lora tipped her head and waited as my thoughts coalesced.

"What we have left couldn't pay for established talent to do a landscape the size I'm after, but we could offer a scholarship that might make the difference for some budding artist to go to school. To learn and grow and one day command the same prices. We get the artwork to fill the house and get to help further the dreams of an up-and-comer. Win-win."

"I freaking love it." Lora flashed her perfect smile at me. "This is why you're the queen of creative thinking."

"I'll have to run in by Alys. There might be legal stuff involved especially if we're dealing with minors."

The main business line rang and Lora moved off to answer it while I jotted notes on my idea in an open document.

"It's Alys," Lora covered the phone with her hand. "She wanted to know if we've heard from Sibby."

I shook my head. "Not a peep."

Lora relayed the message and then held the cordless out to me. "She wants to talk to you."

I took the phone and Lora picked up her purse and headed into the bathroom. "What's up, Alys?"

"I need Sibby's help." Her voice lowered a bit. "Nate's here and he's in bad shape. I was hoping Sibby could *transport* him before any of the crew shows up."

I straightened in my chair. The emphasis she put on the word transport told me that whatever was going on with the young werewolf was worth risking our using witchery and potentially exposing ourselves to magic hunters. "Did you try her cell?"

"Right to voicemail." Alys huffed. "It's probably dead again. You know she's terrible about charging it."

That wasn't true, especially since Sibby had started communicating with whoever her mystery man was. But Alys was already fretting over whatever was going on with Nate. No sense picking a fight by charging to Sibby's defense.

"How about if I come to get him and drive him home?"

"It'll be faster if Brock and I take him," Alys said. "In case he loses it."

Judging from the amount of worry in her tone, Nate was in rough shape. Though I couldn't fault her logic, I still felt a sting. It wasn't Ms. Priss striking out, but the pang from being shelved. Dismissed as useless.

"I need to stay here, Lys. Someone needs to oversee the inspection." Brock's voice echoed in the background. "If we delay again, it'll cost us at least a week."

"How about if Brock helps you load Nate? I'll meet you in route. You know how *charming* I can be." I wanted to help. I liked Nate, liked all the werewolves.

And I needed to feel as though I could still contribute.

Hesitation. Then, "Hang on."

Alys covered the speaker. I could hear her having a conversation with Brock. When she came back on the line she said, "Okay. I don't want to swing through town though. Meet me out at the Grayson's barn as soon as you can."

Lora emerged from the restroom just as I was shutting down my computer. "Are you heading out?"

I nodded. "Something's come up. I'm meeting up with Alys. If Sibby calls, tell her we're heading to Brock's house."

"Will do."

I hustled out the door, not bothering to zip my coat. I hated the feeling of being confined while driving and was willing to deal with a few moments of frigid temperatures so as not to lose time to zip and unzip.

Traffic was light around Eckhart. Tourism waxed and waned with the seasons, swelling around harvest festivals that brought leaf peepers in the fall or those escaping the oppressive summers at lower elevations. Skiers and snowboarders were everywhere in the winter. Luckily, we were in that phase between Thanksgiving and Christmas and it was mostly full-time residents on the streets.

I reached the meeting spot and spied Alys's Suburban already parked beside the barn. After pulling in next to her, I snagged my bag and then locked the minivan before heading to the Suburban.

"Zip your coat," Alys ordered the second I opened the passenger's side door. "Before you catch your death."

It was easier to comply than to argue with her. Outer layer secure, I climbed into the car and looked in the backseat.

Nate, in wolf form, lifted his lip in a warning snarl.

I shrank back from the threat. "What's wrong with him?"

"He's stuck that way," Alys blew out a breath. "He tried to change but couldn't. Brock says this happens sometimes when they've endured trauma. According to him, the wolf rises to the foreground to protect the human's fragility. The longer the wolf is in the driver's seat though, the harder it is for the human to wrestle control back. Brock's been giving him tasks, things that he can control, but he didn't realize how bad it was until Nate couldn't change. He said the best place for him is the cage."

She reversed the Suburban. Cut the wheel sharply and then headed onto the road. The sky grew darker, and the wind picked up as the first few flakes drifted down.

Having a not fully in control werewolf at my back made me nervous. I shifted and then yelped when Nate stuck his nose against my neck and sniffed. He had the same glazed expression in his eyes as the people at the doctor's office the day before.

I'd enchanted him.

Alys's shoulders relaxed. "I was hoping you would be able to do that. Brock wasn't sure what would happen with the wolf being ascendant. We didn't know if your gift worked on animals."

"Go lie down." I used the same tone of voice that I used on Gimli and Grogu when they were being pesty little imps. Unlike the corgis, Nate followed instructions. He circled once, then again, and finally flopped down, his bulk taking up the entire back seat. His gaze remained focused on me, waiting for my next command.

I released a slow breath. "Okay. So you were saying something about a cage?"

"It's in the basement. For any of the ones that go too far in the wrong direction." She cast a worried glance at the rearview mirror.

"But he's going to come out of this, right?" Nate was so young, practically a kid.

"We hope so." Alys's tone was quiet. "In the meantime, the cage is the safest place for him."

"He doesn't seem dangerous right now." Normally the sight of one of my enchanted minions made me feel as though I had done something wrong. But my influence over the werewolf was different. Maybe because he seemed so dog-like. I reached back and scratched between his ears.

"Oh, believe me, he is."

At my sharp look, she said, "Not to us. Brock never would have let us drive him home if he thought Nate would hurt us. We're considered pack now."

"Really?"

She smiled. "Yup. Normally they don't let mortals in. But after our help finding Leah when she was lost, we have been invited to be official pack members."

"That's actually kind of cool," I said. "I always wanted to be part of a werewolf pack and a witch coven at the same time."

Alys laughed. "I didn't, but I have to admit—

A deer leapt out into the road. Alys braked hard to avoid hitting it. The Suburban fishtailed as the heavy back end skidded on the icy pavement. The smell of burning rubber and the sound of glass breaking, metal crunching as our momentum carried us into a huge tree. I was thrown against my seatbelt.

"This is going to be bad," the knowing whispered.

There was a pitiful whine from Nate, almost drowned out by Alys's shriek.

Then impact robbed me of awareness.

SIOBHAN

I woke to the niggling sensation that something was wrong. I sat up and the chunky chenille blanket that had been draped over me fell away.

There was a note on the glass coffee table in front of me. The penmanship was exquisite, much better than my own chicken scratch. It almost looked like calligraphy. *Called to work. Hope you'll still be there when I return. -S*

My lips curled up and I hugged the note to myself. I couldn't recall when I had fallen asleep. Was actually surprised that I had. Wasting moments with Sebastian seemed almost sacrilegious because there were never enough of them to sate me.

I rose and then stretched, working out the kinks in my back and ignoring the twinge in my bum knee. It was an old ache—from an injury when I'd wrecked my motorcycle years ago. The joint had been badly damaged but with rehab, it was back to about eighty percent of what it had been before. Most of the time I forgot about it or could work around it.

I wondered if Sebastian had anything like that. He was almost too perfect. No visible scars. No obvious defects. I knew he was curious as to why I kept coming over and then shutting him down anytime the conversation turned sexual. But he never asked, never pushed. Seemed content simply to be with me. Must be one of those signs of maturity that Alys kept harping on about.

I wondered how old he was. I'd originally guessed he was around my age, early to mid-forties. But there was a look in his eyes sometimes that made him seem almost ancient.

I glanced around for my phone. Where the hell had I left it? I knew I'd been holding it when I traveled here. Maybe in his bedroom.

I moved in that direction. The bed was made with precise hospital corners. The heavy curtains pulled back wide, revealing the Charlotte city skyline. The Bank of America Building and Hearst Tower dominating the view. The sun was heading to the west, backlighting the buildings. How late had I slept? I glanced around for a clock but noticed something else.

There were no photos. No bric-a-brac. The furniture was like something out of a design magazine on minimalist style. Not something I normally would have picked up on, but in working with my sisters, I had started to pay more attention to the little things about a person's home.

Curiosity got the best of me. I peeked into his closet. Opened a few drawers. Lots of black clothing. It made sense. Black looked good on him. The color enhanced his golden glory. But the more I snooped, the more I realized there was nothing personal at all. No framed photos of loved ones. No books or music.

The kitchen had been well-appointed with cookware but no food. I hadn't found that unusual. Many people survived sans cooking. Just because it was my jam, I didn't expect others to have the same priorities. But no personal tidbits in the bedroom was another matter.

I moved on to his bedside table. No sex toys or dirty magazines. No condoms. Not even a Chapstick or a book or a tablet. Just a blank notepad and two black ballpoint pens. If there had been a King James Bible, I would have sworn I was in a motel by the highway instead of a swanky loft apartment.

All the small hairs on my arm stood on end. The place felt...staged. Like what Maeve did to sell the houses she and Alys flipped. As if it were waiting for someone to walk in, set down a box full of possessions, and start living here.

But Sebastian *did* live here.

Desperate and not understanding why I scurried into the bathroom to continue my shameless invasion of privacy.

The toothbrush in the shiny silver cup holder filled me with relief. The fact that the bristles were damp confirmed that Sebastian Jones wasn't just a product of my love-starved imagination. There was also a little tray for contacts and a bottle of saline solution in the medicine cabinet. I'd thought he wore contacts, but there was the evidence.

That was it. No old bottles of painkillers, Band-Aids, or box of tampons from a previous girlfriend. No condoms there either.

I shut the medicine cabinet door with a frown. What little I knew about Sebastian seemed more like a façade than an actual person. The toothbrush proved he was real. But why were there no mementos of his life? Even I—the rolling stone that I was—carried a few trinkets with me wherever I went. My mother's hairbrush, a tattered cookbook from Aunt Jess, a locket with a picture of each of my sisters inside. The detritus of a life.

Every boyfriend I ever had had signs from his previous girlfriends around his space. Most men were lazy and didn't feel the need to purge on the level women did after a breakup. There was always a stray lipstick or forgotten box of pantyhose somewhere.

What made Sebastian so different?

I couldn't figure him out.

And worse, all my lust was gone. I was stuck in this sterile space without the only thing that made it appealing—Sebastian himself.

My phone was on the kitchen counter, dead as a doornail. Frick. Alys was going to have a conniption that I had skipped out and didn't leave word on where I went. I'd better call her before she blew a gasket.

One of the few things Sebastian did possess was a landline. I retrieved the receiver from the base unit and dialed Alys's number. It rang and rang and then clicked over to her voicemail.

I considered calling Maeve, and then decided she didn't need to get dragged into our drama. Alys and I had used her as a buffer too often in the past. In investigating support groups about MS the term "spoonie" had come up. People with chronic illness had fewer energy spoons because the illness demanded great amounts of their reserves. The last thing Maeve needed was to play go-between for her sisters on the heels of her diagnosis.

Instead, I called *Silver Demo and Design*. Lora picked up on the first ring.

"Sibby, thank goodness."

The relief in her voice jarred me. "What is it?"

"There's been an accident. Alys and Maeve were taken to the hospital."

I gripped the phone tightly. "Are they all right?"

"Alys is, she called me. She sounded mostly upset."

"And Maeve?"

Keys rattled in the door and I looked up just as Sebastian

walked in. He was carrying a briefcase and a brown paper bag that smelled like marinara.

His shoulders lost a touch of stiffness when he spotted me, but then his expression morphed into one of concern when he saw my face.

"What's wrong?" he asked.

I shook my head and focused on the phone. "Lora, what about Maeve?"

Her three-word answer made both of my knees—good and bad—collapse under me.

"You should hurry."

CHAPTER FIVE

Siobhan was too quiet. Sebastian had loaded her into the car and taken off for High Country County hospital at top speed. He kept shooting glances at her.

Her face was pale against her artificially brightened hair. Her puffy pink lips moved with words she didn't voice aloud. Her gaze was trained on nothing he could see and her hands were balled into tight fists. Beneath her tough girl exterior, the youngest witch was extremely vulnerable. Normally, Sebastian would have used that vulnerability to his advantage to attain her magic. With her everything was different.

He was different.

"What's the point of having magic if I can't use it when I want?" Siobhan asked.

He shook his head, not knowing what to say.

"I can't be turned on all the time. No one can." Her gaze was locked in the distance.

A few weeks ago, he would have agreed with that sentiment. Since he met her though....

It wasn't sexual. Well, it wasn't only sexual. Sebastian had talked to her until she'd fallen asleep against his shoulder shortly before dawn. It had happened in an instant, she had yawned in the middle of a sentence, then leaned into him and closed her eyes. He had kept talking, telling her about the plot of a movie he had seen on television, wondering if she would drift off.

She had. A strange feeling had expanded in his chest. Like a balloon being inflated and shoving everything else out of the way. He had stroked her hair, not understanding what compelled him or how to sort through the miasma of feelings being with her evoked.

He wanted her. To carry her to his bed and wake her with a kiss like one of those ridiculous mortal tales about a princess put under a curse. He didn't dare.

This obsession was driving him mad. Making him forget who he was and what he was supposed to be doing. As a changeling, a child left out to die by superstitious mortal parents centuries ago, Sebastian had no magic of his own. He'd been born sick and hadn't thrived. His parents already had too many mouths to feed and left him at the base of a fairy hill, an offering to the fae in hopes that the tricksters wouldn't plague them.

Normally, the fae left such children to die or fed them to the beasts of the Wild Hunt. He had been adopted by a bored fae royal. Treated as a novelty, an amusement. A sort of pet to kick and abuse by the queen and her courtiers. They liked to see how much pain he could withstand.

He used to envy the thralls, those mortals who'd been ensnared by fae essence. At least they had no recollection of the ways they were abused. Sebastian recalled all the slights. Each indignity was seared into his brain. He recalled every strike with perfect clarity.

It wasn't until he became a magic hunter that he attained respect. Through fear and ruthless pursuit, he had risen through the ranks until even the council of elders knew his name. The dark fae changeling was the best hope to keep magic hidden from humans.

That was their purpose and within the guild of magic hunters, Sebastian had found his.

New witches like Siobhan and her sisters were dangerous not just to the fae, but to all creatures that wielded magic. The mortals and their weapons had grown into a real threat. If magic was discovered by the mortal governments...

Well, there was a reason the magic hunters guild was sanctioned by the council. The members provided motivation for magic wielders to fall in line and play by the rules of society.

Sebastian knew his job was important, essential to the existence of all magic wielders everywhere. He had never hesitated before Siobhan. Had never cared what a woman thought of him. He didn't want to see her hurt in any way. Her feelings mattered to him. Another new concept. He despised seeing her so worried over her sister. Hated it so much he was about to break another of his's kind's rules.

To never teach a new magic wielder how to use her abilities.

"Perhaps," he made his tone deliberately thoughtful. "Perhaps there is another way for you to tap into your gifts."

Siobhan shifted and he caught a whiff of her warm vanilla scent. "Alys proved there is. She can call her magic when she's angry, scared, or turned on. Maeve and I haven't managed to do that yet." The last words were said in a small voice, as though she were ashamed of her lack of progress.

Sebastian waited, again pretending to mull her situation over instead of burping up a zealously guarded truth. "It could be that you need to overcome a block in your primary emotional trigger before you can...." He removed one hand from the wheel to gesture as though at a loss for words.

"Level up?" Siobhan's brows drew together, the metal of her eyebrow ring glinting as they passed under a streetlight. "I think you're right. Alys was so angry at everyone and everything. Mostly she was angry with herself. She had to get past that and forgive herself. And Maeve is so scared of losing Kal and her kids and of what having MS will do to her family. How can she overcome that?"

"What about you?" Sebastian asked.

She shook her head. "I don't want to talk about it."

Vexing little witch. So stubborn. Sebastian had to clench his jaw to keep from barking at her. She didn't have a clue what he risked by pointing her to her end goal and still, she refused to face her truth.

A light touch on his leg made him start.

"I'm sorry," Siobhan said.

"You don't need to apologize to me, *Annwyl.*"

"*Annwyl?*" She repeated the word, a question in her tone.

"In Welsh, it means the one whom I cherish," Sebastian supplied.

He could feel her gaze on him, questing for more.

As if he hadn't compromised himself enough already. He had no more answers for her.

"*Annwyl,*" she said it again and then squeezed his leg lightly before withdrawing. "I like that."

They arrived at the hospital and Siobhan barely waited for him to stop the car before jumping out. With a curse, he followed his long-legged strides eating up the distance between them.

Side by side they burst into the small county hospital. Sebastian froze the second he sensed it.

Another of his kind. A magic hunter. Here. It could only mean one thing.

The car wreck had been no accident. A predator had

found the sisters. And he had brought Siobhan right into its clutches.

Siobhan was at the desk, demanding answers from the nurse. He had to neutralize the threat. He didn't know why the other hunter had waited. Perhaps it had wanted all the sisters together before it attacked.

Siobhan made it easy for him. "Maeve is in surgery. Alys is in the waiting room. Since she didn't know I was with you, I think maybe it's best if I go up alone."

He bowed his head. "If that is your desire."

"You're not upset?" She peeked up at him through her lashes.

"Of course not. I am here for you."

She stood on her tiptoes and pressed her soft, sweet mouth to his. "Thank you."

"I'll be nearby if you need me."

He watched her stride to the elevator, still in the pajamas she had been wearing when she materialized in his bedroom. Unselfconscious, unaware of the danger.

Sebastian was about to break another rule. He was not only going to save the witches. He would kill another of his kind to do it.

ALYS

My pacing had worn a groove in the threadbare waiting room rug by the time Sibby appeared.

"Where—" I cut off the question when I saw her blood-shot eyes, the wobble in her chin. Instead of tearing a strip off her, I closed my eyes and pulled her into a hug.

"Are you all right?" I asked.

She let out a watery laugh and backed up. "That was going to be my question for you."

"I'm fine."

"And Maeve?"

"In surgery. It was her side of the car that hit the tree. She lost consciousness at the scene and they had to use the jaws of life to get her out."

Guilt was shredding my insides. "I shouldn't have let her come with me."

"It was an accident." Sibby urged me over to the uncomfortable plastic chairs. "Just like my phone dying was an accident."

She didn't tell me where she had been or what she'd been doing and I didn't ask. Sibby was a grown-ass woman.

61

Though she didn't always behave the way I would, she was responsible for herself.

Besides, she hadn't been the one driving.

In my back pocket, my phone vibrated. I extracted it and looked down at the message.

BROCK: HOW IS SHE?
ALYS: STILL IN SURGERY. ANY SIGN OF NATE?

BROCK: I LOST HIS TRAIL. COMING TO THE HOSPITAL NOW.
LOVE YOU, LYS.

"Damn," I hissed and stowed the phone.

"What?"

"Nate's been missing since the accident." I brought Sibby up to speed on why I had asked Maeve to come with us in the first place.

She slid an arm around my shoulders. "It's not your fault, Alys. No matter how many times you tell yourself that you're responsible for everyone everywhere, that isn't really true."

I wanted to believe her. Desperately. But I couldn't get past the idea that all the choices I had made led us to this moment.

"Have you called Kal?" Sibby asked.

"I tried. He isn't picking up either." Unable to sit still, I rose and resumed my pacing. "What the hell is the point of everyone carrying around phones when no one bothers to answer them?"

"Mrs. Stevens?"

I looked up to see a tall man wearing green surgical scrubs. He looked about twelve.

"How is she?"

"Out of surgery. It went well, though there is still a great deal of swelling. I'd like your permission to keep her in a medically induced coma. I see on her chart she has Multiple Sclerosis. We have no way of knowing how that will impact her recovery from the trauma. The best thing to do now is to let her brain heal."

"For how long?" I asked.

He shook his head. "I can't say."

I couldn't be the one to make this call. This was Kal's responsibility.

"Kal would want her to have the best chance of getting better," Sibby whispered.

I turned back to the doctor. "Do what you need to do."

He nodded and my shoulders slumped.

"She'll be okay," Sibby murmured.

Neither of us believed it.

CHAPTER SIX

*S*ebastian tracked the magic hunter into the women's restroom. The space was blindingly white. White tile on the floors and walls. White porcelain fixtures illuminated by the same horrible blue-white lighting the humans favored in their medical facilities. He slipped inside, shut the door, and then turned the lock. Using a precious bit of his waning magic, Sebastian created an auditory shield around the bathroom. No one would hear what was about to happen.

The other hunter was in mid-transformation. A shapeshifter. Bane. He knew the creature only by reputation. Bane was the strongest of the shifters and had been elected to serve the role of magic hunter for their community. The shifters considered it an honor to serve the council.

Bane shimmered, obviously struggling to hold its shape as it morphed into the guise of a mortal female. A nondescript brunette, not thin or heavy but somewhere in between. Selected to blend in, even with a missing appendage. Shifters were like starfish. They could regrow limbs at will as long as they had enough magic in their reserves. Bane's mutilation told Sebastian that killing the magic hunter wouldn't be a challenge.

"Dark fae, what brings you here?" The creature didn't look up from examining its missing limb.

"The same that draws you, I'd imagine. What happened?" Sebastian nodded toward the damage.

Unaware of the danger, Bane related the tale. "One of the werewolves. I turned into a deer to cause a car accident and draw out the third sister. But I didn't count on the aggression of the wolf."

"The eldest is mated to the local Alpha," Sebastian moved closer. "You're lucky it didn't kill you."

"Something drew its attention before it could finish me off." Bane studied the gruesome wound. "Probably another hunter."

Another? "Why are so many after these witches?"

"You mean other than obtaining their magic?" Bane grabbed some paper towels and used them to sop up the blood.

"It's only a percentage." Sebastian shook his head. "The witches are strong but they are coming into their powers. They have protection."

Bane shook its head. "Not a percentage, haven't you heard? The rules have been altered."

Sebastian stilled. "Altered by who? The council of elders doesn't meet for another two seasons."

"The fae queen is dead."

Sebastian had to brace himself on the wall. In the mirror, Bane smirked. "You didn't know?"

He was having trouble breathing but he needed to know. "How?"

"Rumor has it one of her sons struck the final blow. But a mortal with free-floating magic proved her undoing. The mortal magic wielders are growing stronger. And these sister witches are the strongest of them all. The bounty is high because fear is high. And so are the stakes." Bane made a face at the slowly regrowing arm.

Which meant more would be coming. For the glory of the kill as well as the surplus of magic. He needed to move quickly, to shore up his position. "Are you working alone?"

"Is that your way of asking me to team up?" Bane turned to face him, even as the limb pushed out farther into existence. "What happened to your last anchor, dark fae?"

"Allow me to show you," Sebastian called in his net and threw it in a single practiced motion. The shifter stood too close. Injured as it was, Bane didn't stand a chance. The magic cipher net landed atop the other hunter. The shifter's eyes went wide as the unbreakable strands enveloped it. It had let its guard down and would pay with its soul.

There was no escape from Sebastian's net. It would slowly suck the soul out of any being caught within its weave.

"Why?" Bane cried.

"The witches are mine." Sebastian's tone was even. "You got in my way."

"But why not just kill me?" Bane's single hand wrapped around the strands and shrieked as the burning intensified. The soul net glowed brighter, feeding on the shifter with relish. "Taking my magic is against the code of our kind."

"Haven't you heard, Bane? There's no honor among thieves. And that's what we are, no matter the bullshit lines about obligation and glory." Sebastian watched without remorse as the shifter began to lose its shape once more. The limbs molded together into an amorphous blob. A mortal body would've been left behind. An empty vessel. But shifters were magic incarnate. Nothing would give him away, not even residue.

"I promise you, Sebastian. You will regret this."

"I already do," Sebastian murmured. "However, regret is my long-time companion and I have grown fond of her."

The threats of vengeance morphed into wordless cries. Then even the screaming stopped. A minute later the net lay flat on a pile of ash.

Sebastian picked it up, enjoying the thrumming sensation of power that ran through the strands. He would have to take it to his altar. Wring out the soul and transfer the power to amulets or charms that he could use constructively.

Later. For now, he needed to find Siobhan.

Sebastian vanished the net back to his personal vault and then unlocked the door. A slight acrid tang filled the space so he propped the door open to clear the stench. If other magic hunters were lurking about, they would know one of their kind had been slain.

Let them believe it was the witches. The more their reputation grew, the safer Siobhan and her sisters would be.

The fae queen is dead.

He couldn't think about the ramifications of that. Not now.

His phone vibrated in his pocket. He retrieved it and looked down at the message.

SIOBHAN: ALYS JUST LEFT. MAEVE IS IN ROOM 308.
SEBASTIAN: I'M ON MY WAY

ive minutes later, he stood beside her as they stared down at the middle sister inert in the hospital bed. Wires and tubes snaked from Maeve's body to the various instruments that appeared crucial to human healing.

Siobhan had been crying. He could still see the shimmer from the trails the tears had left on her pale skin.

"I can't believe this." She shook her head. "A coma on top of everything. What utter shit timing."

"How long will they keep her this way?"

"The doctor said at least a week." She put a hand over her face. "God, what am I going to tell Kal? Or her kids?"

Sebastian put a hand on her shoulder even as he glanced around uneasily. This wouldn't do. Having Maeve in a public building and unable to defend herself for a week or more. Alys and Siobhan would be coming and going, unaware of the danger. Sebastian was the strongest and the slyest of the magic hunters, but even he couldn't hold them off for long. Not when the sisters were sitting ducks.

"Is there anything you can do...you know...magically?" He intentionally lowered his voice.

Her hands fell away and she stared blankly at the wall. "I don't know. I would have to look in our books."

"Then go look."

Siobhan shook her head. "I can't leave her."

He gripped her by the shoulders. "You won't forgive yourself if you don't."

Her lower lip trembled and he felt like the utter bastard he was by sending her off on a wild goose chase. But he couldn't do what needed to be done with her by his side.

"Okay," she smiled up at him and a bit of her fire flashed in her eyes. "Then kiss me and send me on my way."

Sebastian didn't need to be asked twice. He dragged her around the corner, away from her sister, and then shut the door to the hospital room, before pressing her against it.

His lips melded to hers and his hands roved over her body. Never would he have believed he would have enjoyed touching a mortal magic thief. But the more he did it, the more he craved her.

"I love the way your magic works," he murmured in her ear even as he cupped her full breast through her pajama top. "Use me any time you wish to empower yourself."

Her laugh turned into a moan as his thumb glided over

her nipple and a moment later, she disappeared from his arms.

Sebastian braced himself against the door and tried to catch his breath. He had to focus on his task. But it was damn near impossible when every cell in his body cried out for Siobhan.

His eyes slid shut and he took a long, slow breath before turning back to the bed.

Healing arts was one of the trickiest forms of magic. Because of the nature of his job, Sebastian hadn't learned much beyond basic first aid. How to patch himself up after a battle. How to keep his prey alive when the bounty required it. Healers devoted years to weaving spells to use as little magic as possible while encouraging the body to mend seamlessly with no long-term effects. But not one of them would help him heal an unsanctioned witch.

He didn't possess that deft sort of touch. Sebastian braced his hands on either side of Maeve's head and funneled his magic directly into her. The beeping from the machines around him halted. Technology and magic couldn't occupy the same space at the same time.

He stared down at her bandaged face, her closed eyes, and plunged his power into her. Forcing her body to expedite its mending.

Either she would survive or die directly. Whatever fate had in store, he couldn't change. What would take days or weeks in the mortal realm, Sebastian's magic would accomplish in moments.

He hoped she would survive, for Siobhan's sake. But if she was meant to die, better she do so now. Lingering would only jeopardize her sisters.

The connection formed a bridge into her mind. He saw flashes of her life, images of her and a mortal male. Children. Dogs. Her mother. Alys.

69

And Siobhan. Siobhan as a young child, never walking when she could run. Siobhan on her motorcycle. Siobhan showing up at her door, being there for Maeve.

As he trembled and gave over the final dregs of his power to the task, Sebastian watched the object of his obsession grow from a precocious child to a wild young woman to… who she was. She changed before his eyes. And he saw the hurt there, and the fear. The loneliness.

It took all that he had. Every last drop of power. He braced himself on the arm of the hospital bed as the dregs of his magic trickled into her. He was utterly spent. He couldn't have called a coin from his pocket.

He had given Maeve all he had in him. Drained every amulet. Had it been enough? He needed to go, to siphon Bane's magic so he would be prepared before the next wave of hunters arrived.

"What are you doing to her?"

Sebastian glanced over his shoulder to see that the door to Maeve's room stood open. He had forgotten to lock it. A young mortal in a lab coat filled the doorway and was scowling at him. The doctor.

He opened his mouth, most likely to call for security.

Sebastian may have been tapped out of magic but he was still dark fae. And he had a fae's essence—the defense mechanism that kept mortals from trapping the fae by ensnaring the mortal mind for a year and a day.

Removing the damper on his essence was like shedding a heavy winter coat. He felt the immediate relief of letting it fall away.

Within a heartbeat, the doctor's angry gaze turned blank. The mortal was lost in his thrall.

Sebastian moved forward and gave his new acquisition his first command.

"Here's what you need to do."

MAEVE

"How did I get here? And where exactly is here?"

There was nothing around me. Not a sound or a smell or even a hint of light. Just endless darkness that seemed to stretch on into eternity.

I was alone. But oddly, I wasn't afraid. Maybe because there was no one to enchant. No one to fall under my bizarre uncontrollable spell.

I looked down at myself...and wanted to laugh. I was wearing the pretty floral wrap dress I had on the night I'd met Kal. Well, technically I'd been wearing a borrowed maintenance uniform when I'd met Kal. The dress had been all but forgotten in the middle of the crisis. I hadn't thought about the thing in years. It had been relegated to the back of my closet. Shoved aside for more practical clothes.

But seeing it now reminded me of the young woman I'd been when I'd put it on that night. Full of hope and dreams about meeting her future husband. Wearing it filled me with a giddy sort of joy I'd almost forgotten.

And I had met him. He just hadn't been my date.

I was sick. A wife, a mother, and a business owner. But

when was the last time I'd remembered to be a woman?

"It's funny, isn't it?" a soft southern voice said from behind me. "The things we forget."

My heart pounded harder and I turned, afraid the voice was a figment of my imagination. That she wasn't really there. That I would blink and be alone in the dark again.

But she was there. Laney Silver looked exactly the way she did in my memory. Soft and sweet as sun-ripened peaches at the height of summer. She wore a dove gray dress that flowed around her ample curves and a lightness of spirit she hadn't possessed in life. All the strain around her mouth and eyes was gone. She smiled and extended her arms to me.

I let out a shaky breath and took a step forward, wanting to touch her, to let her hold me. "Mommy?"

"My Evie," she breathed and pulled me in close. She smelled the same too. Like jasmine carried on a crisp breeze.

For an endless time, we stood there. Her arms were around me and I pressed my face against the curve of her shoulder. I didn't cry, though tears clogged my throat. She didn't speak. She stroked my hair the same way she had done when I was little and couldn't sleep.

"Am I dead?" Alys had claimed to see our mother after she had died. The thought filled me with sadness. I didn't want to be dead. No matter how difficult life had become. I wanted to see my children again. Wanted to end the stalemate with Kal.

"No. But you've been injured and the doctors put you in a coma to help your mind heal. That's why I can reach you now." She tucked some hair behind my ear. "Listen to me. You girls were supposed to come into your powers years ago. Jess was going to guide you. She meant for you to drink the brew the full moon before the council of elders met so the risk from the magic hunters would be minimal."

I shook my head, trying to reconcile her words for my

actual life. "That's not what happened. Up until a few weeks ago we didn't know any of this even existed. Drinking the empowerment brew was an accident. And the council won't meet until next spring. I'm the problem. I'm scared all the time because of Ms. Priss."

"Ms. Priss?" she raised a brow.

I turned and before I could blink, the stern-faced woman with the high-necked gown and her sleek black cane appeared before us. She glared at me in her disapproving way.

"She' s putting everyone in danger. Me, Alys, Sibby, Kal, my kids. We're all at risk because I'm always scared of what she'll do next."

My mother moved around Ms. Priss, studying her with a critical eye. The manifestation of my disease didn't lash out at my mother or try to trip her with her cane. She stood still, her back ramrod straight like a soldier being looked over by a commanding officer.

"We were looking for a cure. Some way to get rid of her. Do you know of anything I can do?"

I held my breath and hoped. Laney had been a witch much longer than me or my sisters. She would know things about magic and how best to use it.

Her expression was sad when she finally looked back at me. "I'm afraid not."

My shoulders slumped.

"Then again, I never went looking for anything like that. Jess might know. Or perhaps Ethan."

"Ethan?"

"The spirit who dwells in Jess's cottage." Her smile turned secretive.

My lips parted and I was about to tell her that I didn't know of any spirit at the cottage, but then a memory surfaced.

Literally. The scene breached the darkness and engulfed us like a great sea monster. One moment we stood in the endless void and in the next we were in the upstairs of Aunt Jess's house, in my mother's old room.

There were two lumps in the bed. One was my mother, her hair braided in a loose fishtail and tied with a piece of torn terrycloth. And beside her…

"That's me." I stared down at my young self, asleep and nestled in my mother's arms.

A man sat in a chair beside the bed. He had dark hair and eyes like the underside of storm clouds. He was reading something. I grinned when I realized it was one of my mother's tattered romance novels.

Little Maeve's eyes opened. I stepped away but she wasn't looking at me. Her gaze was fixed on the man.

"You used to sense him." My mother approached the figure in the chair. "When you were little. You always knew when he was around."

I shook my head. "I don't remember him at all."

She gripped me by the shoulders. "You *knew*, Maeve."

The scene faded as did the specter of my mother. Instead of plunging me back into the blackness, another memory faded in. A hospital room and in the bed…

"Kal," I whispered.

He looked so much younger. His body was harder, as was his expression. He stared blankly out the window.

And then…I walked in. Only it was me from twenty years earlier. Wearing pink scrubs. I hesitated by the door. Unsure of my welcome.

My sneaker squeaked on the floor and Kal turned and drank me in like a man dying of thirst.

The energy in the room shifted when their gazes met. I remembered all too well the way my heart had raced. Wondering if he would want to see me in the harsh lights of the hospital.

"Hey," the other me said and even that sounded unsure.

"It's my hero," Kal murmured.

The other Maeve blushed. She was pleased. Oblivious to my presence, she moved past me into the room. "How are you feeling?"

"Like I skied into a tree," he murmured.

"Do you want me to go get your nurse?" Younger me already had one foot out the door. "Maybe your pain meds are fading. I could—"

"Stay," Kal said. He gestured toward the empty chair beside the bed. "Please."

His soft words affected me the same way they had two decades ago. My hand covered my heart as though to conceal the wild pounding within.

"I can't stay too long," younger Maeve informed him as she settled in the uncomfortable chair. "I need to relieve my aunt's nurse in an hour. She has cancer and I don't like to leave her alone."

"I'm sorry," Kal said.

"It probably sounds stupid. All she does is sleep most of the time. But I still don't want her to be alone for very long. I think I'm mostly a pain in her ass."

I smiled at the same time Kal did. I used to be such a ninny, always burping up information or explanations for strangers. It was a sheer impulse. Like the thought of someone not being able to understand my reasons for doing the things I did was a cardinal sin.

Most people didn't care. Kal did though.

"Do you work in this hospital?" he asked.

The other Maeve nodded. "Pediatrics. Mostly I work with newborns and their mothers. You were my first trauma case."

"I hope I lived up to your expectations," he said.

A bubble of laughter came out of the other me. "Trust me, you were better than my wildest fantasies."

I wanted to groan, especially when Kal's eyebrow quirked up. I vividly remembered saying that, feeling mortified because once again, my mouth had run away with me. Then covering with...

"I'm just glad you're going to be all right."

He reached for my hand. "Thanks to you, Evie. I'll be back to work in a few weeks."

"What is it you do?"

"I'm a chef by trade, though I was hired by the resort to do pastry."

"And you like that better? Making deserts?"

He nodded. "Deserts make people happy."

I watched the man who'd become my husband look at my younger self as I crossed my feet at the ankles and self-consciously tucked a strand of hair behind my ear. I knew what the me on the chair was doing. Searching for something to say. A way to get him to talk. To find out if he was interested or if he was just lonely and bored and I was a better distraction than whatever garbage was on cable. Twenty-five-year-old Maeve started prattling about, for whatever reason, skiing accident statistics. As an outside observer, I was able to watch Kal watch me as the verbal diarrhea went on and on and on.

Somebody get this girl some Pepto.

But Kal didn't mind. He never did. He listened and he smiled and made occasional remarks to reassure my dumbass self that he was indeed listening to all of the banalities. And I saw it happen.

I knew the precise moment he fell in love with me.

And a thought emerged. One that was coated in steel and branded itself on my heart.

This is what I'm fighting for.

CHAPTER SEVEN

MAEVE

"Kal," I whispered. My lips were cracked and dry.

"She's coming out of it." That was Sibby's voice.

"I can't believe it you left her alone." Alys's censure came from my other side.

"I told you, I was looking for a magical fix."

"And we'll deal with that later. Go get the doctor," Alys snapped.

"Don't fight, you guys," I croaked. My throat felt as though it had grown scales.

"Maeve? Can you hear me?" Alys put her hand on my arm.

"Where am I?" I'd just been with Kal in the hospital. And our mother before that.

But those were memories.

Alys squeezed slightly. "The hospital. Do you remember the accident?"

"The deer." Bracing myself for an onslaught of pain from the crappy overhead lighting, I cracked an eyelid. But to my surprise, there was no pain. In fact, my head seemed to clear as I looked up at my big sister.

Her face was mottled with ugly bruises, her short hair more disheveled than I'd ever seen it. If Alys looked so rough, I couldn't even imagine the state I was in.

"It wasn't a deer. At least Brock doesn't think so." Her voice lowered to a whisper as she added, "There are magic hunters around."

"So it's a good thing you decided to wake up early." Sibby's tone was chipper. "Are you in much pain?"

"None." The aches and twinges faded as I sat up.

"It shouldn't be possible." Alys studied me closely. "They put you in a medically induced coma not even three hours ago."

That explained my throat. I'd probably been intubated. Perhaps the bizarre dreams as well. Even with all the time I'd spent in hospitals, a medically induced coma was a new one.

Sibby advised Alys, "Doc says she's good to go. Don't look a gift horse in the mouth."

That had been one of our mother's sayings. My brow crinkled as my thoughts flitted back to the scene my mother had conjured. The cottage. The phantom was reading beside her bed. "Ethan. I need to find Ethan."

"Who's Ethan?" Sibby asked.

Alys held me down. "Wait a second. You're fresh from a car wreck and a coma that should have lasted another six days. At least let the doctor make sure you're all right before you charge out of here."

There was a scraping sound as the curtain around my bed was yanked aside. "You're all set, Ms. Silver."

"Doctor, are you sure she's all right?" Alys was glaring at the young man in blue scrubs. "You said a week. What about her MS and the trauma?"

"She's as healthy as she was before the accident. We've

done multiple scans. No sign of swelling or additional lesions. I personally called to check in with her neurologist. There's no reason to keep her here."

"And every reason to skedaddle," Sibby added, nudging Alys in the side. "Agic-may unters-hay."

"The nurse will be in shortly with discharge papers and something for you to wear." The doctor smiled, though it was an odd sort of expression that didn't reach his unfocused eyes. Had I enchanted him?

No, I couldn't have. He was talking and not crowding me the way the people I enchanted usually did.

My big sister was glaring at his back with the same expression she wore when a subcontractor's work failed to live up to her high standards. "Are you sure?"

"I'm fine, Alys. Really. I would tell you if I wasn't."

Obviously reluctant, Alys allowed the doctor to leave.

I swung my legs over the side of the hospital bed. Alys helped steady me. She watched me with hawklike intensity as I shuffled to the bathroom.

After relieving my bladder, I stared at myself in the mirror. Turned my head from side to side. I actually didn't look as bad as Alys. My hair was a mess, but no worse than standard bed-head. There was some light bruising and perhaps it was a trick of my eyes but it seemed as if it were fading even as I watched.

Concussions didn't just go away. Unless they were magicked away.

A moment later there was a knock on the bathroom door and Alys called. "Scrubs for you."

I opened the door and she handed me some generic pink scrubs, the same sort I had been wearing in the memory about coming to Kal's hospital room.

I gripped Alys's arm. "Kal? Does he know?"

If the hospital had contacted him, they might have

mentioned my MS. My throat closed up as I thought of him finding out that way.

She shook her head. Instinctively she knew where my mind had gone. "We couldn't reach him at home or on his cell. Brock and I were out beating the bushes for Nate and Sibby said she would handle it, but she never did."

"He went to the gym," I grumbled.

"Good for him." Oblivious to my tone, my sister crouched down and held out the pants for me to step into.

"I can dress myself."

She looked up at me. Her blue eyes were intense. "Humor me, I almost killed you earlier."

There was a soft quaver in her voice and it was easier to let her fuss than to fight her.

"That could have been bad," she breathed when I slapped her hands away and yanked the bottoms up myself. "Maeve, you need to come clean with Kal before something else happens."

"I can't go home. Not if there are magic hunters nearby. My only ability is enchanting people. Kal and the kids will be in the line of fire." After shucking the hospital johnny I held my hands out like a toddler and let her slip the shirt over my head. "Mom said Ethan might know of a magical cure. There is someone out there who knows how to heal my MS and I am going to find them."

"Ethan," Alys mumbled. "Mom's boyfriend?"

I blew out a breath and admitted, "I used to be able to see him."

She stared at me for a long moment. "You never said anything."

I untucked my hair from the collar. "Because I didn't remember. I was five, Alys. Everything was always changing. I don't know why I could see him then. All I know is that mom told me he was still there and he's our best source of intel on magic."

"But Maeve, how do we find him if you can't see him?" Alys asked.

"At the cottage. His spirit is tethered to it. Maybe Sibby knows a way to summon a ghost."

When we came out of the bathroom, Becky, a nurse I used to work with, stood chatting with Sibby. "That man you were with was something else."

"What man?" Alys's tone was sharp.

"Tall, blond hair. He had the oddest eyes. Doc came in and spoke with him for a few."

Sibby flinched as Alys glared at her. "You brought a *date* to your sister's hospital room?"

Sibby made a face. I realized that she was still in her pajamas. She must have come to the hospital directly from her tryst. "It wasn't a date. He gave me a ride."

I moved over to scrawl my name on the clipboard and then shoved it back at Becky. "Do me a favor and forgo the whole hospital policy on a wheelchair thing, okay? I want to leave under my own steam and as you can see, I have plenty of help."

She looked back and forth between my siblings who were doing their level best to bore holes into one another with their eyes. "No problem, Maeve. Take care."

The boots I had been wearing were on the floor next to the chair. I tugged them on sans socks and then picked up my coat. "Don't make a scene, you two. Too many people around here know my name and if there are magic hunters on our tail, then we shouldn't leave breadcrumbs in the form of gossip."

Without waiting for them, I headed out into the hall.

Ms. Priss was still with me, but she seemed content to lurk in the background as I made my way confidently out of the ICU and to the elevator. I pressed the button and waited. No sudden numbness or tingling or blurred vision. I felt as though I'd gotten early parole.

Alys and Sibby caught up just as the elevator doors opened. We stepped inside together and took the elevator down to the ground floor, none of us saying a word.

My minivan sat in the parking lot like a faithful hound. I didn't push my luck by asking to drive and waited for Alys to unlock the door before scrambling in the front passenger's side. Sibby hauled her cookies up into the middle of the back seat and Alys got behind the wheel.

"Are you sure you don't want us to take you home?" Alys looked worse off than I did. There were stitches on her cheek and big, dark circles under her eyes. "You should be resting."

"I need to find Ethan."

Sibby and Alys exchanged a look. "What about Kal? And the kids? Isn't tonight Bella's dance thing?"

Shit. I'd forgotten all about it. "I'll call him when we get to the cottage."

Alys went to insert the keys and dropped them. Her hands were shaking.

I put a hand over hers. "Want me to drive?"

She shook her head quickly. "I'm fine."

Sibby and I exchanged a glance in the rearview mirror. If you asked Alys, she was always fine. Which was why we didn't usually ask.

Sibby squeezed between the seats. "Move over, Alys. You were in an accident too."

Alys slapped at Sibby's backside as it came in for a landing in the same seat Alys was occupying. "I said—"

"I know, you're fine. That's why those big gray storm clouds are gathering over the horizon, right?"

A rumble of distant thunder echoed around us.

Alys let out a huff but then relinquished the keys. "Fine. You drive."

"Don't mind if I do." And Sibby, clad in her pajamas, drove us back to the cottage on the dirt drive our mother had named Witch Way.

"*H*ello?"

I winced when I heard Kal's voice on the other end of the line. My sisters had said they'd been trying to get a hold of him for hours but he hadn't picked up. I thought I could just leave him a voicemail. I hadn't mentally prepared myself for the conversation. "Hey... you," I said and wanted to smack myself. Hey you? What was I, sixteen?

"Evie? Is everything all right?"

"Not exactly. Alys and I were in a car accident earlier. She hit a deer."

"Are you hurt?" Kal's tone sharpened.

"I'm fine." *Now*, I mentally tagged on.

"Where are you?"

"Back at Aunt Jess's house."

"Do you want me to come and get you?"

"No," I barked and then winced. Exhaled and retrenched. "What I mean is no, I want to stay with my sisters tonight. She's really shaken up."

It wasn't a lie. Alys did appear visibly rattled.

The other end of the line was silent.

"Kal?" Had we gotten cut off.

"Bella's recital is tonight."

"I know." She had been practicing it for weeks, I'd been helping her with her timing. Had driven her to all the practices. She was just another flower in the garden but it was her debut. A part of me screamed that I couldn't miss it.

The other part of me knew that I could live with missing the recital, but not if a magic hunter came after my family.

"What's going on, Maeve?"

"It's complicated."

"You used to talk to me." His tone was quiet, almost hurt. "You used to tell me everything."

"Yeah and that's always the way it worked wasn't it? I talked to you, but you never open up to me."

Silence.

I hadn't intended to pick a fight with Kal. But when my back was to the wall, I came out swinging. And more often than not, I drew blood with my verbal rapier.

"I need to go," Kal said. "The kids will be home soon."

I nodded though it was stupid because he couldn't see me. "Tell her I'm sorry I'm missing it. And give her a big kiss."

"I will," Kal vowed and then hung up.

I set the phone down. The numbness I felt had nothing to do with Ms. Priss. It was a defense I realized. A way to balance out the reality of my very shitty situation with the unfortunate circumstances that were keeping me away from my family.

It was a vicious cycle. Something happened to me. Magic, MS, a car accident that led to a brief hospitalization. I didn't want to tell Kal because he would worry. The secret festered between us, grew tentacles, and pushed us farther apart.

It hadn't been this rough since I'd been trying to get pregnant. I'd kept a happy face on for Kal, even as I was being emotionally shredded every month that it didn't happen.

Seven years, ten months, and four days. Two miscarriages. By the time I gave birth to a set of healthy fraternal twins, I couldn't believe it was over. The constant strain, the guilt I felt every month when my period came like clockwork. It was over and I had won.

But that's the kicker of life, isn't it? You never win for

long. I had those babies and now I couldn't be with them for fear of putting them in danger. And my fear was the greatest threat to everyone I loved.

"Maeve?"

I looked up to see Sibby standing in the doorway. "Are you okay?"

"Best that can be expected," I told her. "Did you find something?"

She nodded and gestured for me to follow. Carefully, I pushed myself off the couch and then shuffled through the kitchen toward the greenhouse.

The air was warm in the greenhouse, full of familiar loamy scents of damp soil and rich with oxygen. Being in the space calmed my frazzled nerves.

Sibby gestured toward the battered three-legged stool that sat before the workbench. I lowered myself onto it then asked, "Where's Alys?"

"Outside talking to Brock." Sibby jerked her chin toward the foggy glass panels through which we could see Brock's red pick-up. "Do you want to wait for her?"

When I shook my head she set the book down in front of me and pointed. "See there?"

"I don't even know what I'm looking at."

Sibby sighed and tapped the book again. "That symbol. It's the sign for a medium. Mom had the same symbol on a necklace. She used to wear it along with this." She held up a familiar clear crystal pendant.

"Her scrying crystal."

"Mom was a medium. That's how she could communicate with Ethan as a ghost."

A medium. I frowned. "But why could I see him when I was little if I'm not a medium like her?"

Sibby shook her head. "I'm not sure really. But I do know that we can borrow other witches' gifts. If we etch this symbol onto a mirror, we should be able to communicate with Ethan directly."

I blew out a breath just as Alys walked in.

"Any word about Nate?" I asked her.

She shook her head. "He's in the wind. What's going on here?"

Sibby brought her up to speed.

"We need to use more magic," Alys made a face. "It's so risky."

"It is." I agreed.

She held my gaze. "And do you really think that this Ethan will be able to help you?"

"I don't know. I hope he can. Mom thought he could."

I could see it in her eyes, the temptation to connect with a link to our mother, even if he was just a ghost.

"I vote yes," Sibby said.

I looked at my big sister. "I want this."

She closed her eyes and then nodded. "Okay. I'll go find us a mirror."

CHAPTER EIGHT

SIOBHAN

"Stop looking at me like that," Maeve said from her position on the stool.

"Like what?" I asked. I knew she was talking to me. Alys, who had the steadiest hand out of all of us, drew the symbol on the antique mirror she'd found in our mother's room. All her focus was on the task.

"Like you're worried about me."

Deliberately, I looked down at the book in front of me, at the medium symbol. Maeve was right, I was worried about her. Not just because she was fresh from a car wreck either. She should be home with her husband and kids. Bossing them around in that way she had that was full of equal parts love and well-meaning censure. Maeve wasn't a control freak like Alys. I always thought of her more as a general who dispatched her troops to get the job done. She took into account everyone's needs and distributed resources efficiently.

That was her place. The way I thought of her. Yet there was something otherworldly about Maeve as she perched on the stool in the greenhouse. Something more than the mom who was battling a chronic illness or the interior designer who could pinch a penny and still come up with beautiful results. She fit here too, but differently, in a way that I didn't really understand.

I would never say it out loud to either of my sisters, but seeing her in that hospital bed had really freaked me out. I knew she was sick. I'd driven her to many of her appointments over the last few weeks. But afterword, she went back to work, or back home, returned to her efficiently managed and very full life.

Maeve let out a breath when Alys held up the mirror. "Does this look right?"

I studied the symbol and then glanced down at the book. "I think so."

"Now what?" Maeve leaned forward eagerly.

"Now set the mirror down here. Make sure the top part of the symbol faces east." I'd cleared space on the workbench for the mirror and had five candles set around it to mark the circle.

Maeve pushed back from her stool. Her movements were careful but not stiff.

I would have to thank Sebastian for that.

I'd been over it in my head a hundred times since the doctor told us that Maeve was all healed with no brain swelling or trace of damage. I had traveled to the cottage and left Sebastian alone with Maeve. And the next thing I knew, I was getting a call that she was coming out of her coma.

And Sebastian was nowhere to be seen.

He must have magic. Why else would he still be hanging around me even after he'd seen me travel? Why else would he live in such a sterile space?

Like Brock and his werewolves, Sebastian belonged to the

supernatural community. He had done something to help heal my sister and then vanished.

Why hadn't he told me he could help? And why had he disappeared again? I'd sent him a few texts but they all remained unread.

"So now what?" Alys's voice broke me from my reverie.

I leaned forward and started lighting the candles, again starting at the one to the east. "With any luck, our ghost will appear in the mirror."

"No chanting or anything?" Maeve tilted her head.

"Not according to this." I lit the last candle and then backed up.

"Nothing's happening," Alys grumbled. "Maeve, do you see anything?"

Maeve squinted into the candle closest to her. "No?" Her voice went up at the end as if asking a question.

"No," she said again, but more firmly. "But I can feel something."

All the hairs rose on my arms. I felt it too. There was a sudden chill in the climate-controlled greenhouse. "Alys, are you doing something to the atmosphere in here?"

"No. Look." She pointed to the mirror which had fogged over.

I moved closer. The symbol, which Alys had drawn in black permanent marker was completely obscured. The old glass was dark once more, the symbol gone.

As one, all the candles died.

"Sibby?" Maeve asked. "What's going on?"

"I don't know." I shook my head, reaching for the book again. An uneasy feeling twisted my stomach. I reread the instructions. We'd done everything we were supposed to do. The symbol. The mirror. Moving from east to west. "It should have worked."

"It did, Sibby," a deep voice said from the mirror.

I jerked my head up and met a pair of stormy gray eyes.

"It's you," Maeve breathed. "Ethan."

He smiled at her. "Hello, little Evie. I've missed talking to you."

"What happened?" Alys asked. "Why were you able to talk to her before but not now?"

"It's the binding." Ethan was studying Maeve's face. "You looked so much like her. You all do."

My lips were parted but I couldn't utter a sound.

Maeve was bolder than me. She reached out and touched the glass. "How long have you been here?"

He smiled sadly. "I wish I knew. I was here long before you girls and your mother arrived. Long before Jess or even the structure, you're standing in."

I studied him and realized he was wearing a uniform of some kind. Alys must have recognized it too. "Were you a soldier?"

He looked down. "I can't remember."

"That's a Union uniform," Alys said.

She was right. The dark blue color was hard to make out in the dim lighting.

"That's what your mother thought too. She was trying to figure out who I was and what brought me to the house when she died." There was no mistaking the sadness and longing in his voice. "I had hoped that she would stay here with me always. That death would bring us together forever. She belonged here in life. But that wasn't her path."

My heart went out to him. The lost soul who spoke so fondly of our mother. What must their relationship have been like with him dead and not knowing who he had been and her, a displaced middle-aged witch and mother of three?

"You said there was a binding on me," Maeve whispered. "What exactly is that?"

Ethan's stormy gaze focused on her. "It's a charm that

inhibits your ability to practice magic. Jess did it. Right after your mother died. She bound all three of your powers. She told me it was too dangerous for you to inherit such powerful magic so young. You needed to be seasoned, to live your lives before you were ready to face all that waited for you. I understood though I worried how it would impact you. Especially you, Maeve."

"Me?" She asked.

Ethan smiled sadly. "You didn't have the strength of your mother's gift but you could always sense my presence. Could tell when I was here or when I was drawn back into the convergence."

"What's a convergence?" It was the first time I had been able to speak. Something about seeing this man who had loved our mother, who still loved her, drove every thought out of my head.

"It's a place where ley lines intersect. A place of power. This house was built years ago by a witch on top of the convergence in hopes that that structure would collect the energy of the lines."

"And does it?" Alys asked.

Ethan closed his eyes. "Not in the way they hoped. There is no more magic in this building than anywhere else. But what exists here is sharper, more focused, and easier to utilize by those who know how. It also acts as a buffer for most magic. As long as you're within the convergence, the magic hunters won't be able to sense your unique abilities, only the power of the convergence itself."

"Too much background noise to filter out," I muttered.

He nodded. "Exactly."

"You know about the magic hunters?" Alys asked.

"I am here, though not all the time. I've heard things you've said. Watched as you've grown." His gray gaze turned sad as he focused on Maeve. "Your mother would be so proud."

No, that wasn't at all creepy. Even still, it brought tears to my eyes. I pretended to be such a badass, the authority on magic but for whatever reason, I wasn't handling this situation as well as my sisters.

MAEVE

I shifted, uncomfortable with the idea that my mother's dead lover knew all about my chronic illness. There was something familiar about him. His accent was soft Southern, even though he wore a Union soldier's uniform from the Civil War. What was his story?

"It will be all right, Evie," Ethan's tone was reassuring. "You can handle this."

My gaze flew to the mirror. Only Kal and our mother had used that particular nickname. But then Ethan knew our mother, had known us when we were children and if he was to be believed, had watched us grow up.

"So, if we stay here until spring, the magic hunters won't find us?" Alys asked.

Ethan nodded.

"That's months away," I told her. "We can't just hide out here and be witchy the whole time. My kids will forget what I look like."

"Then we're back to needing to find a way to keep your magic reigned in," Sibby said. "Ethan, do you know of any way that Maeve can suppress her enchantress gift?"

He shook his head. "No. But you could try the midnight market."

"Midnight market?" Alys repeated. "What's that?"

"A place where magical beings go to buy and sell what they need. Many of the vendors are immortal and have forgotten more about magic than you will ever hope to know."

I leaned in closer so I could see him better. "Where is this market? And how exactly do we get there without attracting magic hunters?"

"I don't know. I wish I could do more to help." Ethan's lids lowered and his forehead crinkled as though he were in pain. "I'm sorry. I need to go."

"Wait," I said and reached out. My fingers touched only cool glass. "Ethan, Mom said you might know a way to cure me."

Those gray eyes were sad. "I'm sorry, Evie. I wish I could help you."

I blew out a breath and watched as the glass fogged over. When it cleared, Ethan was gone.

Alys put a hand on my arm. "I'm sorry."

I shook my head. "I didn't really think there was a way. After all, if magic could cure illness, Aunt Jess wouldn't have died from cancer."

Sibby already had her nose buried in a book. "I'll see if there's any mention of the midnight market."

Alys was halfway to the door. "I'm going to call Brock. He might know something."

I headed toward the stairs. "I think I'll go lie down for a while."

I could feel my sisters staring at me as I ascended the stairs. The thoughts I hadn't voiced echoed around the space.

I'll stay out of the way. Hide out and miss my daughter's dance debut. Be at my pity party if anybody needs me.

I stretched out on my mother's bed again. My thoughts should have been on her and on Ethan. Instead, they wandered back to Kal. The husband I had practically abandoned.

Was that why he was talking with Harper? Because I kept running out on him? Who was she to him? Was she the reason for his sudden interest in going to the gym? Was he getting in shape for her?

Was he planning to leave me?

I turned on my side and let the tears fall. *This really sucks.*

I hadn't been this miserable since before the twins were born. I shut my eyes and tried to focus on happier times. Like when he'd been the one in the hospital gown.

Visiting Kal had quickly become part of my routine. After I finished my shift, I would stop by his room. Sometimes if I managed a lunch break I would sneak in to see him them. He never had any visitors, which I found extremely sad.

"Where's your family?" I'd asked him at one point.

"Canada." His answers were usually one or two words. I could count on one hand the times when he spoke in complete sentences. I don't know why but his reserve gave him a quiet sort of dignity. Even with his leg suspended in a cast.

"Did you tell them about your accident?"

He shook his head no.

"Why not?"

"It's complicated."

Back off, Maeve. That was essentially the message he was sending.

I didn't pry. Instead, I had changed the subject. "What brought you here?"

"The job, mostly. And the climate."

My brows lifted. "The climate?"

"I can't stand the heat."

That made sense. High country summers, while still sometimes humid, were nowhere near as extreme as the rest of North Carolina. A hot week was over eighty degrees Fahrenheit. "I went down to Charlotte to visit my oldest sister last August. It felt like breathing through a wet dishrag the whole week."

He smiled and nodded, but it faded fast.

I put a hand on his arm. I wasn't sure when it had happened that I had become comfortable touching him. It just did. "What's wrong?"

"I don't know what comes next."

"Well, you have another week here and if the X-ray looks all right, the doctor will release you."

He gave me that little smile as though I'd amused him, but it didn't erase the worry in his dark eyes.

"Oh, you're talking about after you're released?"

He nodded. "The job's been filled."

And with it, his temporary housing. The lodge expanded its staff in the winter for the ski season. Kal would be healing for most of the rest of it. I wanted to ask again about contacting his family. After all, my sisters could be difficult but they would still show up for me when the chips were down.

But perhaps Kal wasn't so fortunate.

Thought of my sisters, specifically Alys, made me realize I might have a solution. "You could stay at my house."

His eyebrows shot up and I realized how that sounded.

"I didn't mean it like that." I huffed out a breath and retrenched. "My oldest sister and I are in the process of renovating a house. It's vacant, but structurally it's sound."

Plus, it was on my way to and from the hospital. I could check in with him, bring him groceries and help with anything he needed. See him. Spend more time with him. The more I considered it, the more I liked it.

"You don't even know me," Kal said.

"You told me you were a pastry chef. I know you well enough to let you stay in an empty house." Of course, Alys probably wouldn't feel the same way, but I kept that nugget of info to myself.

I gestured to his leg. "Besides, how much trouble are you really going to get into like that?"

His lips turned up and something about the way he stared at my mouth sent a ribbon of heat straight to my core. "I'll think of something, Evie."

Feeling oddly uncomfortable, I stood and reached for my coat. "I'd better go."

"Thanks," he said the way he always did. As though he were truly grateful for my presence.

As I headed down the hall and to my car, I wondered what had changed between us in that odd moment. One thing was certain. I wasn't about to let Kal leave without a fight.

CHAPTER NINE

ALYS

I stopped in the middle of pacing my bedroom when someone tapped on the window. Rushing forward, I unlatched the hook and pushed them open so Brock, in all his naked glory, could climb inside.

He must have been changing in the bushes for several minutes. I shook my head as I studied the dirt on his hands and feet.

"Why didn't you tell me you were coming over?" I reached out to secure the window before rounding on him. "And why the hell didn't you scratch at the door? You could have changed in here where your dangly bits wouldn't freeze off."

"I didn't want to disturb your sisters." Brock smiled as though he found me amusing and then reached for me.

I spied blood under the grime on his hand and caught his wrist before he could touch me. "You cut yourself."

"Sorry," he winced. "I didn't realize what a mess I was."

"Like I care about the mess. I'm worried about you, fool." I towed him toward the small master bath where my first aid kit was stowed in the linen closet.

"I must have stepped on something when I was on Nate's trail. Other than calling to check in on you, I've been a wolf all night."

"Any sign of him?" I asked as I examined the puncture in his hand. It didn't look as though it needed stitches. Thank chocolate for small mercies. I'd had enough of hospitals for one day. After dumping half a bottle of rubbing alcohol over the wound I guided his hand under the running tap water.

"How's Maeve?" Brock asked.

"Stubborn," I snapped.

With his free hand, he tucked a lock of hair behind my ear. "I meant physically."

I dried his palm gently with a dark blue bath towel. "Physically, she's just as she was before the accident. And I'm glad about that. I am."

"But?"

I paused in bandaging his wound and met his golden gaze. "It shouldn't have been possible. Cranial swelling doesn't just go away. Unless...."

"Unless someone magicked it away." He nodded.

"Right. I could almost believe that Sibby and I had healed her. Just by wanting her better. It's not something we've ever done before, but really, I don't know how far my mother nature gift goes. So maybe it's possible."

"Except?" Brock raised a brow, again picking up on the unspoken word. It was almost eerie how well he knew me.

I leaned against the sink. "Except for the fact that the doctor went along with it. Like it was no big deal that a patient who had been in a medically induced coma decided to wake up on her own. Healed and whole. I look worse than she does. You would never know by sight that she was fresh from a wreck."

Brock used his uninjured hand to stroke my cheek. "I'm sorry I sent the two of you off with Nate. He's my responsibility. But he's bonded to you. I thought maybe you could help him."

"It's not just on you. I wanted you at the house. You can't be everywhere at once, Brock. Not like Sibby."

Sibby, who had brought a freaking date to the hospital. I hadn't confronted her about it yet. Both of us had been caught up with Maeve's miraculous recovery and meeting Ethan. But a reckoning was coming. We were both tiptoeing through an endless minefield. Eventually, something was going to explode.

Brock shivered. The motion pulled me out of my reverie and made me realize that he was unclothed and my ponderous mood was adding a chill to the bathroom. Fog seeped under the door. He didn't complain though. Just like he hadn't complained at my less than gentle ministrations on his hand. That much alcohol should have stung.

"You should take a hot shower."

He grinned at me. "Only if you join me."

"Are you kidding? My control may be better but my mood is volatile right now. If I get in there with you, I might scald us both."

He tipped my chin up until our gazes locked. "You won't."

He had so much confidence in me. What had I ever done to earn unwavering loyalty from such a steadfast man?

Whatever it is, keep it up, Alys. The thought made me smile.

I reached up and wrapped my fingers around his wrist. "Go get cleaned up. I'll get you some clothes."

He didn't fight me on it. That was the greatest thing about Brock. He accepted every little bit of me. My sour moods as well as the good ones. He didn't try to change them to make himself more comfortable. He didn't question my thought process or badger me into seeing things his way. He just existed by my side so we could ride out the storm together.

I left him in the bathroom and strode purposefully toward the battle-scarred armoire. Like everything else in the cottage, the massive antique white piece fit the décor because it didn't look like any other piece of furniture in the space. The frame of the bed was iron scrollwork portraying climbing ivy. There was a Chinese screen depicting a heron standing before blooming Sakura branches in the far corner. The chest at the foot of the bed was vintage mountain carpentry.

French provincial met Gothic met the Far East met Appalachia. Because why the hell not?

I paused with the armoire door open, my hand on a pair of navy sweatpants. Then I looked around again. What if it hadn't been just Aunt Jess being thrifty with her cash at yard sales? I never recalled her going shopping for anything but food and things for the greenhouse. Yet items had appeared over the years.

Like magic.

These things seemed to belong in the cottage, together. Like students in a class.

I'd been living in the cottage for months. And while I repaired homes for a living and appreciated a clean, well-put-together aesthetic, the hodgepodge always felt homey to me. Like I belonged here too.

Curious, I headed out into the main room. To see if the theory held true.

The couch caught my eye first. Overstuffed and covered with cabbage roses. Beside it sat a tan wicker end table. Across from that, a squat corduroy chair. An old painted rocking chair sat beside the woodstove. The Victorian-era hutch at the foot of the stairs held hurricane lamps, a few books, and my laptop bag as well as a silver dish for keys. The knotty pine dining table sported an octagonal glass fruit bowl that had yet to see an apple.

Different styles, different materials, different eras. None of it matched. It should have clashed, but it didn't.

These things belong here. As mismatched as they are, they belong here together.

Intersectionality. That's what the space was filled with. Things from all over the world, joining together at one point. A convergence.

"Alys?" Sibby poked her blue head out from the greenhouse. "What are you doing?"

"Looking at the furniture."

She waited for a beat. "I'm afraid to ask."

"None of it matches."

"You're just figuring this out? Maeve told me that when she was fifteen."

I swung my gaze to her. "She did?"

Sibby moved all the way out from the greenhouse and leaned against the dining room table. "She looked. Not a single piece in the whole house is from the same style or era. It fascinated her how such mismatched stuff fit together so well. She called it "belonging design." Things that shouldn't go together but just do."

Maeve had never said anything to me about it. Then again, when Maeve was fifteen, I was in college and rarely around.

"I'm really worried about her," Sibby murmured.

When I looked over at her she pushed off the table and began pacing. "It's not the MS. Or not only the MS. She hasn't been coping well. I overheard her on the phone earlier. Things between her and Kal sound strained."

"She's keeping several big secrets from him. It would be more of a surprise if things between them weren't strained."

"Your marriage wasn't like that."

"No, it wasn't. Kyle and I weren't close the way Maeve and Kal are. Not even in the same universe. Comparing one to the other is like comparing a muddy puddle to the ocean."

Sibby smiled but it faded quickly. "And now you have Brock. If you were in Maeve's place, would you be afraid to tell your significant other about what was going on?"

I took a deep breath. "You know, I was just thinking about how utterly accepting Brock is about all of me. My moods, my powers. He just rolls with the punches. Plus, he's already in on the supernatural shenanigans. Kal's human."

She tipped her head to the side. With her blue hair, she looked like an exotic bird. "You don't think Kal would be accepting?"

I wanted to say yes. I wanted to say that Maeve's fear was all irrational and that she had nothing to worry about when it came to Kal. But she wasn't the woman he'd married any longer. She was a witch with a chronic illness. Maeve knew Kal better than I did. I wanted to believe he was just like Brock. We couldn't be sure though.

Magic was in our blood. I'd fought it at first and fighting had done more harm than good. Sibby had embraced it. I wondered where Maeve fell on the spectrum.

Sibby seemed to read my thoughts. "She was doing better before the diagnosis. I think...even though she knew what was going on she kept the possibility alive that maybe she was wrong. Maybe it would go away and she could go back to normal."

I nodded grimly. "Even normal looks a lot different than it used to."

Sibby shifted her weight. "About the guy I brought to the hospital."

The pipes rattled in the wall behind me as the water shut off in the shower. I held up my hands. I couldn't get into it with her. "No more, Sibby. I'm at my limit for tonight."

Disappointment filled the space between us. It was thick.

A choking miasma of things unsaid. Guilt threaded through me for shutting her down, but I really couldn't handle my youngest sister's justifications, rationalizations, or explanations. She didn't say anything as I retreated back into my bedroom and shut the door.

Brock emerged and stabbed his legs into the sweats as I slid beneath the covers. A moment later the covers lifted and he slid in next to me. His skin was warm and I sighed as I snuggled up against him, letting the scent of his skin and the feel of his body chase away the last tendrils of ice. After a moment of basking, I got on with business.

"Tell me what you know about the midnight market."

MAEVE

"According to Brock, the midnight market is an open-air bizarre and *the* place to buy all things magical." Alys paused to sip her coffee. "The werewolves don't practice much magic outside of the shift so his knowledge is limited. But everyone knows about it."

I gripped my own mug. "Does he know where it is?"

"It's not a matter of where," Alys said. "It's a matter of how to get there. We need to cross an in-between at exactly midnight."

"An in-between?" Sibby frowned. "What is that?"

"A transitional space that separates one place from another. A doorway. A tunnel. A bridge. The place doesn't matter as long as the intention to travel to the market is clear."

I stared at her. "So, you're saying we could walk through the front door at midnight and wind up in this magic market?"

She nodded. "He has no idea how we get home again though."

"Well, that's easy," Sibby stood and headed toward the fridge. "I jump us home."

Alys's perfect eyebrows formed a deep V as she stared at our youngest sister. "Have you forgotten there are magic hunters on our tail? Ethan said any use of power outside of the convergence will attract their notice. Maeve enchanted Nate yesterday and we almost died."

I flinched.

Alys looked immediately contrite. "Maeve, I didn't mean that the way it came out."

"I know. And you're not wrong. I can't control my fear." I stared out the window. The sky was full of dark, pregnant clouds. "I should go home. The weather forecast is calling for snow later and Kal has to work. I need to be with Bella and Philip until he gets home."

"But what about the magic hunters?" Alys straightened her already stiff posture.

"I learned my lesson yesterday about overextending myself. I'm going to stick to my simple routine and just have a snow day with my kids."

It would be easier without Kal at home. We could bake cookies and play in the backyard with the corgis, then snuggle up and watch a movie. Nothing that would make me afraid or trigger my enchantress gifts.

Alys looked like she wanted to argue but Sibby shut the refrigerator door with a thud. Her hands were empty. "I'll go with you,"

"Sib," I began.

She leaned against the refrigerator. "Just in case anything happens. I can be your emergency ride back here. We can bring Bella and Philip. Even the stupid dogs if you want."

My lips parted but no words came out. She could transport all of us? Since when? I wanted to ask, but Alys was already speaking.

"What if you can't trigger your magic?"

Sibby stared at her. Something passed between them, a current I didn't understand. "I can. It's not as effortless as it is for you, but I know how to trip my own trigger."

Alys nodded slowly. "Fine. I'll call Lora and have her close the office. If there's a snow day, she'll want to be home for her son. Brock is coming for me at eight, so I'll check in with the crew at the Mid-Century Modern and then we'll head out on the Nate search again. Remember, an in-between at midnight."

We nodded and after washing our mugs, Sibby and I headed out to my minivan. I made a beeline for the driver's side door. Alys would have argued but Sibby just headed for the passenger's side.

"It's nice to know we have a safe place to practice our magic," Sibby said as I drove us past the *Welcome to Eckhart* sign. "Like having a home base for witchery."

I checked the rearview mirror and then looked over at her. "Is that how you've gotten strong enough to transport so many at one time? You've been practicing?"

"Yeah," she said. "I try to make one trip every night, increasing the weight. Last week I traveled with my motorcycle to your project house. Then drove it home."

I wanted to chastise her for using magic so freely. We hadn't known about the home base rule then. But Sibby caught enough flack from Alys. She didn't need me to nag her.

"So, who's your muse?" I asked instead.

Her teeth sank into her lower lip.

"Sibby, you might as well tell me."

"It's Sebastian."

I blinked. "Sebastian Jones? The attorney? That's who you've been sexting with?"

"It's not sexting," she grumped as I turned onto my street.

"It's just talking."

I pulled the minivan to a stop beside Kal's car. "And that's who was at the hospital with you?"

"I was at his place yesterday," she explained. "I was too panicked after I heard about the accident to travel. He drove me. I know what you're thinking, but he already knows about us and he's coming to terms with it."

I wanted to ask her if she really thought it was a good idea to get involved with him, but I held back. Sibby was a grown woman. She'd lived on her own most of her life. I needed to trust her judgment.

"Just be careful," I told her. "I don't want you to get hurt when he decides you're too much witch to handle."

"Is that what you think will happen with Kal? That you'll be too much for him to handle?"

I shut off the engine and listened to it tick for a beat.

"Maeve?"

"I think Kal's having an affair."

Sibby made a sound. Like a choking snort. I turned and looked at her. Her lips were pressed together and her shoulders shook.

"It's not funny."

"Oh, it is. All the years I thought Alys was the neurotic one. Turns out it's you."

I huffed out a breath. "I am not neurotic."

"Yes, you are. Kal would *never* cheat." Her faith in my husband was absolute.

"How do you know?" I clung to her surety like a woman lost at sea and tossed a life preserver.

"Because it's Kal," she said simply. "Besides, I told him on your wedding day that if he ever hurt you, I'd cut off his balls and feed them to the pigs right in front of him."

I snorted. "You did not. Besides, where would you even find pigs?"

Sibby waved that pesky detail away. "I'd be singularly motivated to figure it out. Trust me Maeve. And hey, here's a thought. Maybe you should *freaking talk to him.*"

I sighed and popped my car door. "You don't understand."

Sibby hurried around the van to my side. The walkway had done the classic North Carolina black ice shuffle. The intense sunlight melted the ice during the day yesterday and the water refroze overnight to create even more slippery conditions. Kal had tossed some rock salt down, but I still appreciated the assist even as I resented the need for it.

"You're right, I don't understand," Sibby said. "I've never had someone stare at me with the dopey look on his face Kal gets when he is focused on you. A little lost and full of wonder. The man may not say much but he is very easy to read."

"He's hiding something from me though. I can feel it."

"Can you? Or are you just projecting because of all the shit you're hiding from him?"

I shook my head. She didn't understand. Besides, it was cold and I wanted to hug my children, who I hadn't seen in two days.

This conversation could wait.

"Hello?" I called as I opened the front door.

"No!" A door slammed upstairs and a moment later Kal appeared at the top of the stairs. He was dressed for work in his black and white checked chef's pants with a white long-sleeved t-shirt that he wore beneath his chef's coat. The shirt strained over his belly, something I always thought was a hazard of the job as a brilliant pastry chef.

I loved his dad-bod. It wasn't perfect but it was mine.

At least it had been before Harper.

"School's been canceled," Kal said.

"I figured." My throat closed up as I stared at him. I wanted to say something snide, ask him how the gym was and where was he yesterday when my sisters had been trying to get a hold of him to tell him I was in the hospital. But that would lead to more questions than I had the energy to answer. "How was the performance?"

Kal came down the stairs. "I'd better let her tell you."

That sounded ominous. Guilt tightened my throat. Before I could say more, Kal turned to Sibby. "Could you give us a minute?"

Sibby glanced at me and widened her eyes. I could practically hear her voice in my head. *Tell him, Maeve.*

I couldn't. The timing wasn't right. He was on his way out to work and it sounded as though Bella was struggling.

"Sure," Sibby said and headed up the stairs. "I'm just gonna take a quick shower."

Kal waited until the bathroom door shut behind her. "I need to talk to you about something."

"I'm right here." I forced a smile even though my heart was shriveling in my chest.

"Are you, Evie?"

I licked my lips. "I'm standing right in front of you."

"And will you be here tonight? So we can talk?"

I opened my mouth, wanting to say that I would. Then I recalled the midnight market. "I have to go out late."

His expression didn't change but something shifted. He didn't ask me where I was going, or what I thought was more important than him and the kids. But I could feel the questions circling like buzzards.

"I'll see you later." Kal reached for his parka and then eased past me to the door. No kiss goodbye. No, I love you.

He pulled the door shut and my heart broke at the final click.

CHAPTER TEN

"Go lie down," Sibby took the towel I had been using to halfheartedly dry the corgis out of my hand and then pointed.

"Are you talking to me or the dogs?" I asked even though I knew.

"I've got this," my stubborn sister insisted.

My beautiful image of the snow day I would spend with my children had shattered. Bella was upset I had missed her performance. She had tripped on one of the background props and fallen on her face. Humiliated and betrayed by my absence, she was punishing me in her own way. She hadn't liked any of the suggested activities I had planned. No to sledding down the big hill behind the house. No to ice skating on the duck pond. She had only wanted to read in her room. Code for sit around and sulk.

Philip had been out and he had taken the G and G wrecking crew with him. But he had forgotten their waterproof slickers—which were more like sausage casings with leg holes. By the time Sibby and I had caught them and dragged them back into the house, the impish canines were soaked down to their matted under-fluff.

Instead of hot chocolate, my nose was filled with the aroma of wet dog.

"I'm fine," I said to Sibby. Even though I wasn't. It's programmed into women at birth. When someone expresses concern, it's our job to reassure them that we're okay. Even when we're struggling.

It's the polite thing to do.

"Bullshit," said Sibby, who never really took to the idea of polite society being anything but a pain in the kiester. "You're dead on your feet."

I opened my mouth but she interrupted before I could speak.

"How many spoons do you have left?"

It had become a code. Since long before my diagnosis, Sibby had joined online communities for loved ones of people with chronic illness, aka spoonies. The term "spoonie" referred to the number of energy spoons a person had on any given day. When a body is constantly fighting itself, as is the case with an autoimmune disease, the fight alone takes several of the spoons that an abled person can use for cooking or driving or writing the great American novel. People with chronic illness get fewer spoons and have to budget how they expend their energy very carefully. Borrow too much from a future day and a spoonie crashes. Hard.

Sibby started asking me about my spoons when she'd returned to Eckhart. Her asking the question meant I had to take a minute, assess my physical state regardless of what was going on around me, and responded honestly.

I wouldn't be surprised if she had a list somewhere where she recorded and tracked my responses. It was such a very

Alys sort of thing to do, but Sibby was more like our big sister than she knew.

Of course, telling her that would only piss her off.

I shut my eyes and took inventory. No pain or numbness, though there was some stiffness in my neck. Energy-wise...

"I'm on my last spoon." It was painful to admit. I felt as though I ought to be able to do more than wander around for a few hours before falling back into bed, exhausted.

Only a year ago, I had been capable of doing my job, attending all the soccer games and dance classes, keeping the house clean, making love with my husband, and even reading a book now and then.

Where had that woman gone?

I looked down at the mess of saturated towels and the still damp corgis. "They need to be blow-dried. There is no way that is a one-person job."

The dogs were afraid of anything that made noise. It sent them into hiding mode. Kal had used the vacuum on the stairs last week and they'd both gotten stuck under Bella's bed where they'd belly crawled to quake in terror.

"I'll get Philip and Bella to help me." Sibby put her hand on my shoulder and gave me a little shove. "Go rest. We'll deal with the corgi mess."

Feeling useless, I trudged up the stairs. I paused at the door to Bella's room. She lay on her bed, the latest in a children's mystery series featuring a dog and cat detective team was open on her chest. They were simple mysteries, a few reading groups beyond what Bella was reading in school. She had always loved stories, the same way my sisters and I did. I could tell Bella was going to be an avid reader. Her gaze was focused not on the page, however but out the window at the still falling snow.

"Knock knock," I said and then winced. Who says knock knock instead of simply knocking?

She looked over at me and her woebegone expression broke my heart.

"Are you ready to talk to me yet?" I asked.

She shook her head in mute defiance. Unlike her father and brother, Bella loved talking. Would prattle on and on and on for as long as you would let her.

"Okay, well, Aunt Sibby needs some help with Gimli and Grogu. Grab the hairdryer out of the hall bath for her."

She put the book aside and stood up. Still young enough to do what she was told even when she didn't really feel like it. Her teenage years were going to be hell.

"Where are you going?" She asked when she emerged from the bathroom, dryer in hand. I had been headed in the other direction.

My teeth sank into my lower lip. "To take a nap."

"You take a lot of naps, mommy." And with her verbal arrow still sticking out of my heart, she headed toward the stairs.

I crossed the threshold to our bedroom and shut the door. The curtains were still closed, a sure sign that I hadn't slept here the night before. I preferred light and air while Kal slept best in total darkness. Out of habit, I moved to open them but then wondered why I should bother if I was just going to bed.

Maybe I would never bother to open them again.

"Stop," I spoke the word out loud. "Feeling sorry for yourself won't get you anywhere."

It wasn't exactly a rousing pep talk.

My phone charger sat on the tall dresser next to my jewelry box. I stared at the ornate wooden box as I plugged the phone in. When was the last time I'd even worn jewelry? Other than my wedding ring, which I stowed in a zipper in my purse whenever I had an MRI, I usually didn't bother with necklaces or earrings. Alys always had tasteful pieces on, when she wasn't working with power tools and Sibby had funky studs and hoops that displayed her personality.

Did I have any personality anymore? Or was I just the sick sister?

I shucked my outer layers and bra, too fatigued to bother with pajamas. Kal had always wanted me to sleep naked. Eventually, my utter laziness might grant him his wish.

Would he even care?

"You're spiraling, Maeve." I didn't like all the things I was feeling. I had wanted nothing more than a simple fun day with my kids to take my mind off the impending conversation with Kal. Instead, I had gotten moodiness and mess. I resented Ms. Priss for making spoon counting a necessary activity. I resented the kids for wasting my precious spoons. Then felt guilty because no decent mother should ever resent her children. Especially when she had waited so long to have them.

I was forty-five and felt as if I were a hundred and five.

After sliding between the sheets, I let out a soul-deep sigh and shut my eyes. Sleep eluded me. Before Ms. Priss, I hadn't known a person could feel so exhausted but not be able to sleep. I rolled onto my side, then flipped onto my back. My legs were restless, the muscles aching from inactivity.

I should do some yoga. The thought surfaced and was joined by others. *Stretch the muscles. Move and be present in my body. Be kind to my fucked-up, betrayal-filled carcass.*

That's what all the advice on the internet said. *Be kind to yourself. Go easy.*

The internet was full of it.

The yoga mat was downstairs. It might as well have been on the moon. The thought of getting dressed and going down there was too much.

So I rolled onto my other side and squeezed my eyes shut.

And I thought about bringing Kal to our project house from the hospital.

He had been a much better patient than me. He did what he was told without question or complaint when he had been discharged, including sitting in the wheelchair while I carried his crutches out to my beat-up Jetta. Though the winter wind whipped around us, Kal wore loose-fitting shorts. There wasn't enough room for his big frame plus the cast in the front seat so I helped ease him into the back, propping his leg up with two overstuffed down pillows I had brought for just that purpose. The crutches had to be angled into my trunk along with the duffel bag one of his coworkers from the resort had packed for him.

I slammed the trunk shut and then bent down by the open door to check on him. "You good?"

Kal was struggling with his seatbelt. His positioning meant the buckle was beneath his injured leg.

"Here, let me." Without waiting for his invitation, I placed my knee between his and climbed into the car, and reached for the belt. I had to slide my hand along the length of his bare thigh to find the buckle and then pulled the strap at an angle across his body to engage the safety harness without choking him in the process

I was so focused on my task that the intimacy of our positioning didn't register until I met his penetrating stare.

"Evie," Kal murmured. He reached out with one of those big hands. I don't know if he wanted to touch my face or maybe comb his fingers through my hair. My heart pounded and I backed hastily away, not ready to believe the promises the big, quiet man made with that soulful gaze.

I shut the door. And then took a few deep breaths of piercing mountain air, hoping it would clear my head. All it did was make my lungs burn and my fingers turn blue, so I got behind the wheel and shut the door, and then cranked the engine over.

When I checked in the rearview mirror, I saw Kal had his eyes closed. His face was pulled tight.

"Are you in much pain?" I asked. On my way to collect him, I'd stopped by the pharmacy to pick up his prescription. I could see the white paper bag where it had been deep-throated by my enormous purse. I didn't have anything for him to drink but I could always run to the hospital cafeteria for a bottle of water if he was really hurting.

Without opening his eyes, he shook his head.

Okay then. I shifted the Jetta into gear and we were on our way. Not wanting to blather in case he was trying to sleep, I clicked the radio button. The volume was on low, tuned in to the oldies station. Radio signals could be spotty in the mountains but the oldies always came through strong. It was easier to keep listening to the Righteous Brothers and Frankie Valley and the Four Seasons than to fight an intermittent signal on my commute twice a day.

"I like this music," Kal said from the backseat.

Otis Redding was crooning the opening verse to *Sitting on the Dock of the Bay*. I didn't know if he meant the song itself, which was actually kind of sad in my opinion, or just oldies in general.

"The song or the era?"

"Both," he said.

I thought about the song. Its mellow tune was lulling but the lyrics were what unsettled me. "It's about a guy who wanders across the country looking for a place to fit in but never finds it. So, he just sits still and watches as things keep going on without him."

"Right," Kal breathed the word like a prayer. "He's just chilling."

"Just chilling," I repeated and tried to imagine a world

where just chilling would be enough.

It was great in theory. But there was so much to do, always. Every minute of every hour of my every day was booked up. I had Aunt Jess's care to oversee. I had my job and my project houses with Alys. Basic stuff like dentist appointments and vet appointments and car maintenance. Occasionally tracking Sibby down to find out where she was and what was doing with her life. I barely had time to sleep some days.

"It actually sounds nice," I admitted after a time.

In the rearview mirror, I saw Kal smile. He didn't say anything. The man was so stoic. He behaved like words were at a premium.

I took the turn that bypassed the town and led to the project house. Otis transitioned to Bobby Darin's *Beyond the Sea* and Kal and I sat together and listened in mutual silence.

It was the most relaxing drive I could remember. My thoughts weren't leaping about like frogs dumped out of an aquarium. I was focused on my task but at ease.

Huh, maybe that's what the Otis Redding song is really about. Not being lonely or not fitting in. Being okay with where you are in the moment.

The thought that came right on the heels of that epiphany stole my breath more efficiently than the winter wind.

What if it could always be like this?

I dismissed the notion before it could plant seeds. Kal had no job. No connections to the town. He wouldn't stay in Eckhart forever.

So why was I letting him use the project house?

Before any answer materialized, we reached our destination. I ran up the walkway and unlocked the door, then retrieved Kal's crutches.

"This is your house?" Kal studied the A-frame on the hill.

"For now anyway. I don't love it as much as the first one we did." Why had I said that? There was no good reason for me to go running off at the mouth, yet I couldn't seem to help myself.

The kid we paid to shovel had done a decent job but the walkway was steep. Kal hefted himself out of the back, balancing on one leg until I could stick the crutches beneath his armpits.

"Take it at your own pace." I cautioned him. He had practiced on the crutches on the smooth hospital floors. It hadn't prepared him for the steep incline of a slippery gravel path.

My teeth sank into my lower lip. I hadn't thought about the challenge of the approach, only the accessibility of the house itself. Kal didn't complain though. He positioned his crutches and hopped. Position, hop, position, hop.

I stood behind him every step and watched his steady progress. Though he was so big that there really wasn't much I could do other than give him something soft to land on if he did tip over.

The thought reddened my cheeks as much as the stinging wind.

Finally, he made it inside. The house was semi-staged for showings. At the peak of the roof, the open floor plan was divvied up into the living room and eat-in kitchen. Down the hall were the three bedrooms. The two smaller rooms were connected by a jack-and-jill bath but the primary bedroom had its own shower.

"Living room or bedroom?" I asked Kal.

"Whichever is closer." His lips were compressed together in a tight line.

"Living room it is." I gestured him forward.

I had rented several pieces to make the house feel lived in and welcoming. There was a comfortable sectional sofa in the living room positioned before the fireplace. A faux bearskin rug covered the floor in front of it, but that was the only obstacle in the space for Kal to navigate around.

Kal studied the gray sofa and then proceed to maneuver himself to the center pie wedge of the sectional. After the hill, I wasn't surprised that the rug gave him no trouble, but I felt the need to ask. "Do you want me to move that?"

He took his time settling his body onto the sofa and propping his crutches along the shorter end within easy reach. Then he looked down at the faux fur before meeting my gaze. "It's your house, Evie. I won't mess up your design."

"I'm much more worried about you than the design, silly man." I shucked my coat and draped it over the far end of the couch, then fetched a fleece blanket out of the hall closet and checked the thermostat before returning to him. "Unless you're in the market for a cute little A-frame?"

He shook his head and began wedging cushions beneath his cast to elevate the limb. "I couldn't afford it."

Since his crutches took up the short end of the sectional, the only place for me to sit was on the end by his propped-up leg. After shaking out the blanket and draping it over him, I lowered myself on a separate cushion so I wouldn't jostle him.

"Neither can I. At least not without my sister. Alys is the brains and drive of our operation. I pick out stuff like that." I gestured to the cluster of four black and white photographs that depicted several different mountain scenes in all seasons. The lake with the wind ruffling its surface to create ripples of sun-kissed water. A waterfall shrouded by greenery. The raw bare branches of a tree against the backdrop of a hill covered in fallen leaves. A pole barn coated in snow.

"I thought they give you a sense of time and place. You know where you are. What's come before. What to expect." I explained my design choice to Kal. It was something I was sensitive about. With no formal design training or fancy degree, I was just a nurse with a little bit of taste.

"Beautiful," Kal commented.

When I turned to smile at him, I found his gaze was already focused on me. He wasn't talking about the photos.

I stood and reached for my bag. "Let me get you some water so you can take a pill."

He reached out and grasped my arm before I could move past him to the kitchen "Don't."

"Don't what?" My brows pulled together. "You have to be in pain. It's important to stay ahead of it. The meds will be less effective if you wait too long."

He didn't deny it. Instead, his eyes pleaded with me for understanding.

So I knelt on the rug before him. "Kal? Is something wrong?"

He took a deep breath as though steeling his resolve. "Addiction runs in my family. All kinds of addiction. I don't want to risk it."

"These aren't opioids," I put my hand over his. "They aren't addictive."

"I don't even take aspirin," he said. "I palmed the meds at the hospital after the IV came out. They're in the get-well bouquet from the resort. If not for what they gave me for the surgery I would say I've never had pain medication before."

"Why didn't you tell me?" I stared at him in disbelief.

He smiled slightly. "You haven't exactly seen me at my best, Evie."

I understood that. A man had his pride. But I also didn't like the idea of leaving him here alone and in pain. If he had mentioned it before there might have been something I could have prepared to help him.

"Please take the pills away." He closed his eyes as though shutting out the temptation the bag offered.

I swallowed and then nodded. "Okay Kal. Whatever you want."

There had to be another way to help him.

CHAPTER ELEVEN

SIOBHAN

"*H*ey," I said to Kal when he walked into the kitchen at ten to six. "Maeve thinks you're having an affair."

And she was going to kill me deader than dead for telling him.

My brother-in-law stilled. At well over six feet tall and massively built, Kal was a big dude. He didn't move quickly or speak without intention, probably a technique he had picked up when he was younger and had found that his size intimidated people. But he still communicated something to me. It was a feeling, a vibe I picked up off of him that radiated hurt and confusion.

Good, that meant he was innocent and I didn't have to cut his balls off.

"I told her she was crazy," I added. "But I thought you should know what you're up against."

"Will you tell me what's going on with her?" Kal asked. "The truth this time?"

I winced. Kal had made overtures a while back. He was intuitive and knew there was something up with his wife.

And not just because Maeve sucked at hiding things from the people she loved. But I couldn't tell him about the magic or the MS. Maeve would figure out how to resurrect my already dead carcass just so she could kill me again.

"You need to talk to her," I muttered. "I'll take the kids out for pizza. Give you two a little breathing room. You have to deal with the dogs though. I have had all the corgi I can handle today." How could such cute little creatures be such a pain in the ass?

"The roads are slippery. Be careful." Kal didn't thank me and I didn't blame him.

I wasn't much help to anyone.

Kal headed upstairs and I went into the living room where earlier, Philip and Bella had made a blanket fort. It had been assaulted by corgis and the blanket drooped in the middle. Bella and Philip were fighting the classic sibling war over possession of the remote control.

"It's my turn," Philip said making a grab for it.

"It's not. Snow day rules. You got to watch your dumb show on the last snow day."

Apparently, both Bella and Phillip's favorite cartoons were on at the same time. Maeve had sorted it out by making them take turns. According to Bella though—and she could have been BSing me—snow days meant all bets were off. Philip didn't argue with that point of logic. Then again, he was only six. I'd left them to sort it out. The argument hadn't progressed much since I'd departed to snag five minutes of peace in the kitchen.

I loved my niece and nephew. But their nonstop bickering was grating on my last nerve.

"You guys want to go out for pizza?" I asked.

One of the dogs, I thought it was Gimli but couldn't be sure, lifted his head up and stared at me.

"Not you," I told him and then felt like an idiot for talking to the dog.

"No, thanks." Bella had her mother's stubborn streak. I almost felt sorry for Philip.

Then I realized what she said. "Are you seriously turning down pizza?"

"It's my turn." Bella set her jaw.

Philip appeared torn. He wanted the pizza but letting go of the remote was like admitting defeat.

I'd miscalculated. Whenever Maeve wanted them to do something, she told them. I should have said, "We're going to get pizza." By giving them the option, they had the choice to refuse.

"Fuck," I muttered.

"That's a bad word," Bella said. "You need to put a coin in the swear jar."

"I'll get right on that," I said and retreated again.

I pulled out my phone and shot a text to Sebastian.

Siobhan: This parenting gig is harder than it looks.

I hit send and then scrolled through the other six texts I had sent him earlier. No response.

Seven unanswered texts doesn't mean anything. I told myself so I would feel a little less pathetic. It didn't work.

I wondered where he was. Court maybe. Wasn't that how television always showed them? High-priced attorneys in fancy professional suits spent most of their time in court. Or in their polished offices.

I tried not to consider the possibility that he was avoiding me. He had healed Maeve, I was certain of it. That meant he was like Brock. Maybe not a werewolf but he definitely knew about magic. The staged apartment, the fact that my using magic in front of him hadn't freaked him out the way it would a human guy who knew nothing about the hidden world.

Maeve was sick. Kal was upset because she kept him in the dark and her offspring were on the verge of killing each other. I should not be obsessing like a lovesick tween over a boy not calling me back.

But he had healed my sister. I wanted to say thank you.

You already did, Sib. In two separate unanswered texts.

"Gimli, no!" Bella shrieked. Several seconds later. "Aunt Sibby. Gimli peed on the couch."

With a sigh, I stowed the phone and went to get a bucket of water.

 he buzzing sound pulled Sebastian from his stupor. He blinked his eyes open. They itched as though he had forgotten to remove his contacts before going to bed.

Only he wasn't in his bed. He lay sprawled on the floor of his workroom.

It came back to him slowly, like fog rolling in from the water. The shifter, Bane. Killing the other magic hunter. Pouring raw power into Siobhan's sister to heal her from her injuries. Unleashing his fae essence to enthrall the doctor.

Had the healing worked? Sebastian had dumped raw power into her with little finesse. Almost too much. He'd been delirious when he had staggered out of the hospital room with barely enough power to travel back here. The last thing he remembered was setting the net in the sieve so the magic could be strained out.

He must have lost consciousness.

Siobhan.

He pushed himself up and then reached into his pocket

for his phone. The buzzing that had awakened him was the notification of an incoming text message. He remembered how to breathe when he realized that it was from her.

Siobhan: This parenting gig is harder than it looks.

His lips turned up in an involuntary smile. Something that had never occurred before he met her. Maeve must have recovered. He doubted she would be so lighthearted if her sister had died.

Did she suspect something was amiss with him? She was clever but he was counting on her joy for her sister's recovery blotting out the suspicious timing of his disappearance.

He wanted to go to her, to see her and assure himself that she was really all right. If she and her sisters had retreated back to their dwelling on the convergence, they would be safe enough.

Sebastian considered how best to respond to her latest message. The urge to apologize for being out of contact for—he checked the time—nearly twenty-seven hours rose up, foreign within him. He had never had to justify his absence to anyone before. Sebastian went where he wished when he wished and no one dared to question him.

But he could tell from the little bubbled messages on his screen that Siobhan had...missed him.

And he gave into the impulse as he typed.

Sebastian: Sorry it took me so long to get back to you. I was wrapped up in a project.

Her reply was almost immediate.

Siobhan: Were you in court? Because I was picturing you in court. In a fancy suit making a killer impression on the jury.
Sebastian: There is no jury with the dissolution of marriage. You watch too much television.

Such a fae answer. Deflecting and distracting to disguise the fact that he hadn't answered her question outright. The dark fae could lie. They weren't true fae after all. A dark fae could lie from sunrise to sunset with no repercussions. It was part of the reason they weren't trusted within the magical world.

Yet he didn't want to lie to Siobhan outright. Doing so felt...wrong.

The phone buzzed in his hand, indicating an incoming call. He knew who it was, and not because he had just been communicating with her. For a moment he considered not answering. What if she wanted to travel to him? His eyes darted around the workroom.

He hurried into the kitchen and shut the door between what had been the garage and his location before he picked up. "Siobhan."

"I don't watch television at all." She huffed and then before he could answer corrected herself. "At least, not usually. We grew up without it."

"So did I." Television hadn't been invented for a few centuries after his birth.

"Did you go overboard in your twenties too?"

In his twenties, he had been scrounging for food and trying to keep his head down to avoid being beaten. "No."

Her laugh was light. "I felt like I was missing something so I gorged on it. That was before binge-watching was a thing. So yeah, I watched a few back-to-back seasons of Law and Order. *With* commercials. I'm almost ashamed to admit it."

He closed his eyes, absorbing her words, the self-deprecating tone. He loved that Siobhan laughed at herself. Joy was her natural state. The fae and magic hunters alike took themselves far too seriously. He found he felt lighter in her presence.

"You haven't asked how Maeve is doing," Siobhan said, effectively popping the bubble that had lifted him so high.

He scrubbed a hand over his face. "I was about to—"

"I know it was you."

All the small hairs along the back of his neck rose. "I don't know what you mean."

"Look, I'm kinda up to my elbows in Corgi urine and my niece and nephew are standing by the door waiting for me to take them to get pizza so I can't go into it now. But I just wanted to say that...whatever you are. Thank you."

Whatever you are. His stomach was in knots. "Siobhan."

"I have to go. Love ya"

Then nothing.

Sebastian stared at the phone, absorbing all that had just happened. Even though his vision blurred through the dry contacts he could read the words *call has ended*.

But the message did nothing to erase her final two words.

Love ya.

She said so easily. With no real effort on her part. Did she mean it?

Sebastian set the phone down. For her sake, he hoped she didn't.

MAEVE

The sound of the shower running penetrated my dream. I rolled over and looked at the closed bathroom door.

Part of me wanted to go over to it, open it and go into the bathroom. Not for anything sordid, but just to talk. I used to talk to Kal all the time when he was in the shower. I'd brush my hair and teeth, all while chattering away. The subject didn't matter, only the connection did. Sharing a moment and space in time.

But the words were too heavy. They dragged me down, held me in place. Those soft, fluffy conversational bits escaped me. The only ones I still held would crush us both if I tossed them up in the air.

So I stayed where I was, in bed, like a human lump.

I wished I could go for a walk. But the sidewalks would be covered by refreezing ice melt. This was my life now. Every day realizing what a challenge the simplest task presented. My body trapped me and held me prisoner as much as the words I hadn't said.

I wasn't happy at the cottage. And I wasn't happy at home. Could I be happy anywhere anymore?

The bathroom door opened and Kal emerged. He wore a green bathrobe I'd bought him on our first Christmas together. The hemline hit his knees and below that, I could see the surgical scar from the accident that brought him into my life.

He spoke first. "You okay?"

"No," I said because I couldn't lie to him.

His eyebrows pulled together. "Why are you in bed? Are you sick?"

What a loaded question. Was I sick? *No. Yes. Sort of.*

I stared out the window at the purple haze of twilight. The days were so short now and still, I was sleeping them away.

I wanted to speak my truth to Kal. *My body is fighting itself to the point of utter exhaustion. I can't stop it. Nothing can stop it.*

But I chickened out. "I'm tired."

"Can I get you anything?"

The question brought tears to my eyes. He was always so good to me. He never once complained about being sent out to buy maxi pads or tampons when I needed them. He took care of me, no matter what.

And that was the hardest part to accept. That my needs were growing overwhelming. It was easier to think that he would leave me when he found out. For Harper maybe.

The anger blotted out the fear, tamped it down before my enchantress magic could sink its claws into him. "No, thank you."

"You've been avoiding me." He lowered himself onto the bed. "Why?"

It was such a simple, straightforward question. Why couldn't the answer be so to the point?

"Sibby said you think I'm having an affair."

"I'm going to kill her." Flatten her maybe. With a steamroller.

There was a smile in his voice when he spoke. "I think she knew that."

Somehow, I found the courage to look up at him. "Are you?"

He just looked at me, his expression almost pitying. I shifted, not liking the way that penetrating gaze made me feel.

"I think we should seek help."

I blinked at him. "Help?"

He nodded. "A marriage counselor."

"That's the last damn thing I need, another frigging doctor." I could envision how it would be. Kal not talking. Me not talking and paying someone else to listen to us not talk to each other. I didn't need a third party to unearth the issues that were causing the rift between us. I knew damn well what they were.

I just didn't know how to fix them.

"What do you mean?" Kal asked.

I moved to throw off the covers. When he didn't budge, I speared him with the sort of nut-shriveling glare Alys used on shady real estate agents. "I need to get ready."

"Evie?" Either Kal was made of sterner stuff or I hadn't gotten the glare exactly right because he didn't budge.

So I lashed out verbally. "How long has it been since we had sex? Because I can't remember."

A lesser man would have deflected. Put it back on me never being in the mood or being gone all the time. Both of which were accurate statements.

But Kal didn't. "Halloween."

My lips parted I remembered that night. Alys and Sibby had taken the kids out trick-or-treating. I'd been feeling sorry for myself that I was left at home missing out on the fun and doing candy detail and had gotten a little tipsy. When Kal had come through the door, I'd attacked him.

"So you knew. You knew it's been over six weeks. And you haven't said anything?"

He shrugged. Shrugged!

Shame and outrage filled my belly. "So what, are you not attracted to me anymore? Am I too fat for you now that I've had your kids?"

"You know better."

His quiet tone just made me madder. There is nothing worse than totally losing your shit in front of a completely rational person. "Is there something I'm not doing for you? Some need or fetish that we haven't explored? And here I was thinking we'd been pretty damn thorough."

He sat there, through my attack, just...taking it. All the crazy I was unleashing on him. Not getting angry, not running away.

He endured it all. Would endure it all.

It wasn't fair.

I closed my eyes, let out a breath. "I need to get ready."

"Where are you going?"

"You wouldn't believe me if I told you."

No response.

I crawled across the bed and headed into the bathroom, making sure to lock the door.

Not that I thought he would follow me for more abuse. Even a great guy like Kal had his limits.

CHAPTER TWELVE

MAEVE

"Y ou ready?" Sibby cast me an assessing glance as she stowed her phone.

"Ready to cross directly to a magical marketplace? I have no idea how to answer that." I shrugged.

I wore fleece-lined jeans and the bright red parka Kal had picked out. He always liked when I wore red. Heavy tread boots on my feet, plus a scarf, earmuffs, and gloves. Sibby was a little less bundled, wearing her motorcycle duds. We stood at the threshold of my front door, waiting to cross to the midnight market. Kal and the kids were asleep.

"Is Alys good to go?" I nodded to the pocket of her black leather jacket where she'd deposited the device.

She made a face. "Alys thinks this is stupid."

"But she's doing it, right? She and Brock?" I needed the support of my big sister.

Sibby nodded. "Under protest, but yeah, she'll be there."

I let out a breath and reached for the door. "Go over the traveling thing one more time for me."

"It's all about intention. The day is shifting and we can shift our energy. Just focus on the end result. We need to chant in unison, *take me to the midnight market*. Eleven times as the hour tolls. On the final toll, we cross the threshold."

I exhaled and cast a glance up the stairs. Gimli and Grogu lay at the top, their dark eyes watchful. "Okay."

Sibby slid her ungloved hands into mine. "It'll work, Maeve. You have to believe it will work."

I nodded and forced a smile. The clock in the hall let out a soft chime.

Sibby reached for the door. It was pushed open and a swirl of powdery snow drifted inside.

Our eyes locked and as one we chanted, "Take me to the midnight market." *Bong.* "Take me to the midnight market." *Bong.* "Take me to the midnight market." *Bong.*

We fell into a rhythm and as one, we broke eye contact and turned to face the open door.

"On the count of three." Sibby took a deep breath and raised her right foot, ready to take the leap. My sister had no doubts. She believed in magic, that when she took the step we would not be on the other side of my door, but in some fantastical marketplace for people who bought and sold magic.

Bong. "Take me to the midnight market."

Sibby squeezed my hand. "Last chime. On the count of three. One, two,"

"Evie?"

I looked back and saw Kal standing at the top of the stairs. His brow was drawn down and he stared at us as though wondering what the hell we were doing, poised on the threshold, letting all the cold air into our warm house. Time seemed to slow and stretch, warping around us. I wanted to explain. There wasn't time. Sibby had to cross because Alys would be there and without Sibby, she couldn't get home. And I was the reason for this trip. The hunt for the cure to send Ms. Priss packing.

Kal would see us vanish. Would it frighten him?

I should have told him when I'd had the chance. Now it was too late.

Bong. I turned away and said, *"Take me to the midnight market."*

I'm doing this for you, I thought and then took the step.

My foot hit sand, not the expected slick concrete. Muscle memory was thrown off and I staggered. If not for my grip on Sibby, I would have fallen on my face.

"Are you okay?" She helped pull me upright. It was too dark for me to truly see more than the shadows of her features.

I nodded. "You?"

"Not to be all I told you so but," she gestured to our surroundings.

The night sky was full of stars. It looked like a million pinpricks in a blue-black cloth that was being held up to a light source. They shone so brightly they made my eyes water to stare at them. Even in our small town, it was hard to see stars like that.

"But where's the market?" I scanned the surrounding area. No signs of life anywhere. Just rolling dunes.

"Listen," Sibby murmured. And that's when I heard it. Music. It sent a pulse through me, pounding in my blood, beckoning me onward.

"It's coming from over there. Come on."

The night air was chilly but not cold and I immediately began regretting my wardrobe choice. I shucked my jacket and draped it over my free arm as we trekked up the side of a sand dune. Sweat trickled down between my breasts and made my hair stick to the back of my neck as we climbed. It seemed to take hours but when we crested the rise, we saw the midnight market laid out before us.

The market undulated in winding paths that must have

stretched on for close to a mile. A snaking line of tents and tables and people. So many people. Hundreds. All in the middle of the desert without any way to tell how they got there. No cars or sounds of engines, no hum of electricity. But there was light. Light from fires, from what looked like a million candles, and from little floating orbs that pulsed with crackling energy. In the distance, a great bonfire blazed and I could make out small figures as they moved in time to the beat of the pounding drums.

Something deep inside me pulsed to that primal sound. I *knew* it. Even though I had never heard it before, it made me want to move. To join the dance.

"This is where you belong," the *knowing* whispered. *"This is the path you must follow to become whole."*

"Alys!" Sibby called.

I jolted as she shrieked in my ear, pulling me out of whatever trance the music had lulled me into. *The knowing* had never spoken to me in actual words before. Was it because I was in this place where the modern world seemed far away? Or had something broken free when I had stepped over the threshold?

When I'd left Kal behind.

"I should text Kal. Let him know we're all right." I said to Sibby when she tried to tug me down the hill. When I pulled out my phone, the screen remained blank.

"That's weird. I just charged it before we left. I'm sure of it."

"Magic and technology can't exist in the same space," Sibby said. "Something about conflicting energy draws. Neither works well in the other's presence. Come on, Alys didn't hear me and she looks fit to be tied."

Sure enough, Alys's familiar straight-backed figure paced in front of a lit brazier at the entrance to the market. Brock stood by her, his gaze threating any who veered too close to his mate. He touched her shoulder as she passed and pointed in our direction. I saw her shoulders relax slightly when she spotted us.

"I was worried you were lost out there," she said as she gave me a hug. "We should have all left from the cottage. It brought us right here."

"Good to know for next time," Sibby said, her eyes bright. "Come on. Let's explore."

She strode toward the gate, chin up and unafraid.

Alys caught my arm when I made to follow. "Are you sure you're all right?"

I looked over at her. "Yeah. It's just…Kal saw us leave."

To my surprise, she actually smiled a little. "I bet that threw him for a loop."

My jaw dropped. "Alys! The man just watched us disappear in front of him. And I can't even text him to let him know we're okay."

My big sister threaded her arm through mine. "It's good to keep surprising your mate. That way he'll never take you for granted."

"If the shock of it doesn't give him heart failure." Though the words were snide, I found myself smiling. The call of those drums had infected my blood and the urge to explore blotted out even my worry about Kal.

There was nothing I could do about him anyway. Not now. I might as well make the most of the market while I had the chance.

Spices and an air of festivity filled the air as we passed booth after booth. The midnight market didn't look much different than a standard craft fair. Booths and tables and in a few cases, just big blankets spread out on the sand. There was a festive air surrounding the marketplace.

I noticed a display of evergreen wreaths and pointed.

"It's almost Yule," Sibby explained.

"The market is always busier around a Sabbat," Brock added.

I cocked my head at him. "Sabbats? Dare I ask?"

To my surprise, it was Alys who answered. "The Sabbats are the eight pagan festivals that make up the wheel of the year. Yule is the next one and marks the longest night of the year."

"I'm impressed," Sibby said. "You've been studying your witchery."

Alys shrugged. "It was in several of Aunt Jess's books."

"What are the other festivals?" My gaze fell on a display of crystals in all shapes and sizes.

"Imbolc or Candalmas follows Yule in mid-winter. Then Ostara is on the Spring Equinox, Beltane, Litha or the Summer Solstice, Lammas, Mabon also known as the Witches' Thanksgiving, and Samhain marks the start and end of the year."

"So, does that mean that since we're all witchy now, we have to stop celebrating Christmas?" Sibby asked. "Because I got to tell you, my Amazon wish list could choke a donkey."

"Why not celebrate both if it makes you happy?" Brock advised.

"I like the way you think, Hottie McNibblet." Sibby winked at him.

"Stop calling him that," Alys warned. "I mean it, Sibby."

There were no hoary wart-covered witches visible. The pathways were lined with completely normal-looking people. Some were even model beautiful. I found myself staring at one man with golden hair and sapphire eyes. Something about him seemed oddly familiar though I was sure I'd never seen him before. He was with a plump but pretty brunette around my age. When he caught my gaze he winked.

"Do you know who that is?" I asked Brock.

The werewolf turned in the direction I indicated. "He's a fae prince. Or rather he was."

"And the woman?" I studied her curiously. She looked so normal, like a mom I would meet at a PTO fundraiser, not the kind of chick I would expect to run across at a magical bizarre.

"She's the mortal who tricked him out of his powers." Brock grinned. "Undid centuries' worth of his bargains. She's something of a legend in the community. Would you like me to introduce you?"

I was about to say yes, but Alys was tugging on my sleeve. "Do you see Sibby?"

I scanned the crowd but at five foot four, I was at a serious disadvantage. "I can't."

"She's down the end of this row," Brock threaded his fingers through Alys's and tugged her forward. She had a grip on my sleeve and I was forced to follow.

Sibby stood in front of a booth that looked to be constructed mostly out of driftwood. *Seaside Healing* was hand-painted on the front of the booth. The tabletop was covered with sea glass amulets, ropes of seaweed, barnacle encrusted line, and jars of sea salt in every color. Two braziers stood with flickering green flames from a driftwood fire. As we grew closer, I could swear I caught a whiff of low tide, even though the ocean was nowhere in sight.

The man behind the booth was short and stocky with sausage-like fingers. He held up a bottle full of blue-black minerals for Sibby's inspection. "A collection of sands from beneath the seven seas. Perfect for increasing stamina."

"You can't run off like that," Alys hissed at Sibby.

"I'm not a wayward child, Alys." Sibby shrugged her off and returned her attention to the vendor.

Alys cast a nervous glance around. "We need to stick together."

I *knew* how she was feeling. Nervous, exposed, out of her depth. Alys didn't like being forced into situations she couldn't control. Even with Brock by her side and us within her sight, she couldn't wait to get out of here.

Not me. My eyes slid shut and I breathed it all in. Being at the market felt...right.

A flash of memory surfaced. A booth with a green and gold cloth. Bunches of dried herbs hanging from the support that held the canopy up. Mugwort wands, bunches of sage for smudging, calendula oil and rosehip infusions. Bottles of dried herbs and spices. I recalled the silver crescent moon ring she wore when filling out the price tags. "Aunt Jess brought me here."

Alys stared at me. "What? When?"

I shook my head. "I don't know. It's like the memory with Ethan. It's buried deep down. I think maybe she used to sell her herbs here."

"I've got just the thing for memory spells." Having overheard us, the vendor reached beneath the counter and pulled out a fishbowl full of aquamarine-colored crystals. "Gemstones from the deepest trench—"

"Thanks, but we want to keep on task," Sibby said. "We need a cure for chronic illness."

"You be needing a Healer then. One of them who've been trained at the temple of the Mother Superior of Magic."

"The Mother Superior of Magic?" I repeated the title. "She sounds like the big time."

"Oh that she be. If she even exists." The vendor had a raspy chuckle.

"What do you mean?"

The vendor of all things sea turned to look at me and I noticed his eyes were larger than normal and almost egglike in shape. "Some say she's a legend. She's never been seen. But the Healers from her temple are second to none. It's rumored that if they work together, they could command death itself."

"Where can we find the healers?" Alys asked.

"They're usually by the bonfire." Another customer approached and seeing as we weren't interested in buying his trinkets, he turned away from us.

"Have you ever heard of this Mother Superior of Magic?" Alys asked Brock.

"It's like he said. Rumor mostly. No one knows who she is or where she came from. There's a temple was constructed in her honor. All official healers are said to have studied there."

"How will we recognize them?" I asked.

"They wear navy cloaks embroidered with stars over white robes." Brock hesitated and moved us away from the passing crowd of people. "Healers often work directly for the council. It might not be the best idea to reveal your identity to them while there is a bounty on your magic. We could come back after the Beltane rites. When you've been officially accepted into the magical community."

Both Sibby and Alys looked at me. They didn't say anything but I knew they were waiting for me to make the call. Beltane was the spring festival. A season away. By that point, it would have been more than a year from the onset of my initial symptoms.

But could I ask my sisters to keep risking themselves for me?

"I want to see if they are here," I said. *The knowing* was like a fishhook in the center of my body, pulling me to the bonfire.

"We're already here," Sibby said hesitantly. "The damage has already been done."

Alys nodded. "In for a penny and all that. We're here for a cure. So we're not leaving until we've exhausted all of our options."

Tears stung my eyes. "I love you guys."

"Okay, don't get all mushy." Sibby cautioned. "We'll draw a crowd. Better if we head down this row toward the bonfire and—"

She paused and broke off.

"What is it?" Alys followed her gaze.

Sibby shook her head. "I thought I saw—" she shook her head. "Never mind. Let's go find us some healers."

The heat grew more intense as we drew nearer the bonfire. Flames licked upward toward the sky as tall as my house and twice as wide. I was mesmerized by the movement and the way the dancers seemed able to instinctively move in unison with the powerful element.

Sibby shucked her motorcycle jacket. The metal of her eyebrow rings glinted in the firelight. "This is…they do this every night?"

Brock nodded. "Though the dancers change. It's whoever is called to move with the spirit of the flames. They show up when the market opens and dance until the fire is extinguished. It gives thanks to the element and signals welcome to all who come in peace."

As I watched some of the dancers stripped off their clothes and moved even closer to the fire. "If they're not careful they'll—"

The fire consumed them.

Alys gasped and I clapped my hands over my mouth, staring at the place where they had been. Sibby laughed.

"They're fire fae," she said as she moved forward. "I read about them. Don't worry. They're fine. Look."

Sure enough, the dancers swayed out of the inferno, seemingly without so much as a single singed hair.

Alys and Brock stepped closer to the fire.

I let out a shaky breath. "I don't know how much more of this heat I can take. I'm going to wait over there." I pointed to a spot several yards away from the dancing.

"Do you want me to come with you?" Alys asked.

"Nah, I just need a minute to collect myself away from the heat."

"Okay, well, keep your eyes peeled for any healers in blue cloaks."

I gave her a jaunty salute and watched as she threaded her fingers through Brock's and moved closer to the magical blaze.

I scanned the crowd but didn't see anyone wearing an ensemble like the one Brock had described. I pinched the bridge of my nose. We should just get out of here before—

A hand clapped over my mouth and dragged me into the shadows.

CHAPTER THIRTEEN

here had been one moment where the crowd at the market had parted and Siobhan's gaze had landed on him. Sebastian had gathered the shadows to him and muttered a blending spell then hurried away. With luck she would believe the sighting was no more than her imagination.

He was swathed in a voluminous robe and his eyes were unshielded by the contacts that muted his natural color, but he knew she had recognized him. The same way he had been able to easily pick her out from the crowd. Something about her drew him like he was a magnet.

She was his true north.

Siobhan knew he had healed her sister. She'd admitted as much on the phone. What else did the intuitive little witch know?

And what the hell is she doing here?

Sebastian had lost count of the number of times he'd asked himself that question. The answer eluded him. The werewolf alpha was with them. Surely Brock had warned them of the danger?

144

Sebastian had already spotted three other magic hunters in the throng. One of them was the Headhunter. No one knew his true name. In a world of mystics and magic, he was one of the secrets that no one could discover.

No one living anyway.

Had the Headhunter followed the witches to the market? Or was his presence an unlucky coincidence?

When a mutual contact had reported that the sisters were at the midnight market, Sebastian had donned the robe and traveled to the spot directly. The magic he had lifted from Bane hadn't been fully absorbed into his talisman, but it was enough.

Siobhan and her sisters moved toward the great bonfire. He saw her clap her hands in delight at the fae fire dancers that wove in and out of the flames.

"I'm surprised to see you here, Sebastian," a lilting voice said from behind him. "Rumor had it you were dead."

Blanking his expression, Sebastian turned and stared into the sapphire gaze of Robin Goodfellow. "And rumor held that you and your mate had given up magic. So much for trusting to rumor."

"It's true, my mate has given up magic." Robin smiled dopily at the mortal woman who stood at a table haggling with a stoop-shouldered vendor. "But the female does enjoy her little trinkets. Her curiosity is insatiable."

Sebastian sincerely hoped he didn't look as ridiculous when gazing upon Siobhan. "And you indulge her? Even though you know the sort of scum that lurks around this place? And who they report to?"

Robin kept his gaze on his female as he muttered, "She's dead, Sebastian. My mother can't hurt us anymore."

It was as Bane had said then. It took all of his strength of will to hold his position when his knees threatened to turn to water.

"Who?" The word came out as a croak.

Robin nodded to his female.

Sebastian looked at her again. The woman looked as unremarkable as so many others. "Impossible."

"It was Andreas who struck the final blow. But he wouldn't have had the opportunity if not for Joey."

"Then she's the new fae queen."

Robin shook his head. "I told you, brother. Joey doesn't want to rule."

"I'm not your brother," Sebastian snarled. "I was your mother's plaything. Until she grew bored and discarded me. That doesn't make us kin."

The expression Robin wore looked suspiciously like pity. "We were forged in a mutual fire, Sebastian. If you ever have the need, you can call on me."

Sebastian tilted his head to the side. "That's it? An offer, not a bargain or power-play? You have changed, Robin Goodfellow."

"For the better, brother. If you'll excuse me." Robin moved toward his mate, who triumphantly brandished a ring with a sapphire stone. As Sebastian watched, Robin slid a protective hand over her midsection.

She was with child then. A mortal and a fae could conceive only one sort of child.

One like Sebastian. A changeling.

Yet Robin didn't look appalled at the idea. He appeared proud.

The fae prince truly had changed.

Witnessing so much open affection made Sebastian uncomfortable. He turned back to his goal and scanned the beings around the bonfire.

Alys and her werewolf were dancing to the beat of the drums but there was no sign of Maeve or Siobhan.

If he were hunting the sisters for their magic, this would

be the perfect opportunity to pick them off one by one. Separated, no one would notice they were gone until after the deed was done, the soul lost for eternity.

It was how the best magic hunters worked. And after Sebastian himself, the Headhunter was the best magic hunter in the business.

Sebastian plunged into the crowd and prayed to the gods that had forsaken him long ago, that he wasn't too late.

MAEVE

I struggled against the confining grip, glad for once that my panic would trigger my enchantress magic. Then, whoever had me would submit to my will in that trance-like way.

Except even as my panic spiked, the grip on me didn't relent. I struggled harder, adrenaline pumping through my nervous system by the bucketful. Nothing changed. My captor dragged me away from the life and light of the fire and around a bend. My feet sank uselessly into the sand that didn't seem to slow the brute down at all.

The hospital had once brought in a self-defense instructor, to help train those that worked the night shift. The memories were buried deep, but I had gone to every lesson and while my brain was hazy, my muscles recalled what they were supposed to do.

The heel of my boot stomped down on the instep, even as my elbow drove back into my abductor's solar plexus.

A *whoosh* of air escaped and the arms that held me relaxed. I wriggled free and got ready to run, praying Ms. Priss wouldn't decide to trip me up as I made my escape.

"I've been searching for you, Maeve Silver. It is not safe for you here."

The smooth feminine voice came from the shadows. I hesitated and the brute that had grabbed me straightened.

"Enough, Deck," the woman with the soft voice moved into the light in a graceful, gliding motion. "Maeve is to be treated with the utmost respect. It is Her will."

I saw the blue robe embroidered with silver stars. She wore a silver necklace with a pentacle between her breasts and a crescent moon was suspended between her brows with a silver chain. She was older than I would have assumed, based on her voice. Her hair was long and gray with only a few strands of jet threaded through.

"You're a healer?" The garments were exactly like Brock had described, yet I wanted to be sure.

"Yes. I came here tonight to find you in Her name."

"Her who?" I asked.

"The Mother Superior of Magic." Her eyes were dark brown flecked with hints of moss green. "She has been watching you and your sisters since you were young. You are awakening into your strength. And she has a gift for you."

"What sort of gift?" The woman sounded like a zealot. Like the nutters that hung around airports chanting and spreading the word. It wasn't *at all* creepy that her mysterious She had been quote "watching over me" like some sort of stalker.

"A healing amulet that will help end your struggle for good."

My lips parted. "You can cure my MS?"

She shook her head. "I cannot, no."

"But you have something that will?" I wanted to reach out and grip her by her bony shoulders and shake until she coughed up whatever magical item it was that promised to give me my life back.

"The amulet of healing is locked deep within Her sacred space. No one but the bearer may claim it."

"And where exactly is this sacred space?"

"The Amazon River basin."

My lips parted. "You want me to go to South America? To the rainforest?"

The priestess appeared surprised. "Not I. The Mother Superior of Magic. You must come to her. Your journey will reveal all and you must appear unto her before the new moon. Let your soul guide you to the place you need to be."

I let out a breath. The Amazon. "I have problems with the paved walkway outside my house some days. I can't go tearing off through the jungle on my own."

"Trust that She will watch over you. Use the gifts at your disposal and she will provide the rest." The priestess glanced away. "Leave this place, Maeve Silver. It is not safe for you here."

"Wait," I reached out. She couldn't leave me like this, baffled and needing more information.

The priestess turned away and put her hand on the brute's shoulder. They took a step and the shadows seemed to reach out and engulf them.

I stood there, stunned and shaken. The Amazon. There was no way I could make that happen.

"Maeve?" It was Sibby's voice that carried over the drums.

"Here." The word was faint as I had no will to call out. But Sibby heard me anyway.

"What are you doing here all alone?" Sibby asked.

I just looked at her.

"Come on. I think it's time we all went home." I let Sibby tow me away from the shadows where the priestess had been.

The Amazon. There was no way.

✳

"There's no way," Alys said as she paced the confines of the greenhouse. "We have no idea who this so-called Mother Superior of Magic is or what she's after. That healer could be one of those damn magic hunters for all we know."

I looked over at her. "If she was a magic hunter, why didn't she just suck out my soul then and there?"

Alys looked flushed. Sibby and I had found her and Brock dirty dancing in front of the bonfire. If I hadn't still been in shock, I probably would have remarked on her uncharacteristic behavior.

Sibby had stepped up.

"Grind on your own time, you two." My youngest sister had snagged Alys by the arm and then transported us back to the cottage. Brock was out in the living room and the three of us had retreated to the greenhouse where I had done my best to explain the inexplicable.

"Maeve, we're talking major travel here. The heat can exacerbate your MS, never mind what the stress will do to you. And the Amazon River basin is massive. It spans half a dozen countries and the whole width of the continent. If it's a sacred protected temple it's not like we can stop and ask for directions. How will we know where to go?"

"With this," Sibby held out her hand. In it was a clear quartz crystal attached to a silver chain. The pendulum had belonged to our mother and worked well with maps.

Alys huffed out a breath. "It's a bad idea. Do you even have a passport, Maeve?"

I shook my head. I'd never been out of the continental US.

"Hello, witchcraft?" Sibby held up her hands. "My mode of transportation doesn't require us to go through customs, Alys."

Alys rounded on her. Hand planted on one hip, the other with a finger raised in warning. "Don't be glib about this. There are other considerations too. Supplies, vaccinations, transportation to the location. We have a business to run. Maeve has a family that will know she's gone. And have you forgotten about the magic hunters?"

"Hey, I wasn't the one who was getting all frisky with McNibblet in the middle of the midnight market."

Alys blushed to her roots. "We were just dancing."

"You were about six seconds away from orgasming in public." Sibby lifted her chin as though daring Alys to contradict her.

"It's the full moon," Alys said. "And the drums. It ...did things to him."

Sibby held up her hand. "As much as I want to hear about your werewolf's monthly cycle, we have a decision to make. So let's vote. Do we trust this healer and go to the Amazon?"

Alys shook her head. "We still don't know if we can trust this woman not to lead us into a trap. I vote no."

"I vote yes," Sibby said. "It's worth the risk if it cures Maeve."

They both turned to look at me.

I had always been the tie-breaker. The one who made the call when the unstoppable force met the immovable object. If I said we should do this, then they would both come with me. Would risk themselves.

I stared out at the full moon. Part of me wanted to refuse. To wait. As eager as I was for the cure, I didn't want to put my sisters in danger of having their magic stolen and their souls obliterated.

But the healer had said I needed to be at the temple by the new moon or I risked losing the cure forever.

I looked up and held Alys's gaze. My cautious older sister saw it as her job to keep us safe from any harm. "I vote yes."

Alys closed her eyes and nodded. "I'll make the arrangements then." The greenhouse door opened and shut, leaving me alone with Sibby.

Sibby drew me into a hug. "Brave Maeve. I'm proud of you. Want me to pop you home so you can talk to Kal?"

I shook my head. "I'll call him."

She pulled back. "Are you sure? One more trip can't hurt anything."

I shook my head. "If I see Kal, all of my resolve will melt away."

She nodded. "Okay, I'll give you some privacy."

I waited until the greenhouse door shut behind her and then pulled out my phone. It was after three in the morning, but I knew he'd be awake.

Kal answered on the first ring. "Evie."

"I'm sorry," I said. And then winced. I hadn't meant to begin with an apology. It sounded as though I had something to feel guilty about. "I needed to go right then or it wouldn't have worked."

"What wouldn't have worked?" His voice was low and soft. No condemnation.

I took a deep breath. "The magic."

Kal said nothing.

"I'm a witch. So are my sisters. We're the latest in a long line of them, apparently. My mom was, too. We just found out a few weeks ago." I took a breath. "I'm so sorry I didn't tell you sooner. I've been…processing."

"A witch," Kal said slowly.

"It's kind of a big deal," I gripped the phone tightly. "When I'm scared it triggers my powers. I'm an enchantress. When it activates, it turns people into mindless zombies. I didn't want that to happen to you or the kids."

"And that's why you've been staying away? Because you

154

were worried about enchanting us?" There was a note of hope in his tone.

How to answer that question honestly. "That's a big part of it."

"What's the rest?"

"Kal," I ground out, frustrated because of course one huge life-altering reveal wasn't enough. I could never give to Kal in half measures. He demanded my all. "I just revealed a huge secret here. If this got out, my sisters and I could be in serious trouble."

"Did you really think I would tell someone?" His tone was full of hurt. "That I would run off to the tabloids?"

"Of course not," I reassured him. "I trust you."

"Do you?" His tone wasn't snide. Kal didn't do snide. It was a simple question with a very complicated answer.

My chest felt tight. Wasn't confession supposed to be good for the soul? But instead of feeling unburdened, the truth about Ms. Priss smushed me down even harder.

I let out a slow breath. "Look, I need to go away for a few weeks. With my sisters. More magic stuff."

"When?"

My throat closed up. "Tomorrow."

He didn't ask where I was going and I didn't offer anything else.

"I'll tell Bella and Philip in the morning." He sounded resigned.

"Kal?"

"Just promise me something, Evie."

"What?" I whispered.

"When you come back? Come all the way back."

The breath shook as I exhaled. "It's a deal."

CHAPTER FOURTEEN

SIOBHAN

"Maeve's asleep," I said as I returned to my seat in the front of the private jet. Alys had chartered it for our trip to Brazil. I had to give her credit. When Maeve made the decision to venture to South America, Alys had made it happen. She'd called Lora and arranged for her to put *Silver Demo and Design* on standby. Brock would continue to oversee the updates on the Mid-century Modern. And then there was this jet complete with pilot, copilot, and one very helpful flight attendant who had shown us the private bedroom where Maeve could rest and prepare for whatever came next.

Sometimes I forgot exactly how much money Alys had at her disposal. Considering she lived in Aunt Jess's cottage and was never flashy or ostentatious with her money, it was easy to overlook. The fact that with just a few phone calls she could set all this up blew my mind.

As if Alys by herself wasn't intimidating enough.

"How much money do you have?" I asked.

She rolled her eyes. "A bit."

I gestured around. "This isn't nest-egg money, Alys. Come on, just between us. What's your net worth?"

"If you need money, Sibby, just tell me."

I turned my gaze out the oblong window. The ground was invisible from our altitude. "I don't need money."

I started when she put her hand on mine. "What do you need?"

I looked up into her clear blue eyes. She had a few fine lines that winged out from the corners, but otherwise, my oldest sister didn't look half a century old.

But there was something wise about her. Especially since she'd taken up with Brock. He had softened her rough edges.

"When I figure it out, you'll be the first to know."

She let it drop and pulled back her hand. "So, this is the largest town to the river," Alys said as she considered the map displayed on her tablet. "It's about a forty-minute trek via Jeep from the closest landing strip."

I studied the map. "We need to get downriver."

"I've chartered a boat which will head deeper into the jungle." She scrubbed her hand over her eyes. "I still say this is a bad idea. We don't speak Portuguese."

"Actually," I said. "I do."

She blinked at me. "When did you learn that?"

"I worked in a restaurant in San Francisco. The owner was Portuguese. She taught me the language. And how to make the best tomato rice you've ever tasted."

"Still, there'll be inconsistencies. I doubt Brazilian Portuguese is exactly the same."

I leaned back in my seat and closed my eyes. "Would you relax? We're as prepared for this trip as we can be, considering the circumstances."

She huffed out a breath. "I'm worried."

I craned my neck and lifted my lids. "About Maeve? I think she's holding up pretty well."

"About all of us." She darted a glance to the front of the plane to make sure we wouldn't be overheard. "The only way we'll find the temple is by using magic. And using magic will draw the magic hunters down on us."

"If that happens, I'll jump us home. I don't see what the problem is."

Alys opened her mouth to respond but her phone rang. "It's Brock. He might have news about Nate."

She rose out of her seat and headed toward the front of the plane. On impulse, I reached for my own phone and turned it on. I was used to keeping it in airplane mode when I traveled but if Alys could talk to her McNibblet, I could send Sebastian a quick text.

Siobhan: Heading to Brazil. Do you want me to bring you back anything?

Three dots appeared immediately and a moment later my cell buzzed with an incoming text.

Sebastian: What's in Brazil?

Siobhan: The Mother Superior of Magic. You ever hear of her?

It was a risk, asking him about her. I still didn't know how Sebastian tied in with the magical world. Or why he hadn't told me. But some instinct nudged me to reveal our destination to him.

"Sibby," Alys snapped. "Turn off your phone before we crash."

"You're on the phone," I pointed out. "Why is it okay for you but not for me?"

"I'm talking, not texting. And this phone was provided by the pilot."

"Of course it was," I grumbled and powered down my phone.

She made a face then said, "Brock, I have to go. My sister is being difficult."

I turned back to the window. "It's the only way I know how to operate."

MAEVE

I knew it was a dream the second I looked up from the medical text and spied Aunt Jess. Part of me was very aware that the woman who had finished raising us, my mother's best friend, had been gone for almost two decades. But I smiled when I saw her bundled up in her favorite pashmina, a gold and burgundy wrap that complimented her dark skin. She was supposed to be with me at the moment. I accepted her presence and let my awareness of the dream fade.

"Every time I see you, you are working." Her creole heritage was thick in her voice, even though she had been in Eckhart since before I was born.

"What are you doing? You shouldn't be out of bed." I leapt up to angle the chair at the dining room table so she had an easier time sitting down.

"I'll rest when I'm dead, for true." She shuffled forward, her thin legs disappearing into enormous slippers. She dragged her IV pole along with her. Cancer had stolen pounds from her once supple frame and she appeared more fragile than I could ever remember seeing her. Ovarian cancer was a fast-moving thief. She seemed to have withered overnight.

"Actually, I'm researching." Once she was settled, I returned to my seat and lifted the book so she could see the spine.

She squinted and then shook her head. "Homeopathic pain management? I'm fine, you. The doctors have given me the good stuff. Plus, I've got a few tricks up my sleeve."

I knew she was talking about the greenhouse. On the rare occasion that the hospice nurse had to leave before I got home, I'd found Aunt Jess puttering around her former workspace. I'd guided her back to bed but she'd eaten a little and seemed to sleep easier. Did I want to know what she did in there? Not really. I'd just been glad that whatever it was, it gave her some relief.

"Believe it or not, not everything is about you," I winked at her.

Jess didn't have hair on her eyebrows, not since the chemo took hold. But she had me draw them on so she didn't look lopsided. I'd done my best. Her penciled-on brows rose at my words. "You've got a patient more difficult than me?"

"He's not difficult. He's resolute. And he's not a patient. Not my patient anyway."

"Is this the boy you rescued like a superhero out of the movies?"

"He's not a boy. He's a man." A stubborn one. Kal was just starting physical therapy. Though the bone break was still healing, Kal needed to move as much as he could so his muscles didn't atrophy. But because he wouldn't take pain meds, the work left him sweating and shaking in agony.

It broke my heart to see. And he had another session scheduled for the afternoon.

"A man." Jess tipped her head to the side and narrowed her gaze on me. "You're falling for him, for true."

My lips parted and half a dozen protests surfaced. I barely knew him. Sure, I admired Kal. Even his conviction that it was better to suffer than risk addiction was admirable. Everyone I knew avoided pain as often as possible. I was just helping him out because he seemed so alone. Because something about him spoke to me.

But I could never lie to Jess.

"Yeah, I think I am. And I really want to help him."

"That's your gift, Maeve. You're a natural-born healer. But some things you can't fix."

I squeezed her hand, figuring she was talking about her cancer. "Is there anything you can think of? Any sort of homeopathic remedy?" Aunt Jess had been a botanist with a specialty in horticulture. She had forgotten more about plants and herbs than I ever hoped to know.

She smirked at me. "I do know one thing that works, for true."

"What is it? I'll do anything."

"Pleasure. There's nothing more homeopathic than that."

My mouth fell open. "But—"

"You wanted to know. Said you would do anything." She was having too much fun with my discomfort.

A knock sounded on the door and Barbara, the hospice nurse, let herself in. "Hello? I see someone is feeling better today."

"Better is a relative term." Aunt Jess was starting to slump forward a little, her body spent from her trek to the dining room table.

"Help me get her back in bed." Together, Barbara and I half carried Jess and her IV pole back into her bedroom. Once she was settled, I tucked the blankets up around her and was about to turn to go when she gripped my arm. "Bottom drawer of the nightstand. The blue bottle."

I opened the drawer and found the bottle. It was sealed

with red wax and there was no label on it. "What do you need this for?"

"Not for me. For your young man. It's a special oil. Dried calendula with hints of vanilla and clove. Works best when applied with a loving hand." Her eyes were wicked.

"You're incorrigible," I said and dropped a kiss onto her headscarf. "Try to rest. I'll see if I can find a male prostitute to service you."

She snickered. "Trust your gut, Maeve. It won't do you dirty."

I considered her words all the way to Kal's. She wasn't wrong. An orgasm would release endorphins and help Kal relax and ease the discomfort. But could I bring myself to suggest it?

My cell phone rang just as I pulled up in front of the project house.

"Hello?"

"Hey," Alys said. "Sorry, I haven't had a chance to return your call. Work's been crazy."

"No problem." I winced at myself in the rearview mirror. I'd intentionally been leaving vague messages when I knew Alys would be busy because I hadn't wanted a confrontation about Kal. But it looked like the time had come.

"So you said you had some news about the house? Nothing bad, I hope. I was a little worried about the pipes freezing with no one living there."

I cleared my throat. "Actually, I sort of solved that problem."

"Really?"

"Yeah, I have someone living in the house. Temporarily."

"Like a house sitter?" Alys sounded skeptical. "Because you know we should really draw up a contract in case anything happens and they decide to sue—"

"Not a house sitter. A guy I met."

Silence.

"He was in an accident and he needed a place to stay," I told my sister. "I'm checking on him every day and it's only temporary."

"Who is he?"

"Kal."

"Give me his last name." I could hear the distinctive click of keys on a keyboard. "I'll hire a PI and run a background check. Make sure he doesn't have a record."

"He doesn't have a last name."

"What sort of person—"

"He's Inuit. His tribe doesn't believe in family names." I huffed out a breath.

"How convenient," Her voice dripped scorn.

"Don't you trust my judgment?"

"Maeve," Alys said patiently as though I were a simple-minded child. "He could be a con artist."

"A con artist who intentionally broke his leg on the off chance that I would feel sorry for him and let him stay in the house that didn't close when it was supposed to?"

"You never know."

My sister lived in a very dark world. Every stranger and most of the people she knew posed a threat.

"I do know. He's a good man, Alys. And it's only temporary until he heals up."

"Maeve," she said, sounding as though she were mustering her last shred of patience. "I'm coming up next Friday. We'll talk about it then. Now I'm late for a meeting."

I hung up and then thunked my head back against the car seat. Damn it, I hated when she talked to me in that tone. Like I was a few bricks shy of a load. She was always so sure and I....

Well, truth be told, I winged it. A lot.

Alys's doubts made me doubt my instincts and every gut

decision I'd made. Even though I knew Kal didn't pose a threat, I still found myself eyeing the house.

Trust your gut, Maeve. It won't do you dirty. Aunt Jess had faith in me. I should have a little more in myself. But I didn't know if I had enough faith to boldly announce to Kal that he needed to orgasm to suppress his pain. It sounded like the world's worst pick-up line. Just the thought of that conversation had my cheeks heating.

Maybe I could…suggest that it would help. Just give him the bottle of oil. Then he could take care of matters himself.

Dollars to doughnuts he was already taking care of business. Men were like jackrabbits when it came to masturbation, weren't they? That's why internet porn was so popular.

Okay, so saying something was probably redundant. I had myself well and truly talked out of even mentioning it by the time I picked my way up the path to the front door. I knocked three times before using my key.

"Kal?" I asked as I stepped inside. "Are you ready to go?"

Normally on PT day, he was dressed and waiting for me in the living room. But the space was dark, with no sign of him.

I heard the groan from the back bedroom and hurried down the hall.

The shades were drawn but there was enough light to see. Kal was sprawled in bed, his face pinched with pain. He wore black sweats but the skin of his chest and arms along with his forehead was dotted with sweat.

"Kal!" I rushed to his side. "Did something happen? Did you fall?"

His dark eyes fixed on my face. "No. I couldn't sleep."

I read between the lines. Fatigue made the pain worse. If he couldn't escape into sleep, and I knew there was no way he would take a sleeping pill to do that, he would just continue to feel worse and worse. Without the physical therapy, his recovery would take longer, which could lead to depression, less sleep, more pain.

The blue bottle was still in my pocket.

Trust your gut, Maeve.

Slowly, I extracted it and placed it on the bedside table. "Will you let me try something?"

"No meds," he rasped.

"No meds," I agreed and took off my coat. "Here's what we're going to do."

CHAPTER FIFTEEN

MAEVE

Someone shook my shoulder. The motion startled me out of my dream/memory of Kal. "Maeve. Wake up. We're here."

"Where's here?" I cracked an eyelid. "And when did you dye your hair purple?"

She held up two fingers. "To answer your first question, technically, here is in the air above the private airstrip outside Tabatinga, Brazil. Because we're trying to fly our brooms under the radar, we can't go through the international airport."

"And the hair?"

She shrugged. "There wasn't anything else to do on the trip other than listening to Alys fret. Besides, my roots were showing."

"Can't have that."

My mind was foggy from too much sleep and I had been too caught up in everything that had happened to ask questions or give input. "Why Brazil?"

"Alys will explain it all when you're strapped in for landing. Now hop to so we can get the hell off this plane. I'm going stir-crazy." She bounced up and then exited through the curtain that led to the main cabin.

I moved much more slowly. Half of my brain was stuck in the past, with Kal and the first time we'd been intimate. The rest of me was soon to touch down in Brazil and go hunting for a hidden temple in the Amazon rainforest.

"Get it together, Maeve." I breathed and then got to my feet and headed for the front of the plane.

Alys glared at Sibby's fresh dye job and then gestured for me to take the seat near hers.

"So, where exactly are we? The Amazon is huge and spans several countries.

"I know." She pulled open a map. "We are here. The private landing strip is about thirty miles from Tabatinga. It was as close as I could get us without going through an international airport."

"Tabatinga?" I repeated.

Alys nodded. "Tabatinga borders Peru and Columbia and while the main language is Portuguese, there will be some native Spanish speakers as well so my college language requirement might help me muddle through."

I had taken the same two semesters worth of language. "All I remember is *Dónde está el baño,*"

Sibby laughed. "Well, it is always helpful to know where the nearest bathroom is."

Alys gave her a level stare. "Don't tell me. You speak Spanish too."

Sibby held her fingers about an inch apart. "*Muy poco.*"

"Very little." I made a face. "This is going to be a disaster."

"Stop that," Sibby snapped. "The last thing we need you to do is manifest negative energy. Here, I made these for all of us."

She handed me a necklace on a black cord. It had a single dark stone, smoothed and polished tethered to the cord with copper wire. When I held it to the bright light streaming through the window, I could see striations within ranging from a deep amber hue to gold to brown.

"Pretty, in a witchy kind of way." Alys studied hers. "What's the stone?"

"It's onyx. The stone is supposed to give focus to help achieve goals, give physical vitality, as well as offer protection." She tied a knot in her own necklace cord and then slipped it over her head. "All stuff I thought would come in handy. There's an affirmation, too. *I will stay the course and accomplish my goal.*"

I wanted to laugh. Three necklaces and an affirmation up against the world's largest rainforest, Ms. Priss, and a ticking clock.

I didn't though. Sibby was doing what she could to help me, as was Alys. It wasn't their fault I wanted to follow the wild goose of a priestess into the dark heart of the rainforest. After taking a deep breath I muttered, "I will stay the course and accomplish my goal. Thanks, Sib."

Alys returned to studying her map. Sibby dug through her bag for gum. Instead of wearing her stone as a necklace, I wrapped the cord around my wrist so I could see it more clearly. A reminder that I had some awesome sisters, even if they were completely unhinged.

My ears popped several times as the jet cut through the clouds. The "airstrip" was more of a long stretch of dirt where the jungle had been cut back and away just enough to give the plane clearance to land. There was a sleek metal hanger on one end, large enough to hold a few other aircrafts.

Sibby was out of her seat the second the jet stopped rolling and she beat the flight attendant to the door. My legs felt shaky and Alys gave me a worried glance as she noticed my struggle.

"I'm fine," I told her.

She held out a hand. "Promise you'll say something if you aren't?"

I met her gaze and nodded. "I promise."

The heat hit me like a wet dishrag to the face. Within the last twenty-four hours, I'd endured a mountain winter, a desert night, and now the humidity of the rainforest. At least I'd had the presence of mind to change out of my fleecy jeans. Instead, I wore a black tank top beneath a white button-down shirt and a pair of lightweight cargo pants that Sibby had retrieved from my house in an old knapsack. I'd kept the boots though and added a few extra changes of socks as well as tampons and pads because of frigging course my cycle was due soon. Just to add another level of challenge to our journey.

Sibby handed me my pack and then put on her own. She pulled a dark blue baseball cap over her purple hair.

I had no doubt that Sibby's bag was full of witchy items as well as her clothing. Alys had a first-aid kit, the map, our mother's crystal, a compass, and potable water as well as protein bars. I knew because she had an inventory list she had gone over before we'd left for the airport. Her trekking through the jungle ensemble was all khaki and came with one of those funky dome hats.

There was a jeep waiting for us in the hanger and a driver who introduced himself as Paulo. Alys helped me climb in, she sat next to Paulo and Sibby scrambled up next to me. A few minutes later we were heading up what looked more like a mule trail than a road on our way to Tabatinga.

Not wanting to mention magic in front of Paulo, I focused on the scenery. My natural affinity for plants hadn't prepared me for such wonder. An odd sort of giddiness replaced my trepidation. We were in the freaking Amazon!

Everywhere I looked teamed with life in all different

cycles and phases. The canopy was thick overhead, making it feel more like late evening rather than noon. The towering Kopack trees stood head and shoulders above the rest. Brazil nut trees, palms, and the infamous Hevea trees, the sap of which was instrumental in the Rubber boom days of the nineteenth century.

"Look, there's a macaw," Sibby had clapped her hand over her hat to keep it from flying off as we bumped along over ancient root systems.

I turned in the direction she was pointing and spied the brilliant yellow and blue feathers of the gorgeous bird a moment before it took flight. A feather the color of sunshine drifted down and Sibby reached out a hand as Paulo slowed the vehicle to crawl over uneven terrain. The feather landed in her palm as though that had been its intended destination all along.

Sloths hung from limbs and insects zipped about. I spied at least three hummingbirds and several spider monkeys.

And the flowers. I could have spent weeks documenting them all. Bright red heliconia, also known as the lobster claw flower. Delicate orchids in colors I had never seen and could barely process as we bumped along. Monkey brush vines, passion flowers, Bromelia flowers that would eventually yield pineapple. Coffee plants, cacao, passion flowers. No one would starve in the Amazon if they knew where to look.

It made sense all of a sudden that the Mother Superior of Magic had her temple somewhere in the river basin. Between mystical properties of plants that perhaps average humans had yet to discover and the difficulty in reaching the place, the magical healers would have plenty of privacy to learn and practice their craft in peace and relative seclusion.

There had to be a cure. Something in the jungle held the secret to restoring my health. And I was more determined than ever to find it.

ALYS

I had a knot in my neck the size of a bowling ball by the time Paulo drove into Tabatinga. No tarantulas or venomous snakes had dropped into the open-air vehicle and we hadn't wrecked tear-assing through the jungle. If there hadn't been such a damn time-crunch, I would have had us fly into Manaus.

Ours was one of the few vehicles on the road through the river city, which wasn't a surprise. The main thoroughfare in and around civilization was the mighty river. Ferries traveled between the borders of Peru, Brazil, and Columbia taking people about their business.

Paulo pulled to a stop in front of the hotel and unloaded our bags. The meager supplies made me twitchy. A trip like this deserved huge amounts of preparation and forethought. No wonder I felt as though I'd flown out the door and left the coffee pot on.

Brock's handling things. I reminded myself.

He had wanted to come with us. Badly. But Nate was still missing and someone had to keep the work on track at the Mid-Century Modern.

"Can you feel it?" Sibby was staring out at the water, her ridiculous purple hair once again revealed for the world to see.

"Feel what?" I asked.

"It's a convergence." She let out an exhale as though she'd been hauling that particular breath around for the better part of her life.

"Of course it is. Three different countries are in spitting distance of one another." I made a face as I swatted the biggest freaking mosquito I had ever seen. "Didn't I tell you that?"

"It's not just that." Maeve had closed her eyes and tilted her face up to the sun which was once again visible. "It's like the cottage. A magical convergence. I can feel it in my blood."

I stared at my sister in awe. Something seemed very different about her since we'd gotten into the Jeep. I couldn't put my finger on exactly what had changed but something had. She seemed brighter but at the same time a little bit more knowledgeable. Sort of like the meandering river that was the source of life for this community. Deep, treacherous, and full of secret dangers.

It scared me. She scared me. She shouldn't even be here. None of us ought to be. Three women traveling alone. Sibby was the only one who spoke more than just a few stilted phrases in Portuguese. She had fallen into easy conversation with Paulo on the ride about who knew what.

It wasn't safe. We didn't even have time to exchange some cash for local currency or to check in with Maeve's doctor about what she would need to travel.

But if there was hope for an actual cure, how could I deny them?

I couldn't, which was why I was staring at the mighty Amazon instead of my task list for the Mid-Century Modern and that cabin we'd shelled out for.

Paulo said something to Sibby who nodded and then turned to me. "He says that he will be staying with his sister for the next few days and we can call him there if we need him for anything."

I forced a smile and then nodded. "Okay. Tell him thank you."

"*Obrigada*, Paulo." Sibby said.

My teeth sank into my lower lip as he drove off. There went the last contact I had made in preparation for this trip. We were truly on our own. Winging it. I hated winging it. I liked plans and punch lists. This going with your gut thing was for the birds. They could wing it. And maybe take off when shit got critical. Powerful witches or not, the Amazon had gobbled up sterner stuff than the three of us.

I looked at Maeve. "Should we get a hotel room? A place to use as a home base?"

She shook her head, her eyes still closed. "The river is calling to me."

"No swimming in the Amazon," I said.

"Why not?" Maeve opened her eyes and challenged.

"Piranha, caimans, anacondas," I ticked off the natural predators on my fingers.

"Spoilsport." Maeve nudged her in the ribs. "Come on, let's check out the docks."

"Was she kidding?" I turned to Sibby. "Please tell me she's kidding and that she really isn't going to go for a swim in the damn river."

Sibby was staring after Maeve. "Honestly, Alys? I have no idea what she's capable of right now. She's a woman on a mission. The best we can hope for is that she slows down long enough so we can keep pace with her."

Sibby strode off and after a moment, I followed.

No sense in wishing things could be different. We were where we were and there was no way to go but through.

I wish I knew what was waiting for us on the other side.

Sebastian paced his magical workroom, his thoughts in turmoil. Brazil.The Mother Superior of Magic. After an ill-advised trip to the midnight market and a close call with the Headhunter, Siobhan and her sisters had for whatever reason, decided to head into the Amazon rainforest.

Alone. Sebastian had spotted both Maeve's mortal mate and the werewolf in downtown Eckhart.

They were powerful witches. But they were green and worse, they were the top magical targets for the hunters.

And now they were mincing about in the Headhunter's backyard.

Did the three of them *want* to die?

Sebastian ran a hand through his hair. His every instinct told him he needed to go after Siobhan and drag her home kicking and screaming. He had no doubt she would put up a fight.

But how could he explain his presence there? Hell, how could he even *find* her?

Although...

His gaze fell on the pendulum he had taken off his first rogue witch. It was a powerful tool and if he had something of Siobhan's he could use it to find her. To track her down.

And as for an explanation? Well, she already knew he possessed magic. He could gloss over the dark details. As long as he could keep her and her sisters out of the Head-hunter's clutches, he could figure the rest out later.

Now he just needed something of hers.

Tapping into a ley line, Sebastian opened himself to the pull of the nearest convergence. He knew the witches tended to congregate at those magical crossroads and though he had never been himself, he was willing to bet that was the location of their home.

He closed his eyes, allowing his body to dissolve into a state of pure energy. The ley line pulled the bits and pieces of him like a magnet and he went with the current, dipping through the swirls and eddies of pure power.

He felt the shift, the other colors, and patterns that came together up ahead. Instead of letting himself be lost in it, he pulled himself back together and used his force of will to step out of the stream and shift back onto the mortal plane.

He felt it still, the song in his blood. The convergence. So much raw power. If only there was a way to channel it directly from the source. Alas, any who had tried had gone mad. The energy could be funneled through a trained witch, but even the strongest could only hold so much without burning out.

He opened his eyes and stared at the cottage. The structure didn't look like much. But this was her place. Sebastian was like a dog who scented its prey. He knew Siobhan had spent a great deal of time in the structure. Her particular magical resonance had been absorbed into the space. He noticed it from the top floor as well as the glass structure that was tacked on to the side of the house like an afterthought.

Sebastian moved to the greenhouse door. The smartest thing to do was to get what he needed and spend as little time in the house as possible. He unlatched the door.

And the guardian spirit of the house attacked.

CHAPTER SIXTEEN

MAEVE

"*T*here," I stood at the edge of the dock and pointed out across the muddy water at the island. "That's where I need to go."

"That's Santa Rosa," Alys came up beside me and shielded her eyes. "Peru. Are you sure that's where you need to go? Maybe we should find a place out of sight and try scrying...?"

My eyes were on the wooden structures poised on stilts. I knew what Alys was asking. Unlike what I'd seen of the substantial settlement of Tabatinga, the island buildings appeared much more rustic.

Hell, many of them made Aunt Jess's cottage look like a five-star resort.

But I *knew* that island was where I needed to be. Despite my teasing, swimming in the slow-moving Amazon wasn't on my bucket list. But I'd dive off this dock to get to this island if that was my only option.

I nodded to Alys. "Peru, final answer."

"A new country then." Alys bobbed her head as though her logistical brain was crunching through the details.

"Paulo told me customs tend to be pretty lax between the

countries," Sibby offered. "People bop back and forth all day long so if we don't have anything to declare, we can probably just hire a water taxi and go on over."

Alys didn't like it. I could tell by the way she was worrying her lower lip that the idea of coloring outside the lines troubled her. She was a by-the-book kind of girl, even if she had charted us to a private landing strip to bypass customs. Chances were good that she was picturing some Peruvian jail cell where she would be forced to use a smattering of college Spanish to communicate.

"It's fine." I put my hand on my big sister's arm. "If we get into trouble, Sibby can jump us back out. Right, Sib?"

Sibby smiled brightly which did nothing to reassure Alys.

The driver of the water taxi looked to be in his eighties. His deep brown skin had been slow-roasted by the sun over many decades and he had all of three teeth left in his head. But he waved us on board when Sibby offered him colorful banknotes.

"Where did you get that?" Alys gestured to the currency when we were out on the water and heading toward the island.

"I had it." Sibby pulled sunglasses out of her pack to blot out the sinking sun.

"You had what?" I cocked my head to the side to study the colorful bills with faces of historical figures I didn't know. "What exactly is it?"

"It's called Neuvo Sol. Peruvian currency. Though mostly they take the US dollar no problem."

I stared at her. "Sibby, have you been here before?" She'd never spoken of it.

"A long time ago," was all she said.

I swapped a glance with Alys. There was a story there for sure. Sibby always talked about her travels in vivid and sometimes uncomfortable detail. The fact that she didn't want to talk about the last time she'd been in Peru spoke volumes.

I wondered if it had something to do with one of her exes. I would make a point of bringing it all up later. After I figured out my own mess.

The wind was still and the sun had started to dip below the treeline when we got off the ferry and began our exploration of Santa Rosa. The sounds of basic life, the smells of the evening meals being prepared made the island feel homier than Tabitanga had.

There was a certain sort of freedom to traveling without Kal and the twins. No one whining about being hungry or needing to pee. The three of us were free agents. We could eat when we felt like it, move when we needed to, rest when the urge overtook us. The only needs we had to look after were our own.

Sibby's stomach growled and she clamped a hand over it. "Sorry."

"We should find a place to get some dinner." Alys glanced around. "I don't see anything that looks like a restaurant. Maybe we should take the ferry back, get a hotel room and figure out a plan of attack for tomorrow...." She trailed off and frowned. "Uh oh."

"What?" Sibby asked.

"Those guys over there are sizing us up like we're prey."

I glanced over my shoulder and spotted the three men leaning against the supports of one of the huts.

Sibby put a hand on my shoulder. "We need to get out of sight so I can jump us."

"I can't leave yet," I told her.

"Maeve," Alys hissed. "It's not safe. This border being so lax isn't a great thing. There are probably drug runners moving up and down the river and I for one don't want to cross paths with anyone like that."

She was right. Logically, I understood. But at the same time, I *knew* that whatever I had come here to find was nearby. "I can't go yet."

The men called out what might have been a greeting. The tallest of the three began to move in our direction.

"What did he say?" Alys muttered to Sibby.

"Nothing worth repeating." Sibby's eyes were wide.

Alys huffed out a breath and the wind began to rustle the abundant greenery that flanked the river. Leaves turned over even as my adrenaline spiked. My sister's mother nature magic wasn't subtle. If she unleashed lightning directly at these men, word would spread of the three white women who'd been meandering on the island.

But my gift was sneaky. And I was just scared enough to call on it.

"Stop," I said to the man. I didn't know whether or not he spoke English, but the command came from deep within. It transcended language barriers and as my eyes met his, I felt something rip free.

He stopped. His buddies appeared confused but I shifted my focus to them, letting my will penetrate and fog their minds. It didn't feel like a violation the way it did when I enchanted those I had known all my life. These men had meant us harm. I *knew* it. At best they would have taken our bags. At worse, our lives.

I was using my magic on purpose for the very first time.

And it felt *incredible.*

181

SIOBHAN

"My sister's hungry," Maeve said to the men she had so obviously enchanted. They stood there, slack jawed and staring at her. I stared at her, too. She was still Maeve but a version of my sister I didn't recognize. As the sunlight faded she looked eerie and primitive. A witch in the full throes of her magic.

Then her words registered. "What are you doing? You can't make them feed us."

"You wanna bet?" Maeve didn't take her eyes off the men. "It's the least they can do after scaring the hell out of us. A good meal shared between friends."

I looked to Alys for support. She shrugged.

The man who had initially called Maeve an unflattering name turned back to the hut with the thatched roof he'd been loitering under. His comrades followed and then Maeve fell into line behind them, leaving Alys and I no option but to trail along.

Her power radiated out of her like rays from the sun. I could feel the heat even though it wasn't directed at me. Was it this place that was amplifying Maeve's power? Or the threat the men posed to us that had unlocked this new level?

Whatever the case, she was a force of nature as much as Alys but in a much different way.

The men trudged up the stairs to one of the rickety structures and Maeve paused at the bottom. Either she was worried about her balance or her strength was waning. I moved up beside her and without a word, escorted her up the stairs to the hut.

The three enchanted men stood to one side, allowing the three of us to enter the small space. There was a rough-hewn wooden table and four spindly-legged chairs. An elderly woman with a slight frame was carrying a large pot to the table. She frowned when she spied us.

"Who are these women?" She asked the man in Spanish.

"She wants to know who we are," I repeated to Maeve.

The woman's gaze turned to me and spoke in heavily accented English. "Americans yes?"

I bit my lip and nodded. "That's right. Your....son?"

"Grandson," she spat. Then added a few harsh criticisms in her native tongue.

"Grandson was good enough to invite us to your table after we missed the last ferry to Inquiotos."

Her dark eyes were sharp. "That doesn't sound like him. He hates gringos."

"I can be... persuasive," Maeve said.

"We would be happy to pay you for the trouble," Alys extracted a couple of twenties from her wallet in offering.

The woman's demeanor changed, her eyes lighting up with the thought of fleecing a few wealthy gringos. "Come, sit. Eat while it is hot. And you two, *vete a casa.*" She shooed her grandson's friends out of her home.

When she turned to the shelf where the bowls were kept, Maeve took the opportunity to whisper instructions to the other men. They left without a fuss.

We gathered around the table. Since there were only four

bowls, Maeve encouraged our would-be attacker to go wait outside. His grandmother eyed her shrewdly as she doled out the thin stew into battered bowls made from hollowed-out gourds.

The concoction was flavorful though and I was hungry enough to eat the green bananas that had been on display in Tabatinga.

"This is delicious," I said. "Thank you."

She smiled at me, revealing her missing eye teeth, and made her pronouncement. *"De nada, Bruja."*

Witch. I wondered if she was using the term in a tongue-in-cheek manner or if she really suspected our true nature.

Alys had stiffened at the word and I kicked her under the table. I loved my big sister but she would prove to be the world's worst poker player. Maeve wore a funny little smile as though people called her a witch every day and she found it amusing.

"I don't think we've been properly introduced," Maeve pushed her bowl aside and leaned forward. "I'm Maeve Silver. These are my sisters, Siobhan and Alys."

"Brigida," Our hostess held a withered hand to her chest. "Eat while it's hot."

We did without further conversation. I took the time to study the circular structure. The roof was thatched to keep out the weather and mosquito netting lined the glassless windows. The interior was a single room with few creature comforts. There was a raised pallet-style bed to my far right. The mattress looked lumpy as though it had been stuffed with dried leaves. Two hammocks were suspended from beams to my left. Probably the grandson's sleeping area. A line of drying clothes spanned the space behind Alys's head, obscuring my view of whatever lay back there. No bathroom. Most likely there was an outhouse that Brigida and her grandson shared with some of their neighbors. Buckets and a haphazard pile of tools as well as several fishing poles were shoved along the wall. The floor was clean otherwise.

Brigida finished first but didn't move away from the table. "What brings the three of you to Amazonia?"

Alys shifted in her chair. "We're looking for someone we met...." She trailed off, clearly not knowing how to finish the sentence.

"She lives in a place for healers," I added. "But we aren't sure where it is."

Our hostess cackled. "Foolish girls."

I didn't correct her. Probably in her rheumy eyes, we were girls.

"You know where we need to go." Maeve's tone was quiet and though her words posed a question she didn't ask it as one.

Brigida focused on her. "Perhaps."

"How much?" Alys leaned forward.

"Three hundred of your dollars." Brigida nodded to the table. "Plus room and board for the night."

Three hundred in US currency was undoubtedly more than the woman or her grandson made in a year. Did she actually know where the healer's temple was located? Or was she trying to get one over on the gullible Americans? I hadn't been a witch long enough to be able to tell when someone else was magically inclined. The people at the midnight market all felt like people to me.

Alys looked to Maeve who hadn't said much but seemed to sense something about the woman. It was her instinct that had brought us to this place, her magic that enchanted Brigida's grandson and arranged for this meeting. I got that sense that whether she was aware of it or not, Maeve knew what she was doing.

"Twenty for the night's lodging. We already paid for the meal," Maeve said.

"Thirty," Brigida haggled back. "There are three of you."

"Twenty, there are only two hammocks and I doubt you'll give up your own bed, no matter how much we pay." Maeve raised a brow and waited.

"Agreed," Brigida said. The gleam in her eye told me she was impressed with Maeve's shrewdness and still felt pleased about the outcome.

Alys counted out three hundred and twenty dollars, the majority of what she had left. The way Brigida stared at the remaining bills made me wonder what else she would devise to charge us for before we left.

"What is it we need to do?" Maeve asked once the bills were tucked safely in the older woman's skirt.

"Tomorrow at first light, you will take the fast ferry to Iquitos. From there you will need to go upriver to the source."

"The source?" Alys asked. "Of what?"

Brigida grinned wickedly. "Of the Amazon, of course."

Sebastian landed on his ass in the slush. He stared up at the thrumming energy that surrounded the house. A spirit guarded the place.

How careless of him. He should have anticipated it. Witches set protection spells around their homes all the time. Even if the Silver sisters were new to the craft, the cottage had been in their family for many years. Plenty of time for an experienced witch to infuse the place with magic.

He could disperse the ghost. The dead were transmuted energy that clung to the plane of the living. Without a body to contain what they had once been, however, the energy would eventually dissipate. Sebastian knew an incantation that would hasten the process but he didn't want to alert the sisters that he had been in their space. Banishing the guardian would certainly do that. Besides, it would be foolish to expend the magic he had just acquired if there was another way.

Instead, he tried to reason with the spirit. "Siobhan is in danger. I need something of hers so that I can find her before the Headhunter does."

To his surprise, the ghost formed before him. A man with dark hair and gray eyes and an old-fashioned military uniform studied him. "Who are you?"

"I'm Sebastian," he said.

"Last name, fae." The ghost stared him down.

I'm not a fae. Not a full fae."

"Your eyes say otherwise," the ghost pointed out.

Sebastian sighed. "I am a changeling."

Careful to keep his hands where the ghost could see them, Sebastian got to his feet.

"And how did you meet Siobhan?"

If the guardian lurked around the house, he would have heard the sisters talking. He would know how they met. "I'm an attorney. I go by Jones. I represented Alys's ex-husband for a short time."

The ghost didn't relent. "You're one of them, aren't you? A magic hunter."

Sebastian could lie. He wasn't a full-blooded fae and the restrictions that limited them didn't apply to him. "I was. But now I only wish to protect Siobhan and her sisters."

The ghost tipped his head to the side and studied him. He smiled softly. "You love her."

He wasn't about to make that claim. Love wasn't an emotion that ever got anyone anywhere in his experience. But if the ghost wanted to believe that, he might as well let him. "Have you heard tales of the Headhunter?"

"I have. It's said that he can reanimate corpses to serve his will." The ghost looked oddly unsettled by that news.

"It's true. And the last time I communicated with Siobhan, she was heading into Amazonia. His seat of power. I have to get to her before he does." It occurred to him that the ghost might provide information. "Do you know why they went there? What they seek?"

The ghost said nothing. He was obviously loyal to the sisters.

"Please," Sebastian said. "I must keep her safe."

"You healed Maeve," the ghost said. "I detected your energy signature on her when she returned here. For that, I will allow you entry. But know this, dark fae. If you do anything that hurts my girls, I will haunt you until the end of time itself."

With that, the ghost disappeared.

"I understand," Sebastian said and made his way up the steps to the house. He found what he needed in the greenhouse. A strand of blue hair the length of his palm. He wrapped it around his finger and then exited the house, though he turned back to address the ghost.

"I make no promises," he told the empty space. "But know this. I have already given up all I was for Siobhan. My reputation, my kinship to the other hunters, and most of my magic. I am a soul with nothing to lose. Nothing except her."

Without waiting for a reply, he merged his energy with the ley line and headed back to his workspace.

There was magic to be done.

CHAPTER SEVENTEEN

MAEVE

"*A*re you okay?" Alys's face was the picture of concern. We stood in line to disembark the crowded ferry. The colorful river city of Iquitos spread out before us, waiting. I couldn't muster any enthusiasm for it.

I pretended not to hear the question. Why did my sisters continue to ask? No, I wasn't okay. That was why we were here. Dwelling on it wouldn't change our situation. If there was a way to magically take away my fatigue we hadn't found it yet. I had woken up exhausted and aching. My head was full of cobwebs and I couldn't seem to hold a thought.

Ms. Priss was making her presence known.

The twelve-hour ferry ride to Iquitos hadn't helped. The seats on the ferry were full and cramped. Iquitos, we had learned, was the largest settlement in the world that couldn't be reached by road. To get to it one had to fly in or take a ferry.

We'd risen before the sun and made our way, escorted by our hostess.

All the power I had experienced the night before had

vanished. I'd hoped my enthusiasm for being on the river would combat my symptoms. After boarding we'd spent the first few hours by the railing, watching the rainforest world pass by. I'd been on the lookout for more of the indigenous plants, particularly the giant lily pads, Victoria Amazonicas, that reportedly grew up to ten feet in diameter. Alys had been hoping to see giant river otters or perhaps pink river dolphins or even bright beaked toucans. We'd struck out on all counts.

"It's us," Sibby had murmured.

"I'm trying not to take that personally," Alys muttered.

"Not us specifically. People in general." Sibby turned to lean her back against the railing. "Deforestation and the encroachment of civilization has sent what's left of the wildlife into hiding."

Small settlements dotted the river, and a few human inhabitants appeared as they went about their daily business. I smiled as I spotted a group of children using a muddy incline as a natural slide that dumped them into the water, where they splashed around with glee. My kids would have adored the adventure.

"What about piranhas?" I stood up straight as I thought of the dangers the river presented and tried not to panic. "Or those alligator things?"

"You mean caimans?" Sibby shook her head. "Don't fret. Those kids are too big for most of those to tangle with. And piranha is probably a regular source of their diet."

I shuddered at the thought. Bella and Philip's Goldfish crackers and instant mac-and-cheese seemed like a different world.

As the miles passed and the sun rose higher, the muddy water, oppressive humidity, and crush of bodies—many of them unwashed and all packed in like ground pork in a metal sausage casing—rapidly lost its appeal.

"Can't you do something about this weather?" Sibby used the map to fan herself.

Alys snatched it out of her hands. "We're trying to lie low, remember? Reclimitizing the rainforest would be the opposite of that."

Sibby shot a worried glance at me. "Heat isn't good for—"

"I'm fine." My tone was short, much like my temper. Mood swings were par for the course now. I hoped she didn't ask me the spoon question. I'd already run out for the day and was desperately scrambling to steal from tomorrow's allotment of energy. There would be a reckoning.

"I'll see if I can find us a hotel with AC." Alys tapped on her sat phone. "We can stay a few nights if we need to."

A few more nights in the middle of nowhere. A few more nights away from my children. From Kal.

I shifted for the thousandth time in a fruitless effort to get comfortable. The seats weren't designed for the well-fed backside of an average American and it had been impossible to relax. My legs ached and for the first time, I was regretting that I hadn't decided on a course of treatment before taking this trip. Some medications could relieve symptoms of MS. Of course, all medications came with side effects, and just like the disorder affected every patient differently, there was no predicting how severe those side effects would be.

Even Sibby's bright plumage looked somewhat wilted by the time the ferry pulled up to the dock in Iquitos.

We disembarked right away and Alys followed the instructions on her phone's GPS to the hotel. It was surprisingly luxurious and my big sister seemed pleased with herself for having found it.

"It's so cheap," she confided as we rode the elevator to the top floor. "Compared to what we would have paid in Charlotte. And did you see the pool?"

Sibby too had caught a second wind. "They have all sorts

of tours. I grabbed a bunch of pamphlets to see if we could figure out our next move."

Brigida had told us we needed to find the source of the Amazon. But from what Alys had been able to discover with her spotty internet connection, no one could agree on exactly which tributary was the true beginning of the mighty river. Three different rivers and a lake had all been touted by different scholars to be the source of the Amazon. Just one more factoid that the internet couldn't agree on.

The elevator doors dinged open and Alys walked in that purposeful way she had, leading us to our room. We had agreed to stay together, forgoing privacy for safety in case the magical worst happened. Sibby shot me a glance and I tried to hide my fatigue, not wanting her to waste her energy stressing about me.

Two full-sized beds with pristine white linens. The room overlooked the pool. I stumbled to the one farthest in as Alys shut the door.

"Are you hungry?" Sibby asked. "Can we bring you anything?"

I shook my head. "I just need to sleep. Why don't the two of you go out and explore a little? It would be a waste of a trip if you didn't do some sightseeing while you're here."

Sibby took a swig from one of the complimentary water bottles provided by the hotel. "Hey, now that I've been here, I can pop on by whenever I want. After we get our magical carte blanche, of course. Who knows, Iquitos might be my new weekend getaway."

I closed my eyes and listened while my sisters took turns freshening up in the bathroom. I felt like a drag, the boring heel of a woman who couldn't be bothered to get out of bed to go out and enjoy life.

Alys, wearing a short black tank dress and her onyx protection necklace, sat on the edge of my bed. "You sure you're all right, Maeve? Sibby can jump you home if this is all too much."

I rolled onto my back. "I need to be here, Alys. Or there. Wherever the source is. It has to be me."

"I'm allowed to worry about you." Her tone was defensive.

I took a few deep breaths. "I'm sorry."

"What for?"

"For being sick. For insisting we come here. For making you worry."

Alys let out a slow breath. "Maeve, I would worry even if you were completely healthy and tucked safely in your bed at home. It's what I do. So don't apologize for how you are, okay? You haven't done anything wrong."

Sibby emerged dressed in cut-offs and a beaded halter top that showed off her shoulder tattoo of a crescent moon with big pouty lips and a sultry look in her eye. She too wore her homemade necklace. "All right, let's go rustle up some grub."

"You'll call my cell if you need anything. Or if anything strange happens." Alys held my gaze. "Promise me."

"I promise."

"No wild parties 'til I get back," Sibby winked at me.

I let out a relieved sigh when the door clicked shut behind them. I loved my sisters but they were a lot to deal with.

I stared at my own onyx stone, rubbing my fingers over the smoothness and trying to relax.

The dream fell over me like a blanket. Again, I knew I was asleep and was reliving a memory from long ago. Accepted it and merged my consciousness into the young woman I'd once been.

I was with Kal, who was using crutches to navigate the paved walkway behind the soccer complex. The sun was out and the path was dry so when he had said he wanted to move a little, I figured this was a good place. The temperature was in the mid-fifties and the Carolina sun-infused us with much needed vitamin D. Small green shoots were beginning to poke through the dormant grass. I watched Kal's progress with a careful eye but he didn't seem tired as he placed the crutches then hopped forward. He must be feeling better.

I bit my lip as I considered my part in that.

It was the third time I'd taken an, *ahem*, hands-on approach to his pain management. The first time I hadn't asked. He had been in pain and hadn't been aroused at all when I'd started to massage him. Beginning at his temples, I'd progressed slowly to work on his neck, his shoulders, down his arms. I'd yanked the sweats up on his good leg and kneaded the muscles there as well before focusing on his chest. I'd listen to instincts I hadn't known I possessed while touching him. It felt as though a light poured out of my hands and into his body. A rosy glow slowly eased his tension with each stroke of the deep-tissue massage. I didn't hurry. Forgot all about the appointment. Time stretched out as I caressed and molded his flesh with my hands. Let the oil fill my senses and his. My goal was simple. To coax a sexual response from his big body until he could climax either by my hand or his.

It happened sooner than I had thought possible.

"Sorry," Kal had muttered when my hand brushed over the erection that strained against the fabric of the black sweat pants.

"Don't be. Is it okay if I keep going? Or do you want to finish yourself?" He needed to finish. If he didn't, the pain would be worse than before I'd started.

Please ask me to stay. I'd mentally begged. *Please want me to touch you.*

In his deep, soft tone he had murmured, "Keep going."

And with his permission, I had reached inside the sweatpants. Stroked him. Enjoyed the feel of him in my hand. He was so large and hot and heavy in my oil-coated palms. He cried out when his body convulsed and I felt a rush of my own pleasure seeing him that way in such an unguarded moment.

That had been the first time.

After he said, "Thank you."

And what exactly was he thanking me for? The release? Taking away the pain? Something else entirely?

We had yet to talk about it.

A bench sat beneath a naked oak tree in the direct sun. Though Kal seemed to be all right even after the rigors of therapy, I urged him toward it. "It's nice enough now to sit. You should soak up some vitamin D while you can. It'll be below freezing again tonight."

Kal sat. He was a good patient, but not a great one. A great one would say something when he needed help. Kal never murmured a word of complaint. I had no idea if he was giving himself release between the times when I did. He should. It was his pain to manage after all and if the natural endorphins were the only ease he was getting. He should be taking advantage of that.

Plus the line between healthcare provider and patient had blurred. He was my friend, my psedo tenant. And I was touching him sexually. Reliving the encounter late at night in my own bed. It seemed wrong. I'd promised myself I wouldn't do it again.

Yet when I'd found him in bed in much the same state as he had been in the first time, I'd started in on him again. And then earlier today before his appointment.

"Are we going to talk about it?" Kal asked. Obviously, our encounters weighed on his mind too.

"Talk about what?" I busied myself with digging through my purse, pretending to look for nonexistent gum.

"Evie." He gave me a stern look.

I blew out a breath. "I don't know what to say, Kal. I'd like to think I'm helping you manage your pain. All you ever say is thank you. And I don't know what you mean by that."

The skin around his eyes crinkled in amusement. "I mean thank you."

I threw my hands up "For what though? Pain management?"

"That too."

I huffed out a breath. The man frustrated the hell out of me.

"Why are you doing it?" he asked gently.

I scowled at him. "I don't want you to be in pain."

"Is that the only reason?" His tone was soft but I picked up a hint of something darker.

I fidgeted with a loose thread on my sweatshirt. Why did I feel like a letch all of a sudden?

Because you're enjoying it, a little voice whispered. *Because you aren't as altruistic as everyone thinks.*

Shut up, self.

He waited while I wrestled with my conscience. Kal could wait out time itself.

I pushed off the bench and began to pace. "I don't know what I'm doing, okay? I hoped I could help you because I couldn't stand the thought of you being in pain. But if you're asking if my feelings for you are strictly professional, they aren't. I'm not a sex worker, Kal."

Those dark eyes were trained on my every move. "I never thought you were."

I turned to face him. "Look, I have made one bad decision after the next when it comes to you. I don't have a clue if you feel anything for me beyond friendship. So could you maybe just put me out of this super awkward misery and tell me what's going on in that head of yours?"

He reached out a hand and caught my wrist. With a light tug, he pulled me back to the bench. "I want you."

A laugh bubbled up. "Just like that?"

"Just like that. Why do you think your massage always works? My leg hurts too much for me to get fully aroused on my own."

My teeth sank into my lower lip. I hadn't thought of that.

He coaxed me down onto the bench next to him and brushed my hair back from my face. "I want to touch you, too. To kiss you."

"Why didn't you say anything before?"

"Because," he said simply. "I was afraid you would stop."

I licked my lips and his gaze dropped to them before he continued. "But today I realized that you would just keep going on with everything as it was. I couldn't tell if what we've been doing affected you. And as much as I don't want you to stop, I want more from you than that, Evie."

"You do?" My voice sounded breathy all of a sudden.

He feathered his large hand across my cheekbones. "Can I kiss you, now?"

When I nodded, his fingers combed through into my hair until he cradled my face. His lips were warm and soft as they glided lightly over mine. Like the brush of a butterfly's wing.

It felt…right. Perfect. Everything I had imagined when I lay in my lonely bed at night and fantasized about how Kal would kiss me.

At times I wondered if I'd conjured him to fill all the dark corners of my life. To make me whole and happy.

He withdrew and leaned his forehead against mine. "Will you stay with me tonight?"

"We can't…you know." I made a rapid back and forth gesture between our bodies. "Your leg."

Again he stroked my cheek with a whisper-soft caress. "I just want to hold you. Maybe touch you a little. If that's okay."

The breath that escaped my lungs shook. "Yeah Kal. That's okay."

"Okay," he said. "Now that that's settled, let's go home. My leg's killing me."

"Really?" I asked.

There was a wicked gleam in his eye. "Depends."

I threw my head back and pure joy bubbled out of me. "Okay. Let me take you home."

By the time we got back to the house, Kal really was in pain. I could tell by the tension in his jaw. He maneuvered slowly down the hall with me right behind him.

"It's okay to complain," I told him. "Vocalizing the pain might even help."

"Ouch," he said as he shucked his coat and sweatshirt. "Didn't help."

"Keep doing it. You don't always have to be so stoic." Once I was sure he was settled in bed, I went into the kitchen and got him a glass of water.

His lids were closed when I reentered the room, his breaths even. I set the water down on the bedside table and then positioned his crutches off to one side before heading to the door.

"I thought you were going to stay," he murmured.

"You need rest," I told him.

Those dark eyes opened. "I need you more."

My heart squeezed tightly. "No funny business."

"No, ma'am." He agreed.

"Why don't I believe you?" I narrowed my eyes at him.

"Because I'm a damn liar."

I laughed and he grinned. "Come here, Evie."

I was a weak-willed woman because I went. Careful of his injured leg, I curled up on his other side. The dip of his shoulder formed the perfect place to rest my head. His hand stroked through my hair.

"This is good," Kal breathed and then fell asleep as though he had only been waiting for me to curl into him.

"Yeah, it is," I breathed in the clean scent of his skin and settled more deeply into his warmth. "A girl could get used to this."

CHAPTER EIGHTEEN

ALYS

"*S*o what's next, Lys?" Brock's voice echoed through the speakers of my cell and off the ceramic tiles in the hotel bathroom.

I set down my hairbrush and reached for my fitness tracker. "The stupid pendulum keeps giving us different answers. I've chartered a helicopter to take us to Cusco. It's the closest major city to the Andes. We're leaving at noon."

"How's Maeve holding up?"

"She slept about fourteen hours and rested all day yesterday. But she actually looks better today. She used so much magic the night we got here, I think it sapped her strength even before we got on the ferry. Her abilities are so different than mine, but I'm starting to think they're just as strong. She's been keeping a tight leash on her fear and spending most of her time with us. It was a shock to see her use so much magic."

"Be very careful. You're not in your own territory with the pack to run interference anymore," Brock cautioned.

I smiled and picked up the phone. "We were in another convergence, so I don't think anyone could have tracked her.

Sibby and I agreed last night only to use magic as a last resort. You don't need to worry."

"I should be there," Brock grumbled.

"No, you should be exactly where you are. Any sign of Nate?"

He let out a sigh and I had my answer. "I'm sure he'll come back as soon as he can."

"I miss you, love," Brock said.

I missed him, too. While the rainforest was beautiful, I'd never really enjoyed traveling the way Sibby did. Too much time in the car as an adolescent had turned me into an adult homebody. Eckhart provided everything I needed to be happy, including Brock.

"I'll be home soon. The new moon is just a few nights away. So, either we'll find the healers or we won't."

"Call me when you land," Brock said. "Love you, Lys."

"I will. Love you, too." I hung up the phone just as Sibby pounded on the bathroom door.

"Are you almost done in there? Some of us really need to pee."

"Hang on a minute." After stuffing my toiletries back into the carrying case, I unlocked the door.

Sibby pushed past me, hiked up her nightgown, and plunked down on the toilet before I could even exit the space.

She looked like hell, sitting there, mascara smeared down the side of her face, glaring at me through red-rimmed eyes.

"Could you at least wait for me to leave the room?"

"No," she snapped. "If I had sneezed, I would have pissed all over myself."

"You drank too much last night," I said sternly.

She flushed the toilet and then moved to the sink to wash her hands. "It was just a little rum."

"I practically had to carry you back to the hotel room."

And once I had she had flopped face-first onto the cover and proceeded to snore in my ear all night. "What's with you anyway?"

She shook her head. "I just have a bad feeling."

I'd had a bad feeling about the entire trip, but here we were. "What about?"

Sibby reached for a washcloth and worked at removing her mascara streaks. "What if that woman in Santa Rosa lied to us? The healer told Maeve to come to the Amazon, not the Andes."

I'd had the same thought. "What else can we do? The pendulum isn't working. This is Maeve's trip. If she wants to follow Brigida's advice and head to the mountains to look for the source of the Amazon, we need to support her. Besides, it's only a couple of hours by helicopter."

"I know." She dropped the washcloth and headed back into the bedroom. Maeve was up and dressed in a long, flowing strapless wrap that I had seen some of the locals wearing. I'd bought it for her because it looked as though it would help keep the wearer cool in the steamy air. The only jewelry she wore was her wedding ring and the onyx bracelet Sibby had fashioned. With her hair unbound around her shoulders, she looked very different from the woman who drove the minivan to her son's soccer games.

She certainly didn't look sick. Which didn't mean she wasn't symptomatic, only that no one would know about it until she was dead on her feet the way she'd been two days ago when we'd arrived in Iquitos.

"How's school? Have you been practicing your spelling?" Maeve said into her phone. She must have been talking with Philip as she'd been on the phone with Bella when I'd gone into the bathroom.

She smiled at me and gestured to the coffee pot that room service had delivered.

I poured a mug full and sipped while Sibby attacked the scrambled eggs. Most people wouldn't want food with a skull-crushing hangover but Sibby could eat anything at any time. She hadn't batted an eye at dishes like guinea pig or ceviche, raw fish marinated in citrus juices. Maeve and I had been somewhat less culinarily adventurous, sticking to the vegetarian options. *Papas a la Huancaina,* a potato dish in spicy cheese sauce was a particular favorite.

I cradled the mug like a long-lost lover. One thing I had to give to Peru. The coffee was orgasmic. I'd have to buy a bag of the local beans before we headed home.

"Mmmhmmm," Maeve got up and moved out onto the balcony. "And what did Dad say?"

She stepped onto the balcony and shut the door.

"Has she talked to Kal?" I asked my youngest sister.

Sibby had yanked her denim shorts up and was crawling around on the floor searching for chocolate alone knew what. "To my knowledge, not about anything important."

"Does he even know where she is?" It was a funny sentiment for me to have. Brock and I were two entirely independent people. Yet I felt the need to let him know when we arrived at each leg of our journey. I wanted to set his mind at ease.

Not because he demanded to know my every move. But because he would support me in whatever I chose to do.

"Not sure," Sibby was head and shoulders deep beneath the bed.

I sat on the other bed, the one, not strewn with the contents of her backpack. "And what about Sebastian. Does he know where you are?"

There was a thump and Sibby emerged, rubbing her head. "I haven't told him."

I glared at her. She had worded that answer very carefully. "What aren't you telling me?"

"Nothing,"

"Siobhan Eloise Silver."

Her hand fell to her side and she made a face. "I hate when you three name me."

I folded my arms over my chest and waited.

Sibby blew out a breath and sat back on her heels. "Okay, so there's a pretty good chance that Sebastian was the one who healed Maeve."

"What?" I was on my feet in a flash.

"Back at the hospital. He encouraged me to go back to the cottage and see if I could find a spell. I left him alone with Maeve."

Blood pounded in my temples like a churning sea. "You left Sebastian alone with her?"

"In the hospital. Not like I left her at his place or something." Her tone was defensive. "Besides, it all worked out for the best, didn't it?"

"Are you freaking kidding me right now? Siobhan, he's got magic and he didn't say a word about it." I barked. "For all we know could be a magic hunter!"

Sibby shook her head. "There's no way. He's had too many opportunities."

"What opportunities?" I cut her off.

She swallowed. "I've sort of been seeing him. Since a little after Halloween."

A sharp banging sound. I turned to see Maeve, knuckles to the glass. Her eyes were wide and she gestured to the sky outside, where thick, heavy clouds had begun to stack up.

"Shit," I muttered.

"Rein it in, Alys." Sibby put her hand on my neck and began a gentle massage.

I blew out a long, slow breath. Concentrated on relaxing my shoulders and releasing the rage that had spiked so suddenly.

Because Sebastian had magic. And hadn't told us. What was he?

I must have asked that last question out loud because Sibby murmured. "I don't know."

"I don't trust him," I said.

My sister said nothing, which was probably for the best. Getting into a fight with her was not on the day's agenda.

My lips twitched. We always managed to make time for an argument, didn't we?

MAEVE

Alys had appeared much calmer by the time we climbed on board the helicopter. That was a good thing since it was already raining. The wet season had arrived in force.

Our pilot was a silent man with skin the color of Espresso beans. He wore a helmet with a microphone attached to it and he spoke in such rapid-fire Spanish to whoever was on the other end that even Sibby couldn't translate.

As the helicopter lifted off, leaving the city of Iquitos behind, I got my first good look at it. I was sorry I hadn't seen more of it while we were there, but the rest had done me well.

There were two other passengers on the helicopter. Men with dark eyes that showed no hint of expression who seriously gave me the creeps every time they looked my way. I shifted and tried to keep myself calm.

Talking was impossible over the whirr of the rotors. It gave me too much time to think.

I thought about the dreams I'd been having of Kal and how they were such a sharp contradiction to the husband who had barely said two words to me when I'd called home.

In fact, he had said exactly two words. "Hello," when he had picked up and "okay," when I'd asked how things were. He'd handed the phone to Bella and that was all.

It was my fault. The farther I got from Kal, the more the dreams of our earlier selves gnawed at me and the more I realized that I wasn't the same woman I'd been when we had first met. Funny how I believed I'd been unsure of myself back then. But I had handled every situation with swift decisions and the confidence that things would work out. I'd fought for what I'd wanted tirelessly.

Where had that woman gone?

"Something's wrong," Sibby shouted in my ear.

"What?" Alys leaned forward.

"We're supposed to be heading south, toward Machu Picchu. But we're heading north."

The light drizzle and gray fog hid the sun. "Are you sure?"

"I just caught sight of a mountain in the distance and it's on the wrong side of us. We're definitely heading north."

When Sibby nodded, Alys unhooked her harness. "I'll just go talk to the pilot and we can...."

She froze.

"Can what?" I asked and then turned to see what had so thoroughly captured her attention.

The men in the seats across from us each held a pistol. And the one on the left had his weapon pointed at my heart.

Sebastian studied the hotel room. The sisters were gone and judging by the steaming mug still sitting on the low dresser, he had just missed them.

The spell had taken longer to reach full efficacy than he'd wanted. He had arrived in the room still unsure of what he would say to Siobhan. It hadn't been an issue. He'd checked the bathroom, the corridors and even flung open the glass door to the patio. The oppressive heat and gray drizzle of the rainforest had let him know his destination was correct, but Siobhan was nowhere in sight.

Where could she have gone? He checked the room more thoroughly. No bags. They weren't planning to return.

His contacts were dry, making his eyes itch. When was the last time he'd changed them? Sebastian retreated into the bathroom and removed them and then donned sunglasses before heading out on his search.

He sent Siobhan a text, but after several moments it was still marked as unread. He paced along the docks that led to the riverboats but something in his gut told him that wasn't right either.

He was about to head back to the hotel to ask a few questions when all the small hairs on the back of his neck rose. He turned in place. A shadow in an alleyway caught his attention. The second he noticed it, it dipped back inside.

Someone was watching him.

Sebastian hurried to the mouth of the alley, drawing his magic tightly to him in preparation for a fight. He entered the alley and looked around.

Wooden crates filled with green bananas and the pervasive scent of rot were his only companions.

Odd, he hadn't sensed magic use. Unless...

Sebastian looked up. Just as the Headhunter dropped the cage made out of human bones over the top of him.

CHAPTER NINETEEN

SIOBHAN

I waited for Maeve to do her enchantress schtick. After all, what could possibly provoke fear more than having the barrel of a firearm pointed at your chest? But after casting me a wild-eyed look, Maeve did a microscopic shake of her head.

She couldn't get it up.

"Who are you?" Alys barked. The second gunman aimed his weapon directly at her. "What do you want?"

They didn't answer. There was something about their eyes. Some scent hidden beneath the overpowering cologne had grown stronger the longer we spent in the enclosed space. A stench that almost made me vomit.

It smelled a lot like rot. They didn't look angry. In fact, there was no emotion on their faces at all. It was almost as if…

I swallowed. "They're dead," I called out risking a look at the gunmen to see how they'd take my announcement.

"What?" Alys scowled. "What do you mean they're dead? We've seen them move. They're holding guns on us for crying out loud."

"There's no soul in their eyes. And can't you smell that? It's decomposition." That was why Maeve's ability didn't work on them. It was tough to enchant a corpse.

Alys looked angry enough to bring hailstones or lightning down on the helicopter, but that wouldn't keep us from getting shot.

I was our only hope to keep this abduction from proceeding.

Moving as deliberately as I could, I crept one hand toward Alys, the other to Maeve. Those lifeless eyes continued to fix on us but I got the sense they weren't tracking. Could dead men see? Or was whatever force that controlled them winding them up and letting them go, like those little cars Philip left all over the living room floor?

I had never traveled from a moving vehicle before. Even though I could use other emotions like anger and fear—both on tap at the moment—lust was still my primary trigger. I couldn't travel far without it, certainly not carrying my sisters.

So, I focused out the window at the jungle below.

And jumped.

I landed on my ass in a muddy puddle. Maeve was to my left and Alys to my right.

"Holy shit," I breathed as I stood up. Way way way up in the sky above the canopy, I spied the small dark dot of the helicopter. "That was close."

"Are you all right?" I asked Maeve.

She nodded breathlessly. "I think so."

I reached for her hand just as Alys screamed.

I whipped my head toward her and spied the coiled green and black body of an anaconda on the tree branch directly above her head. I grabbed her by the shirt and jumped us all to the far side of the riverbank just as the snake plunged down.

In the trees above us, howler monkeys shrieked.

"Shit," Alys had her hand to her chest. "I think I'm having a heart attack."

"Don't even joke about that," Maeve pushed the hair out of her face. But she too looked shaken. "Sibby, can you get us out of here? Back to Iquitos?"

I shook my head. "Not without lust. And believe me when I say I'm *really* not in the mood right now." Dead men flying in a helicopter and a near-miss with a giant snake.

I'd be lucky if my libido ever worked again.

"What are we going to do?" Alys asked. It was probably the first time in her life she had voiced that question.

I looked to Maeve who was staring warily up at the trees. "We can't stay here. Eventually, they'll land that helicopter and set out for us on foot."

"But where will we go?" Alys glanced around. "It's not like there are street signs. This way to the temple of the Mother Superior of Magic."

My oldest sister grew as tart as a green berry when she was riled. And Alys was definitely riled now. All her money and magic couldn't protect us from the hazards of the Amazon. Our bags were still onboard the helicopter. The scrying crystal, first aid kit, provisions.

All we had were the clothes on our backs.

"The helicopter was traveling northwest. Whatever is that way, I don't want to know about it." I turned to Maeve. "This is your quest, She-Ra. You decide. Which way do we go."

"I say we stick within sight of the river. Maybe a boat will come along." Maeve looked terrified as she took the first step but she flashed me a grin. "I always wanted to be She-Ra."

"I remember. You used to have the arm cuff things and a plastic sword with a mirror sticker that looked like her jewel. That was the only commercial gift I ever remember Mom buying you."

"She was so much cooler than He-Man." Maeve agreed.

Alys had stopped in her tracks and was staring at the two of us as if we'd lost our minds. "What are you even talking about?"

"She-Ra? Princess of Power. We would go over to my friend Becca's house after school to watch it. Her grandma had a VCR so she recorded them all." I frowned. "Does Becca still live in town?"

Maeve nodded. "She owns the bakery up the road from *Silver Demo and Design*. She has a daughter now. She's in sixth grade."

"You guys have the attention span of mosquitos," Alys said just as the largest mosquito I had ever seen landed on her neck. It sank its needle-like nose into her neck and she yelped, jumped a foot in the air while simultaneously slapping at the bug. It left a huge, bloody smear on her neck.

"That was weird timing."

My heart was beating rapidly. "I don't think it was a coincidence."

"What do you mean?" Maeve asked as she began walking again. I noticed her gaze was trained on the uneven ground. Was that because she was on the lookout for more reptiles or was she more concerned with her footing?

How long until she needed mobility aids for basic locomotion?

Then I blinked back that thought and refocused on the eerie-ass feeling. "So you know how I've been getting all up in the witchy shit right? Well, there's something called manifesting. Anybody can do it, not just legacy witches like us. The key is to be in tune with the energies of the natural world and to focus your thoughts. If you put your desires forth, the energies will go out of their way to bring you what you want."

"Are you talking about the Law of Attraction malarky?"

Alys snorted. I did not summon a mosquito just because I said the word—ow!"

I faced her and saw where she had a new smear, this time on her forehead.

"You were saying?" I said sweetly.

She glared at me but didn't argue.

I looked to Maeve. "I think the reason the healer wanted you to come here is because nature is dominant here. You can't ignore her and survive in Amazonia. If you focus on your goal, you'll be able to manifest it. But be careful how you word it or who knows what you'll unleash."

Maeve looked at the bloody smears on our eldest sister. "I will."

*B*e careful what you wish for...you just might get it.

How many times had Aunt Jess said that to me? I had thought it nothing more than an old truism, something you pass on to the younger generation. But if what Sibby said was right....

I wish I could find the Mother Superior of Magic.

The wish was earnest and heartfelt. The only good thing about our current situation was there was no one around for me to enchant. The humidity had grown oppressive and I was slowing my sisters down.

The pretty dress I'd put on, thinking we were going to simply fly from city to city, was impractical for trekking through the rainforest. At least I'd had the good sense to don my boots. Though my feet were well protected, the things were heavy and clunky and between the uneven ground and with the oppressive humidity, my energy was flagging.

We weren't in a great position. No food or water, no shelter or changes of clothing. A fat drop of moisture landed on my nose. The rainforest had decided to live up to its name.

"Over here," Alys gestured to a tree with wide, flat leaves. "Snake-free, I already checked."

"Can't you do something about this?" Sibby bitched.

"Did you forget we're being perused?" Alys snapped. "Why not just send them a text message. Your prey is here. Come and get us before the jungle does."

"You guys," I said tiredly. "Stop."

We huddled together, doing our best to wait out the rain. Were we the most pathetic witches of all time or what?

Sibby stood straighter. "I...I don't think that's the Amazon."

"What?" I turned to look at her. "What do you mean? What other river could it be?"

"Look at how fast the current is moving." Sibby pointed to where the water was beginning to eddy around a large tree. "Don't you remember how wide and slow the river moved the other day?"

"It's a tributary," Alys said with awe. "Dear sweet dark chocolate. We might be in totally unexplored territory."

We all paused to consider the ramifications of that.

My body shook. The tremors weren't due to MS, but more the mental and emotional anguish of our situation. Water came down harder, faster. The rainy season had arrived. The tributary, whichever one it was, was creeping up out of the river bed we'd been following.

"We can't stay here," Sibby tugged my arm. "In a few minutes, we'll be standing in the river. Come on, Maeve. We need to get away from the water."

Tears mixed with the rain as my sisters and I plunged into the jungle. The sun was completely obscured by the clouds. What little light had hit the forest floor through the dense canopy was all but gone. Roots from the trees jutted up and my sisters took turns helping me over each obstacle. The rain beat down, bending the leaves that had been protecting us. The only good news was that the ground began to slope upward. Hopefully, that would put us well above the churning water.

"Over here," Alys called. "There's some sort of structure."

I looked up. Squinting through the rain I spied what looked like a small shack on stilts. The stairs leading up to it were carved grooves of dirt lined with bits of rock to keep their shape.

"Make sure it isn't occupied," Sibby said. "I'm tired of surprises today and I don't know how much more witchy mojo I can tap."

Alys ran forward, her boots squishing through the soggy soil. She sprinted up the steps with ease and then rapped on the door. There were no windows to the hut for her to peek into so she pushed the door open. Disappeared inside.

Sibby gripped my hand so hard it hurt but I was hanging on to her just as tightly. After a moment, Alys reappeared and waved us forward.

"You lead the way," Sibby called in my ear. She practically had to shout as the rain had grown deafening.

I moved forward carefully, well aware that the last thing my sisters needed was for me to lose my balance and cause us injury. We slogged up to the stairs to the hut and then crossed the threshold.

Alys had already removed her shirt and was wringing it out on a bare dirt floor. "It's not much, but it's sound enough. I don't think anyone has been here for some time."

I waited for my eyes to adjust to the dimness. She was right. The place had a stagnant air as though the door hadn't been opened in a very long time. Much like Brigida's home, there were three hammocks along with a line that must be used for stringing up laundry. Some candle stubs sat in a chipped ceramic bowl in one corner. There were cobwebs strung between the charred wicks.

"Strip down," Alys ordered. "The last thing you need is a cold from wearing wet clothes."

I glanced around, hoping maybe I had missed something. "Isn't there anything to put on?"

"It's just us," Sibby said, already half-naked and utterly unashamed.

Of course, she had nothing to be ashamed of. Her body, while not some fit or toned ideal that advertising companies wanted women to buy into, was perfectly feminine. She had muscles and curves. Alys was strong and supple, though she sported the family hips and thighs but me...

"What if the owner comes back?" I tried.

"Then I'll fry him with a bolt of lightning," Alys said. "I'm getting angry enough to zap you so stop being ridiculous and strip already."

There was no getting around Alys when she had that tone.

So I closed my eyes—feeling self-conscious because of my bulbous belly, scars, cellulite, and stretch marks—removed the sodden boots, socks, wrap dress, and underwear.

My sisters weren't even looking at me. Sibby was doing her best to remove as much water from her jeans as she could. Alys had found a couple of pots and set them outside to collect water.

They were right. I was ridiculous. What had I thought, that my sisters would point and laugh at my naked body? There was barely enough light in the hut to see my hand in front of my face, never mind every imperfection etched in my skin from an abundant four and a half decades of life.

"Maeve, lie down before you fall down." Alys took the sodden dress from me and proceeded to hang it to drip dry.

"Quit bossing me around," I said to her even as I shuffled

toward the nearest hammock. I leaned into it, making sure it wouldn't snap beneath my weight. It seemed sturdy enough so I eased my weight onto it and shifted until I was balanced within.

My body was cradled by the ropes and I felt the tension seep out of me as I listened to my sisters move around the cabin.

"Why were you being so reluctant to undress?" Sibby asked as she hung up her jeans to drip dry.

I sighed. "It's been years since anyone but Kal and medical professionals have seen me naked. And the medical professionals are always harping on me to lose weight. Didn't matter if it was the obgyn or the neurologist. "You'll feel better/ have more energy/be able to get knocked up if you shed a few pounds."

"Assholes," Sibby groused. "They need to get a new line. Not everything is about numbers on a scale or BMI. Like women don't have enough shit to feel badly about as it is."

"I agree with you on principle. It's supposed to be about how I feel. But if I'm honest, I don't feel so hot." My smile was rueful.

"It's got to be difficult," Alys must have run out of tasks because she settled in her own hammock. "Getting ten thousand steps a day when each one might lead to disaster isn't really sound advice."

"It's not that I haven't tried to lose weight." I shifted in the hammock. "I put on forty pounds with the twins and I worked so damn hard. Tried every diet. It's been years since I've had anything fried. I've given up Kal's desserts too. But with the kids and work and now Ms. Priss, it takes more energy than I have to keep up."

"Ms. Priss?" Alys asked.

I hadn't meant to say that out loud. "It's what I call the

MS. She's a tough old bird always ready to give me a whack with her trusty cane."

Neither of my sisters said anything. What could they say, really?

I closed my eyes and thought about the one person who actually liked seeing me naked.

Or he used to. Before everything went sideways.

"*E*vie," Kal was shaking my shoulder. "There's someone here."

Dream me woke. I was young again, and in bed with Kal and his broken leg. And someone was hammering on the door. I got up and headed for the door, then flung it open.

"Alys? What are you doing here?"

Alys stood there, an umbrella open above her head, keeping the sleet from messing with her perfectly smooth blowout. "I've been trying to call you."

My heart lurched. "Is it Aunt Jess?" Where was my phone? I always left it on in case Aunt Jess needed to get a hold of me.

Alys stepped inside and then pivoted to shut her umbrella. "She's fine. I checked in on her before coming over here. She wanted me to give your young man her regards, for true."

Even though it was delivered in an acerbic tone, I knew that was a direct quote from my aunt and smiled.

"Where is he?" Alys scanned the front section of the house.

"In the bedroom." It was beginning to dawn on me that there was no real crisis except the one my sister had manufactured. I should have known she would make a point to come up here and raise hell the second she had the chance.

She rounded on me. "Have you found out what he's doing here?"

"He's recovering from a skiing accident."

Alys shook her head and cast me a pitying look. "Oh, Maeve. You don't know this man from Adam. How do you know he's not a con artist?"

My blood pressure spiked. "Don't talk to me like I'm your idiot sister who was sent home for eating paste. He broke his leg. I offered him the use of an unoccupied house until he's on the mend. That's all."

"Is everything all right?" Kal asked from the bedroom door. He looked rumpled from sleep but if he was in pain, he showed no signs.

Dear sweet dark chocolate, I hoped Aunt Jess hadn't mentioned our pain management strategy to my sister. Alys's head would explode like a cartoon character.

"Yes, Kal. This is my older sister, Alys Silver. Alys, this is Kallik." With my eyes, I tried to send her a silent message. *Please please don't make a scene.*

It didn't work.

"What are your intentions toward my sister?"

Alys was like steel wool. Abrasive to her core. She could play politics but most of the time didn't bother. She got down to business and stripped away any sort of exterior polish.

I groaned. "Alys, please don't do this."

"I'm in love with her."

My head whipped toward Kal. "Say what now?"

His words didn't soften Alys one bit. "I've hired a private investigator."

"Alys," I hissed, utterly mortified.

"I'll tell you anything you want to know."

"Last name?" She raised a challenging brow.

"I don't have one. My tribe doesn't believe more than one name is appropriate so we don't have family names."

"How convenient. Where were you born?"

"Alaska. Though my father lives in Canada now."

"Would you give me your social security number?" Her eyes narrowed.

He shrugged. "If you would like." He rattled off a series of numbers.

"Employment history?"

"Stop it," I snapped at Alys. "You're going too far."

"Maeve—"

"No. We decided to go into business together. To buy and fix houses. And yes, I may have overstepped by letting him stay here without asking you first but you're way out of line. Our relationship is our business, so butt out."

"Evie," Kal began but I held up a hand. This discussion was between me and my sister.

Alys scrutinized my face and then looked up at Kal. "If you hurt her, they won't find all the pieces of you."

"I won't," Kal said the words solemnly, as though he were making a vow.

With that, Alys strode to the door, snapped open her umbrella, and then turned. "I'll stay with Aunt Jess for the next couple of days. And I want him out of here and the house ready for the spring market."

I shut the door and then leaned against it. Alys had a way of supercharging the atmosphere in a room. When she left it was as though she sucked all the air out with her.

"Are you all right?" Kal placed his crutches and swung forward.

"Just where do you get off telling my sister that you love me," I snapped.

"It's the truth."

My mouth fell open. "And *that's* how you tell me? In the middle of an argument with my sister?"

He shrugged. The motion awkward with the crutches supporting his weight. "I told you I wanted more."

"Yes, but there's a world of difference between wanting more and love," I argued. "We don't know each other that well."

"I know enough."

"You *can't*," I insisted. "Kal, that's crazy. You can't possibly know enough about me to make that determination."

He tilted his head to the side. "I know that you're beautiful, inside and out. I know you want to heal people and that you fight for what you want. That you have a terrible singing voice. You snore and you like extra cream in your coffee. I know that you're warm and your soul has been as lonely and adrift as mine. I know that when I'm with you, even when I'm terrified or in pain that everything just feels…right. And I've learned to trust my instincts. So yes, Evie, I know enough to be sure that I'm in love with you. Haven't you ever just *known*?

My heart was beating too fast and I had forgotten how to breathe. Kal wasn't big on speeches. Most of the time I was lucky to pry more than one syllable out of him. But when he did decide to use his words….

Haven't you ever just known. I understood his meaning, his emphasis. On the word. It was intuition, a level of surety that radiated from every cell in my body. An inherent understanding.

I'd never labeled it. Never told anyone else about it. But damn it all, sometime I just *knew*.

And Kal was saying he did, too. That his knowing was telling him we belonged together. Could I disrespect or argue with that innate compression?

Maybe if I wanted to. Which I didn't.

I sighed. "What am I going to with you?"

He leaned his forehead against mine. We were so close that we shared breaths. "I can think of a few things."

"No sex," I admonished.

"Not yet," he agreed.

"You should rest that leg."

"On one condition."

The man was incorrigible. He knew I wanted him to be well and was using his psychical health to barter with me. "What's the condition?"

"You take off all your clothes."

CHAPTER TWENTY

ALYS

he rain slowed as if someone was using a wrench to turn a sticky valve. I lay in my hammock and listened as it tapered to a drizzle. Maeve was passed out cold and Sibby had excused herself outside to "use the facilities". I hoped she remembered not to go in the river to pee. There was a type of parasitic catfish that would follow the stream of urine and swim up inside a body where it would gorge on the host's blood. Removing it was difficult because the little bastard had spines that would help it hold its position.

Mother Nature could be a raging bitch sometimes.

I left the door to the hut open in case Maeve woke. I took a deep breath of some of the wildest most oxygen-rich air I had ever tasted. After spending much of my life living at mountain elevation, Amazonia was like having an oxygen mask applied directly to my lungs. I picked my way down the winding dirt and rock steps and looked around at the misty landscape. My fitness tracker told me it was six in the morning local time, but away from the river, the canopy was too thick to give a true position of the sun. "Sibby?"

"Up here."

I craned my neck up at an uncomfortable angle so I could see. Then wished I hadn't because the full moon was out. "You climbed a tree in the nude?"

"I was hungry. Look out below."

I jumped back just as a bunch of bananas landed in the spot where I'd been standing. Sibby shinnied her way down the tree-like she always did so in the buff.

"It's too bad we don't have a blender. There's enough fruit around here to make a truly excellent organic smoothie. Look, I found avocados, coconuts, guava, and even a pineapple. Though I'm not sure how we can eat that without a knife."

I looked at her bounty. It along with the rainwater we had collected the night before would be enough to fill the holes in our bellies. Since none of us had eaten since breakfast the day before and had walked who knew how many miles, a meal was long overdue.

Sibby reached for the bunch of bananas, clearly intending to rip one free and tuck in, but I gripped her wrist. "Wait."

She tried to pull free. "Why?"

I picked up a stick and prodded the bananas. Immediately I saw the same black and yellow legs I'd spied a moment before. Moving the banana aside, I revealed the inhabitant to my sister.

"Banana spider," I said.

"Is it poisonous?" Sibby's eyes were wide.

"Venomous," I corrected. "If you bite it and get sick, that's poisonous. If it bites you and you get sick it's considered venomous. And not this particular one, no." I reached down and extended a hand to the spider.

"What are you doing?"

"It's okay." I let the spider crawl across my hand. "She's an orb weaver. They tend to live in a bunch. It's good camouflage from birds that would eat it. When fruit begins to rot, it attracts bugs, which the spider captures and devours."

"She?" Sibby asked.

"The vivid colors. The male spiders aren't as boldly colored. There are other kinds as well. Look out for the brown ones though, they can be deadly."

Sibby watched as I took the orb-weaver over to the trunk of the tree and deposited her there. "That's downright witchy of you, Alys."

I made a face. "After restoring houses for the last twenty years, I've seen more than my share of spiders, snakes, and all sorts of other creepy crawlies. For the most part, if you didn't harm them, they didn't harm you."

"You weren't so sanguine yesterday when that anaconda was gunning for you."

The image made me shudder. "Don't remind me."

We checked over the rest of the fruit to make sure we didn't have any other uninvited guests before hauling the bounty onto the rock that doubled as a porch for the hut.

Maeve was still asleep so I moved over to her hammock and shook her shoulder. "Maeve. We've got some food and water."

She yawned and stretched and I helped her out of the hammock. She seemed steady enough on her feet and we picked our way outside.

"So, about the dead guys," Sibby began as she bit into a peeled banana.

I groaned. "Really Sibby? We're about to have breakfast."

"We need to talk about it," she insisted.

I knew she was right. "Okay, so what about the dead guys?"

"Someone had to have sent them. Maybe another witch or a different being who possesses necromantic magic."

"Necromantic?" Maeve repeated.

"Power over the dead," Sibby tossed her banana peel out into the rainforest. "Maybe blood magic, ritual sacrifice. Whatever power it is, it isn't perfect. The bodies are decomposing. Eventually, all the magic in the universe won't keep them functioning. Especially in a place like this."

I mulled over what she said as I attempted to peel an avocado with my fingernails. "One of two possibilities then. Either we pissed off the local necromancer or…."

Maeve finished the thought for me. "Or a magic hunter has been tailing us."

I didn't want to accept that. Yes, we had made hasty arrangements for this trip. It had happened faster than I wanted but I had been careful and we hadn't used magic outside of the convergence. Except….

"I lost my temper yesterday," I closed my eyes as it dawned on me. "When Sibby told me about Sebastian. That's how they found us in Iquitos. It's my fault."

"It was an accident," Sibby said. "Alys, we know you wouldn't put us in danger on purpose."

Still, I felt horrible. I was supposed to be protecting my sisters. Instead, in a moment of weakness, my temper had slipped the leash.

"It happens to the best of us," Maeve reached out a hand. "Right?"

I took it and squeezed. Mentally I vowed then and there that I would quit haranguing both of them about lack of control. We were only human. "Right."

"So, what do we do?" Maeve withdrew her hand and reached for a mango. "We're nowhere near the source of the Amazon or the temple. Sibby can't jump us back to Iquitos or home to Eckhart. One day tromping through the rainforest was plenty. But should we risk staying here?"

Sibby shrugged and looked at me. "What do you think, Alys?"

I think I wished I had my purse with a cell phone so I could have sent a message to Brock. I think we were terribly unprepared to take on the rainforest, even with magic. A magic hunter who could control the dead was just one more lethal factor in a world teeming with them.

Maeve looked somewhat better, but she still needed rest. The abandoned hunt wasn't much to look at but any port in a shitstorm.

I looked out over the raw, unapologetic beauty of the rainforest. A parrot took flight, its green feathers lost in silhouette as it crossed the path of the sinking sun.

Was there a cure for Maeve's MS somewhere in this place? A magical talisman to correct the war that raged inside her body?

I exhaled and spoke from the heart. "I think we need to take it slowly. Rest through today and see how everyone is feeling tomorrow."

"And by everyone, you mean me," Maeve grumped.

"I mean everyone. I'm not as young as I used to be either."

She gave me a tight-lipped smile and then headed back inside.

"Where are you going?"

"You wanted me to rest so I'm resting."

"And don't pee in the river," I cautioned. "There's a parasitic catfish—"

"That lodges in the vagina by sinking in little spines so it can suck your blood. I watched the same documentary." She disappeared back into the hut.

I looked at Sibby, who was smirking. "What could possibly be funny?"

"Only that my vagina should come with a warning label.

Abandon all hope ye who enter here. Poor fish wouldn't stand a chance."

"I don't understand you half the time," I told her.

"Back atcha, Alys." Sibby reached for another banana. "Back atcha."

MAEVE

What I didn't tell my sisters was that I enjoyed sleeping more than being awake. A day of rest in the hammock sounded heavenly, even though I worried I was slowing us down and that the magic hunter and his zombie minions would catch up. But dreams embraced me wholly every time I reclined in the hammock. The part of me who'd been a nurse worried that was depression talking. After all, my problems all got shelved when I slept. My stress levels went down and I didn't have to make arrangements or decisions. I didn't have to feel guilty for putting my sisters in danger, guilty for abandoning my husband and children. I didn't have to miss them. Was I avoiding dealing with reality by escaping into sleep so much?

Perhaps but one thing was clear. I couldn't stop.

In my dreams, I was young and healthy again.

I was with Kal again. The old Kal, the one who adored me.

"I want to look at you," the crazy man who had just told me he was in love with me said. "I want to see all of you."

He'd only ever seen me in scrubs or thick winter layers. What if he was disappointed with what I looked like?

"Come into the living room then. In front of the fire." I urged. "It's warm in there, and better to be naked."

He nodded, clearly satisfied. I angsted the entire time he made his way on crutches over to the couch.

"Can I get you anything?" I asked the question to stall. Like he would really want me to fetch him a coffee or something.

"Evie."

"I have a love/hate thing going on with the way you say my name," I told him.

He just smiled.

I fretted as I tried to decide where I should stand. Closer, where he could touch me, or over on the faux bearskin rug so I would be backlit by the flames? The light in the room was low, only a low wattage bulb on the side table lamp and the firelight lit the room. It was cozy and cave-like, the way I had envisioned.

Of course, my design hadn't exactly envisioned this.

I wanted to ask him, or maybe beg him to wait, but that felt cowardly.

I wasn't a coward. I just didn't look the way I wanted to.

That was one way to test his love. If I undressed and Kal went screaming out into the night—broken leg and all—I knew his confession of love wasn't all it was cracked up to be.

"He won't leave. This is the one."

I started at the feminine voice that spoke with authority in my head. *The knowing.*

Kal was waiting patiently, silent once more.

I trusted *the knowing.* More than that, I trusted Kal. Alys would say I was being reckless or foolish, but damn it, sometimes a woman had to go with her heart. Because she *knew.*

I reached down and pulled the sweater up over my head. I placed it on the mantle and then bent over to unlace my boots. I toed them off, and the thick socks as well. I was down to leggings and underwear. There was no fabric barrier to conceal my shape.

"*Move.*" *The knowing* urged me. "*Sway.*"

I swished my hips a little and used my hands to lift my heavy mane of hair. On impulse I looked at Kal over my shoulder, keeping up the slow. sensual rhythm.

His gaze was transfixed on me. Not the boobs spilling out of my push-up bra, or the curve of my ass. He wasn't making a mental log of my physical defects and areas for future improvement. No, the man was drinking me in as though I were an oasis he'd found after days of crawling through the desert.

A woman could get addicted to that look.

His desire was written in his gaze, on his face, in the bulge in his sweats. It emboldened me to keep going. To give in to the primal force that slowly unfurled between us. I pushed the leggings down and flowed into bigger, bolder movements. There was no music but I could swear I heard drumbeats as I danced for Kal in my underwear.

"Come here," he said.

And I moved to him ready to reveal the rest....

The need to pee dragged me from the vivid dream. I woke not knowing where I was or where the bathroom was located.

I sensed the presence of others. The brain fog lifted and my situation registered.

In a hammock, which was actually very comfortable somewhere in the Amazon rainforest. On the lookout for the Mother Superior of Magic and a talisman that would cure my MS.

Dead guys, and magic hunters, and an abandoned hut in the forest, oh my!

My bladder control wasn't great. Whether that was Ms.

Priss or a side effect of middle-age didn't matter. What did matter was that I was about thirty seconds away from wetting myself.

"Maeve?" Alys's voice drifted out of the absolute darkness as I wriggled out of the hammock.

"Need to pee," I said.

"Not in the river," she muttered, still bossy even when she was half asleep.

"Yeah yeah." The thin fabric that made up the sarong style wrap was dry. I swirled it around me. My boots were still soggy, but I wasn't about to go tramping around the jungle in my bare feet so I slid my feet into them.

Half dressed and still groggy, I made my way out to the porch. I smiled when I saw the knobby walking stick. Sibby must've left it for me to find. She was on my case almost daily about getting a walking aid. At home, I fought the idea. The MS wasn't that bad yet. What would I say to Kal or the kids?

In the rainforest, I was grateful for the assist.

The waning moon was a pale sliver above the treetops. Its silvery light was barely enough to guide my steps. I didn't dare wander too far from the protection of the hut or my sisters so I found an area to the left of the path and squatted.

Ah, sweet relief.

Business attended to, I was all set to head back up the steps and get lost in the memory of what I knew came next when a flash of something illuminated by the moonlight caught my eye.

Using my walking stick as a guide, I carefully picked my way toward the thing. It was smooth and round, like a moonstone polished by the river. But it was too large for any moonstone I'd ever seen.

I nudged it with the stick. It moved a little. Not a stone, something much lighter.

I knelt down and then set my stick beside me so I could use both hands to pick it up.

It was cool to the touch but light for an object that size. I turned it over and dropped it.

I stuffed a fist in my mouth as I beheld the empty eye sockets staring back up at me.

A human skull.

What was it doing out here?

The knowing whispered inside my own skull. *"The answers are here. All of them. It is time."*

My hands shook as I lifted the skull again. The lower jaw was missing, but the upper was intact.

"Who were you?" I asked the skull.

It didn't reply. Not that I had expected it to.

I looked up and spied another stark white object a few meters away. This one was oblong and jutted through the ground.

It seemed disrespectful to leave the skull where I found it. Instead, I bunched up the hem of my dress and tucked the skull within, then moved toward the new object.

A femur. Completely intact and sticking up out of the ground. I turned it in the shaft of moonlight and examined it for marks. Nothing to indicate it had been chewed on by a carnivore. Nothing had cracked it open to get to the marrow.

Was it from the same person? How had they died? And how had the femur and skull been left so far apart? The bone was pristine, undamaged. In the pale moon's glow, it looked more like a Halloween prop or maybe something that had been created as an aid for medical school students.

I glanced up and saw another white object up ahead and was halfway to it when I heard my sisters calling my name.

"Over here," I shouted and waited. Was it a wise idea to follow a trail of bones to whatever lay at the end? No. But *the knowing* was urging me forward.

"You can't wander off like that," Alys began.

I shoved the femur at her and the skull at Sibby. "There's a trail of bones. I intend to follow it."

They were silent as I used my stick to move to the next breadcrumb. It was a ribcage, though it was in much worse shape than the other pieces of the skeleton. Several of the ribs were missing and the sternum appeared to be cracked. All the small hairs on my body stood on end. What was this?

"Over there," Sibby whispered. "There's a whole pile of them."

I looked up but couldn't see where she pointed. "Take me there."

I could feel Alys's nervous energy pulsing behind me. Could feel Sibby's excitement. We moved forward slowly until I could see it too.

Not just one bone. A mountain of them. No, a mountain range.

My hand flew to my mouth as I beheld the sight before us. A graveyard full of bones. They seemed to encircle a dark heart that we couldn't penetrate.

"I can see something in there," Sibby breathed. "It looks like—"

Fires blazed from unseen torches. And we beheld the ruin of what had once been a temple. A stone retaining wall encircled the bones. Beneatha our feet was the smooth expanse of what had once been a human made floor.

"Oh my god," Alys gripped my hand tightly.

Slitted red eyes the size of volleyballs fixed on us. We gasped in unison. Sibby's hand was on my arm and I was willing to bet she was preparing to jump us out of this place.

But that was wrong. I needed to be here.

Those mesmerizing eyes appeared to be at chest height but as I watched, they rose up and up and up.

And up.

The coils of the great serpent stretched out around the boneyard. To the walls of the temple. My mind could barely comprehend the size of it.

"Welcome," the voice in my head, what I thought was *the knowing* had taken on a sibilant quality to match the massive snake before us as she spoke in my head. *"Welcome, Silver sisters. I am The Mother Superior of Magic. And I have been waiting a long time for you."*

CHAPTER TWENTY-ONE

*S*ebastian hadn't felt fear for most of his unnatural life. He still wouldn't say he called the sensation that was snaking through his gut fear, but whatever the name, he experienced it when he got a whiff of the Headhunter's camp.

Where the dead walked. Hundreds upon hundreds of animated corpses stood awaiting their master's bidding. All in different states of decomposition. Fresh corpses and ones that were little more than bones and sinew. All responded to the call of the Headhunter.

They didn't speak. Didn't do anything except wait for the next order. Sebastian had been left in the cage of bones, a cage that separated him from his magic. He didn't believe the cage drained him the same way his net did. It just cut him off from the source of his power.

The Headhunter was in his tent. Sebastian could tell because the corpses were all aimed at the lone canvas structure in the middle of the clearing. From the place where the bone cage was perched, he had a clear view of the valley below.

He hadn't been given food or water. Not that he would trust any fare his captor offered him. Who knew how the Headhunter ensnared his victims? He had managed to collect rainwater in a large leaf, but his stomach was gnawing on itself from hunger.

Sebastian knew he was alive for only one reason. Bait.

He'd used the tactic a time or two himself. Capture someone the prey cared for and hold them. Then, when the prey emerged either to bargain or rescue the loved one, the hunter would skillfully ensnare them.

If the Headhunter bothered to speak with him though, he would tell the man that the plan would fail. Siobhan had no idea he had come to the rainforest. And even if she did, she had herself and her sisters to think about.

A helicopter had landed in the clearing a few hours ago. Though the Headhunter remained as silent as his army, Sebastian could sense the man's aura. Something hadn't gone as it was supposed to. *The witches*, he thought.

There was a force protecting them. Sebastian had felt it at the house. Something more than the ghost. It was as if magic itself was working to keep the three of them safe.

No wonder the bounty had been raised. No wonder the Headhunter would risk trapping him, betraying guild law just as Sebastian had done with Bane.

Though it burned each and every time, Sebastian reached his hands forward and wrapped them around the bone cage. Smoke began to rise as his life force met the necromantic magic, but he ignored the pain. Instead, he focused on his task.

"It won't work," A voice said from behind him.

Sebastian gasped and released the bars. "Robin? What the hell are you doing here?"

"I sensed your distress, brother." The fae prince flickered much the same way the spirit had at the cottage.

"You aren't dead?" Sebastian asked. An odd lump formed in his throat at the thought.

Robin shook his head and circled the bars. "Not yet. And I'm not really here either. This is just a projection. One of my holdover powers from the time before. Where are you?"

"Somewhere in northeastern Peru." Sebastian stared at the image of Robin Goodfellow. "Tell me what you know about the Headhunter."

"I'm afraid I don't know any more than you do. He is very old. Born mortal and trained by a witch doctor in Amazonia. He only bestirs himself for large bounties."

"Like the Silver sisters," Sebastian muttered. "But what is his end goal? What does the man want?"

Robin tipped his head to the side. "I could do a little spying for you if you like."

Sebastian was surprised. "Why would you do that?"

"To help you." Robin offered a strained smile. "The way I should have done when you were young."

So, the fae was here to absolve his guilt. Whatever his motivation, Sebastian decided he didn't care. "Find out what you can. I'll just wait here."

Robin flashed him his trademark wicked grin and vanished.

Sebastian sat crossed-legged on the bottom of his cage to wait.

MAEVE

"Did you guys hear that?" Sibby hissed in my ear. "Is the snake actually talking to us?"

Those slitted eyes focused on her. *"I'm mind-speaking you, Siobhan. As I have done almost every day for your entire existence."*

My lips parted even as the snake focused on me.

"You call me intuition. What I am is the source of your magic. Of all magic in the world."

"But why are you're a snake?" I breathed.

The head bobbed closer. *"This is just one aspect of who I am. I am a mother, maiden, and crone. I am your past and your future. I exist in all and all exist in me."*

"The bones?" Alys gestured to the graveyard around us. "Do they still exist in you?"

"Don't be pissy to the big-ass snake, Alys," Sibby whispered.

"It is no longer safe for me to leave this place. They were sacrificed to sustain me, so I in turn could sustain you. Life and death are cyclical. You know this, Alys. As one who has been to the other side."

Alys jerked.

Though the thought that this giant snake was *the knowing* as well as the being I had come all this way to find still hadn't fully registered, I wasn't about to squander the chance. It took all of my effort to step forward, to draw her attention to me. "You *know* why I've come all this way?"

"*I know. I had a vision of you three standing before me long before you ever existed. I have seen your destiny and it is great.*"

Leaning heavily on my cane I asked. "Can you help me?"

Those eyes bore into me, could see down to the last little particles of dust in my soul.

"Please," I fell to my knees. It had nothing to do with Ms. Priss and everything with showing reverence to the one being who might be able to help.

"*You must first defeat your worst enemy before you can become whole.*"

I shook my head. "How can I possibly fight anyone? I barely made it here in one piece."

The snakehead hovered at eye level with me until we shared breath. "*Look into my eyes and see. For you are the enchantress and the seeress who bleeds with the dark of the moon. Look into my eyes and see.*"

I looked. My gaze went unfocused and the world tunneled down to me and the slitted red eyes of the Mother Superior of Magic.

The rainforest around me spun and spun and the last thing I heard was Alys's cry before the world faded away.

"Sebastian."

Sebastian looked up to where Robin's transparent face hovered just outside of the bone cage. "Did you find anything?"

The image flickered. "Yes. He wants to kill the Mother Superior of Magic."

Sebastian blinked. "But she's just a rumor? A fable made up by the healers at her temple."

"The Headhunter believes her to be very real. She is too powerful for him as he is, but according to the missives and maps, he knows where she is, and absorbing all the magic from the three Silver sisters will give him enough strength to best her."

Sebastian gripped the bars of the bone cage. "Where are they?"

Robin shook his head. "He's been unable to track the witches. Apparently, Siobhan vanished them from the helicopter he sent to acquire them."

His knees went weak at the thought of Siobhan traveling from a moving helicopter. She was such a novice, didn't know what she was doing half the time. "She could have been killed. They all might have been."

Robin appeared grim. "She still might. If they went into the dark heart of Amazonia…, there are uncontacted tribes, megareptiles, all sorts of dangers."

Sebastian began to pace the tight confines of his cell. There wasn't enough room but he couldn't be still a moment longer.

"The sisters came down here, looking for a cure for Maeve," he murmured.

"Cure?" Robin asked. "You're sure about that?"

"She has an autoimmune disease. It's been their focus for several weeks."

"Spoken like a true hunter." Robin's tone was wry but Sebastian ignored him.

"What if…?" He frowned. "What if the Mother Superior of Magic knows she is in danger. What if she has brought the sisters here to protect herself?"

Robin sounded dubious even as he said, "I suppose it's possible…"

Sebastian gripped the bars again. "You said you saw the Mother's location. You need to warn them. Get her to safety."

"Are you talking about the Mother Superior or your witch?"

"Just go," Sebastian snarled.

Robin vanished.

Rain began to patter down in the leaves above his head. He walked and walked as he waited for the fae prince's return. The storm let loose, coming down in a steady stream that soaked him to the bone. The ground beneath his feet turned to mud and soon he was slogging through ankle-deep sludge.

Sebastian stopped in mid-step. Looked down. Then fell to his knees and began to dig.

MAEVE

So here's the thing about dreams—especially snake-trance induced ones. Sometimes they are X-rated. At least the best ones are. If reading about the naughty things I did with my husband before he was my husband isn't your jam, skip on over to the next chapter. I'll meet you there. Right after I relive the most erotic encounter of my life.

"Come here," Kal said.

The yearning in his eyes, the hunger. How had I existed without seeing that look? I moved to him, ready to reveal the rest of my body. To let him touch me.

The first contact of his hand on my bare midriff sent a zing up my spine and created a slow unfurling in my core.

I'd had sex before and it was...fine. Nothing special. Usually over much too quickly or not quickly enough. I'd never had an orgasm with another person. After working in the maternity ward, I knew all about the possible repercussions of a one-night stand. Diseases and unplanned pregnancy. And in my mind, that wasn't worth the risk.

But I loved being touched. Craved it. Thought about it more than was probably normal. Touching with a man always led to sex though, so I didn't get anywhere near enough of it to suit my greedy nature.

Kal had agreed we weren't going to have sex. It wasn't safe with his broken leg. He wanted to look and touch. And I wanted him to do those things. So we were on the same page and this encounter would only go so far. I promised myself I would soak it up.

He spent several minutes exploring my body with his eyes and fingertips. They felt like butterfly wings as they drifted over my exposed skin. His hands were calloused, more so than I'd ever expected a chef's hands to be. I tipped my head back and reveled in the feel of harness scraping so lightly across my skin.

"I asked for naked, Nurse Silver," Kal murmured.

"I'm getting there," I breathed. "Don't be so impatient."

"Can't help it." A hand slid up along the underwire of my bra. "I've been fantasizing about you for days. And your little strip tease almost made me faint."

"Not a fan of anticipation?" I smiled down at him. He was so handsome. No real facial hair marked his strong jaw. His dark eyes shone and his full lips were curved in a sensual smile.

He shook his head. "I'm all about instant gratification."

"Too bad. I'll have to convert you to my way of thinking." His healing leg was propped along the length of the couch. I carefully moved into position, hovering over him and letting my breasts dangle enticingly in his line of sight before pressing myself against the bulge between his legs.

"Mercy," Kal breathed.

One of my bra straps slipped down my shoulder. "I think I like it when you beg."

He made a hoarse sound then and his touches grew bolder. Long sweeping caresses from my shoulder to my hip and then back. He stopped and struggled to unclasp my bra himself. It was a quadruple hook underwire. I wished him luck. Half the time I struggled with the clasps.

Acres of smooth skin begged me to explore it. I'd touched him before but hadn't had the freedom to explore for my own ends and took shameless advantage of his preoccupation with my bra.

I loved that he was impatient and fumble-fingered like a teenager in a pickup parked at Lover's Lane. I loved the way he gasped when I bit lightly on the straining tendon on his neck and the way he rocked his sex up to meet mine when I scraped a fingernail over his nipple.

"Are you coming around to my way of thinking?" I asked playfully. "Or should I…?"

He sucked my breast into his mouth. Bra and all. The suddenness of the wet heat made me throw my head back. His teeth found the nipple and worked the stiff point, abrading it against the damp fabric.

The game playing was over. Now I was the one reaching for my bra clasp. Desperate to get the barrier out from between my flesh and his hot, hungry mouth.

One of the hooks was crooked and took a certain amount of finesse I didn't possess at the moment. Finally, I gave up and just pushed the other strap down my arms and peeled the cups away.

He took me in deep again and a sharp cry came from my throat as he laved the tight peak. My other breast ached and his fingers found it, rolling it gently as though imploring it to wait its turn.

My underwear grew damp as with each swipe of his tongue he tightened the coil of my desire. Soon his crotch sported the wet evidence of my arousal. I didn't care as I rocked against him, loving the small contact even as I wanted more.

You can't have more. He's hurt. This is all you get.

My fervor cooled a little as I recalled our limitations. What had given me reassurance moments before now irritated me. I wanted more.

Kal focused on my other breast and I sank my fingers into the silky length of his hair, holding him to me even as I rocked gently against him.

Suddenly Kal broke off and guided me off him.

"What is it?" I knelt beside him. "Did I hurt you?"

He shook his head. "I need more room."

"More room for what?" I asked and then gaped as he crawled off the couch and sprawled onto the bearskin rug.

"For you." Kal nodded at my panties. "Take them off."

My throat went dry. "We can't—"

"Have sex, I know. But I can taste you." He held out a hand.

"Um," I said, feeling ridiculous all of a sudden. "Why would you want to do that?"

He just gave me that Kal look. As though I were ridiculous for even asking.

I delayed a minute by spinning my bra around and dealing with that devil-crooked hook. My heart was beating so hard that I thought it would burst. The logistics of what he suggested were like something out of internet porn. Not only had I never had anyone do that to me, but I was also self-conscious that I wouldn't live up to whatever fantasy he had in his mind.

"Evie," Kal said in a low tone. "I don't like when you get quiet. It means you're thinking too hard about something you shouldn't be thinking about at all."

I glared at him over my shoulder. "You can't tell me what to think."

He held out a hand and reluctantly, I lowered myself onto the rug by his side.

He tucked a strand of hair behind my ear. "Tell me what's wrong."

My breath huffed out of me in a ragged sigh. "It's just that, well, I've never...done that."

"Done what?" He looked blank.

"That. What you want to do to me. I don't even know if I'll like that or if I can..." I trailed off, feeling foolish.

Kal waited for a beat and then pulled me down next to him. "Okay."

I blinked. "Okay?"

He nodded. "If it makes you so uncomfortable, then I won't."

"Oh, but you wanted to." What was I even saying?

He stroked the shell of my ear. "Of course, I want to. There's no part of you I don't want to touch. Don't want to kiss. No part." He repeated and the look in his eyes told me he meant what he said.

My lips parted but I had no words.

"The thing is though that I want you to be comfortable with me. I want you to trust me enough to do all those things. We have time, Evie. So right now, I want you to show me what it is you do like."

My eyes went wide. "You mean....?"

He took my hand and trailed it down over my breast and then let it rest on top of my panties. "Show me how to give you pleasure."

Never in my most fevered fantasies had I imagined this sort of connection. Some distant part of me felt as though I ought to be embarrassed or ashamed to even admit that I touched myself. But why? It wasn't as though Kal were going to judge me. He wanted to pleasure me, wanted to learn what sort of touches would bring me release.

His hand left mine and his fingers trailed those butterfly caresses up my thigh.

"Show me." His eyes were intent on my face.

I slipped my hand beneath the sopping fabric and stroked with two fingers against my tender flesh.

Hie eyes consumed me, heated my blood. Liquid warmth flowed from my feminine core. I rubbed deeper and got lost in the wet sensation.

"That's it, Evie," he encouraged me as I rubbed and circled and rubbed harder. "Does that feel good?"

I nodded jerkily as my hips began rocking up into the touch. Kal squeezed the meat of my thigh between his thumb and forefinger. He wanted more, but I didn't know how to give it to him without breaking contact.

"Take these off," Kal said as his fingers trailed along the waistband of my underwear. "Let me see all of you."

There was no hesitancy this time. I sat up and shimmied out of the scrap of fabric then lay back to resume.

Kal had turned onto his side and had his hand already in place. "Show me how you like it. Use me." His deep voice was a velvet caress.

So I showed him. With my own wet hand, I guided him into the deep rhythm that had me so close to climax.

"Can I touch you inside?" He whispered the question against my ear.

I moaned and arched my hips up, begging him to do just that.

"I love how wet you are," Kal lowered his mouth and licked a nipple, making me writhe on the rug. "You're so damn hot."

No one had ever said such things to me before. I loved it, loved him. The feelings built and built along with the pleasure. The stretching sensation of his fingers within, the heat of his body pressed against mine.

His gaze was hooded as he watched my face. "You're getting close, aren't you?"

"Don't stop." If he stopped, I would die.

"Never." It was a vow he made even as his thumb resumed circling my clitoris.

That one word combined with the gentle touch I had taught him put me over the edge. I arched and cried out as the orgasm threatened to shatter my spine. It went on and on and on and through it all, Kal watched me. Drank me in and touched me deeply.

All the way to my heart.

Slowly, I drifted back down, into my body. His hand cupped between my legs in a proprietary fashion, as though he had discovered treasure he didn't want to let go of.

"That's one," he said.

"One?" I was confused. "One what?"

"One release. You've given me three so far. I owe you at least two more. A real man would make it six."

I rolled my eyes. "Don't be a Neanderthal. I'm not keeping score. That's for pain management."

"Whatever you want to tell yourself, Nurse Silver." Kal brushed my hair away from my eyes and then leaned down to whisper in a way that made all the hairs on my body stand on end. "Now, show me where it hurts."

CHAPTER TWENTY-TWO

MAEVE

"*W*hy are you crying, Maeve?"

"I don't know." I wiped the moisture beneath my eyes and looked up. I recognized the voice but the body….

"More like what you expected?" The Mother Superior of Magic wore a voluminous purple gown that flowed down to her bare feet. Her hair was coiled in intricate braids of every color. Her dark eyes were lined with kohl.

I sniffled and forced a smile even though my heart ached. "Yeah."

"That's the trouble with human dreamers. They expect to see a representation of themselves." She reached out a hand and helped me up. "Why are you crying?"

I swallowed past the emotion that was slowly suffocating me. "It's Kal."

"Your husband?"

I nodded. "The way he looked at me back then. The way he wanted me. The way I wanted him…. It's just…I want it to be like that again. And it can't."

"Why not?"

I snorted. "Because I'm sick. I don't have enough energy to handle my basics some days, never mind have lurid sexual encounters. But I miss that version of me. The one who took risks."

"You took a risk in coming to find me," she pointed out. "Didn't you?"

"I had no choice. Not if I wanted to beat this."

"You mean, beat her." She pointed a finger in the darkness an image appeared.

I sucked in a breath. Ms. Priss. "What's she doing here? I don't want her here."

"She's always with you."

"I thought I had to defeat an enemy," I said. "I thought you were going to help me."

The Mother Superior of Magic waved her hand in the other direction and another body appeared. My body, the me that had just been with Kal.

"Let me ask you a question. If you had the option to go back, to live her life over again, would you?"

I looked into her eyes and then stared at the mock-up of younger Maeve. "I don't...what does that have to do with anything?"

"She is you and you are her. But you are not one and the same." She put her hands over my lower belly. "She doesn't comprehend the feeling of having a child growing inside her. She hasn't experienced the joy of giving birth to not one but two healthy babes. She is the maiden and her time is past. You are the mother. Your time is now. Mother, maiden and..."

She turned her head and slowly, I did the same as realization dawned. "She's the crone. Ms. Priss is me."

"A possible version of you. She is you without Kal. You who is bitter and alone."

I moved closer to inspect her. The lines of her face, the

thin lips. The burning in her eyes as she leaned resentfully on her cane.

I shook my head. "So you're saying I'm going to end up like her. All pinch-faced and stern?"

"Not necessarily. She's part of you. Much as *the Yacumama* is part of me."

I repeated the word.

"It means "Mother of Water". It is what the inhabitants of this land have called the snake aspect that they so fear. I didn't actually eat any of those people. They sacrificed themselves before me as I was helpless to watch. The bones piled up year over year, decade after decade and the legend grew. I cannot leave Amazonia. My physical body is too cumbersome to maneuver. So I have become trapped in my own skin." She raised one perfectly arched brow. "Sound familiar?"

I sucked in a sharp breath and looked back to Ms. Priss.

"She is the aspect that you've manifested to represent something that is a part of you, but also apart from you. And you are becoming more like her every day."

"But I don't want to be like her." It came out as a whine. "She's awful."

"Do you recall what Siobhan said to you, about manifesting your thoughts into reality?" At my nod, she smiled. "What have you been thinking about since your diagnosis?"

I shook my head. "Are you saying I'm making myself sick?"

"Sicker. By concentrating on what you've lost," she pointed at the young version of me, "You are like a stream that cuts its path through space and time to reach its final destination. If you don't wish to be like her Maeve, then choose to be different. But no matter what life throws at you, realize that you are *not* powerless."

This was starting to sound more and more like a pep talk.

Why would the Mother Superior of Magic be giving me a pep talk unless….

The truth peeked out like a sliver of moonlight from behind the clouds. I swallowed and asked the question I was most afraid to voice. "Is there a cure for my MS?"

She touched my shoulder. "No, Maeve Silver. There is no cure. But there is help."

She held out her hand and something appeared within it. A silver crescent moon necklace, with something dangling from the bottom. On closer inspection, I recognized it as a curved snake fang.

I could feel the energy pulsing like a heartbeat as it radiated from the necklace. She moved around me and fastened it around my neck. The second it touched my skin it melded into me. Became part of me.

"What does it do?" I asked.

She turned me to face her and smiled. "You'll find out soon enough."

SIOBHAN

"Maeve?" I tried as the sun rose beside the giant snake. I'd heard the stories of *Yacumama* before. The legendary serpent of the Peruvian Amazon was said to live surrounded by the bones of its victims. But never in my wildest imaginings had I thought that the giant serpent would be magic.

Not just magic, the source of all magic. She was what Maeve had been looking for.

"Can you jump her back to the hut?" Alys asked.

I closed my eyes and pictured the small hut that was far from safe, but at least provided shelter and wasn't within striking distance of a humongous reptile.

Nothing happened.

I tried again. I could feel magic. It was in the air, pulsing all around me but I couldn't access it. "I can't."

Alys swore. It wasn't something she did often, not my classy big sister. The fact that she let out a string of cuss words that could make a sailor blush scared me more than the giant serpent.

"What do we do?" I asked Alys as I stroked Maeve's pale

face. Behind her lids, her eyes flickered back and forth as though she were reading. Or maybe watching a scene.

"Keep trying to wake her up." Alys paused. "I'm going back to the hut. It isn't far from here. We need food and water and our freaking clothes."

"What if she doesn't wake up?"

Alys dropped to her knees beside Maeve and stroked her arm. "She will. Whatever that...thing is doing to her, she'll come out of it. We just need to keep her safe."

She got to her feet. "I'll be back as fast as I can."

"Are you sure you don't want me to go?"

Alys shook her head. "I need to do something productive or I will totally lose it."

She walked out of the clearing and disappeared inside the rain forest. I had never seen my oldest sister so worried and it worried me.

Maeve's status hadn't changed so I looked at *Yucamama*. The Mother Superior of Magic.

The snakehead was lowered, its eyes shut. The spot it inhabited was in the center of the temple, near what looked like a well. In the misty rainforest morning, it was hard to get my head around the fact that the creature was real.

"That is the biggest fucking snake I've ever seen."

Startled, I turned my head to face the man. At least, I thought he was a man. He was tall with shaggy blond hair and eyes the color of polished sapphires. His accent reminded me of Sebastian.

He didn't appear to be solid. In fact, he looked much like Ethan had when we had summoned the ghost of the cottage. "Who are you?"

The man looked down at me. His mouth kicked up in a familiar grin. "My name is Robin Goodfellow."

Wasn't that the name of the fae from *A Midsummer Night's Dream*? "Puck?" I asked, confused.

"Exactly! Hardly anyone ever gets that. I worry about the youth of today. And you must be Sebastian's witch. He said you were a live wire."

"You know Sebastian?"

"He's my adopted brother. He sent me here to warn the Mother Superior of Magic."

"Warn her about what?"

"The Headhunter is going to try to slay her." Robin stared from the snake to me to Maeve. "As soon as he kills you and your sisters."

My head was spinning. "Wait, the Headhunter?"

"He's a magical bounty hunter. And the bounty on the three of you is sky-high. With your magic, he'd be able to kill, well, her I suppose." Robin looked back at the snake with a shudder. "You need to get away from here. If they find you with her, you'll have made his goal that much easier."

"Where is Sebastian?"

Robin looked me dead in the eye. "The Headhunter has him already. He's bait for a trap laid for you and your sisters. But if you don't move your lovely arse, he won't need the bait anymore."

My heart pounded. I looked down at Maeve's unconscious form and then to the trail leading to the hut where Alys had disappeared. "I can't leave my sisters behind."

Robin's face was set. "I was afraid you would say that. I wish I could do more to help you, but I need to get back to my body. It was lovely meeting you, Siobhan. I hope our paths cross again."

And with those ominous words, he faded into the morning mist.

Something rustled to my left. Then behind me. Death's signature fragrance encircled me. I picked up Maeve's walking stick and hefted it like a club, ready to defend my unconscious sibling.

They moved forward in an awkward shuffle, propelled not by muscle, but by magic.

I swung blindly. Bone cracked. A skull flew. But they kept on coming.

"Shit," I breathed as I took a step back and almost tripped over the snake. "Maeve, wake the hell up already!"

ALYS

I smelled them before I saw them. Zombies. Peeking through the openings to the hut, I spied at least a dozen of them.

My temper flared. Though I could tap into my mother nature gifts with both desire and fear, anger still gave the most bang for the buck.

And after the night I'd had I was *pissed.*

Maeve was in some sort of trance and she and Sibby were helpless and exposed in the jungle with some kind of magic dampening field pulsing around them.

So I strode out the front door. Too bad the door was made of sticks and slid along the ground instead of swung on hinges. It would have been so much more satisfying to slam it open in all my badassness.

"I have to tell you," I said to the dead men who stood before me. "I didn't even want to come on this chocolate forsaken trip. And now I have you smelly jackasses to deal with. One star. I do not recommend!"

With that, I turned my hand in a sharp motion. A rumbling sound filled the jungle. The ground split beneath their feet, and water bubbled up.

They didn't scream as the new tributary I had just created washed them downhill and away from the hut.

I gathered the food and Sibby's clothes and boots, which were still damp but better than hoofing it through nature barefoot, and then set off.

The trail of bones was harder to find in the gray daylight. I had to hunt around but finally spotted the path that led to the temple ruins.

Sibby and Maeve were nowhere in sight.

"Siobhan!" I called out.

"They're gone, Alys."

I looked up into the now open eyes of the Mother Superior of Magic.

"Gone? Where?"

"They were taken to him. The Headhunter."

Lightning crackled in my veins. "Is he the one controlling the zombies?"

"He is master of death. Long ago he learned how to steal life and at the same time reanimate the body. The dead are easier to control than the living. If the Headhunter has his way, only corpses will walk the Earth."

"Can't you do anything to stop him?"

"I cannot leave this place." She stared down at me. I never would have thought a snake's eyes could look troubled. But hers conveyed the depth of worry and fear.

"What can I do?" I asked.

"Nothing."

I shook my head. "I don't accept that. There's always something."

"The enchantress is the key. Only she can save us all."

Maeve. "That's why your healer wanted her to come here. To save you."

"Not just me. The world."

"You never had any intention of curing her MS. You let

her put herself in danger, all for false hope." My anger flared and I was a hairsbreadth away from opening a crater beneath the snake. Mother Superior, my pasty white hide. "And you know what really sucks? If you had just asked for her help, Maeve would have given it. No questions asked. That's who she is. Instead, you manipulated her."

The snake stared at me. I wondered if she was thinking about eating me.

Bon appetit, I thought. *I'm bitter as hell.*

"Tell me how to find my sisters." I barked at the enormous serpent, who was a person, who was also a snake.

"If he has all three of you, the Headhunter will have everything he needs to destroy me."

I lifted my chin. "It's a risk I'm willing to take. Tell me where to find him."

She stared at me again for an endless moment. Was she trying to entrance me the way she had Maeve?

But in the end, all she said was. "Follow the river to the north, deep into the heart of the forest. You will find a cave that looks like a giant skull. That is where the magic hunter has taken your sisters."

"Thank you," I said because Sibby was always harping on me about gratitude.

"Have faith, Alys Silver. Things will work out."

I nodded to her and set off. The fate of the world was on Maeve's shoulders.

How much could a woman carry before she broke under the strain?

CHAPTER TWENTY-THREE

MAEVE

*T*he licking flames of the raging bonfire drew me in like a moth. This wasn't my memory. The only bonfires I recalled were pep rallies before football games at Eckhart High. But there were no bouncing cheerleaders in purple and gray uniforms. No letterman jackets or teens perched on tailgates holding red Solo cups.

There was only the fire.

I moved closer until the heat warmed my skin. Wood shifted and sparks flew upward into the vast expanse of night.

The stars were...enchanting. That was the only way to describe the blanket of night. Like in the Amazon and the desert, no light polluted the natural wonder. But there weren't any leaves or tree branches to obscure the view or bulky clothing bogging down my enjoyment of it.

The low rumble of a drum sounded. Much as it had in the midnight market. Only this time...

This time I felt the beat coming from within.

Dancers appeared. Much as they had at the market fire.

But these weren't ethereal creatures of legend. The way they moved was completely human.

Totally alluring.

And oddly, familiar.

There were three of them. All with long braided dark hair and masks that obscured their features. All bare breasted women. They wore long gauzy skirts that were split on either side so as not to impede their movement. Each step was deliberate, coming at the same time as I felt that pull in my belly. Something about the dance, about the way they moved called to me. My feet knew the steps, urged me to take them, to fall into the dance. The second I tried to examine the memory it thinned then drifted away like smoke.

The drumbeats increased and the dancer to the far left raised her arms to the sky. The wind whipped up sending the billows up and curling the smoke into strange symbols.

I stared at the woman. "Alys?"

She didn't answer. She couldn't hear me.

I looked at the other two figures. The one on the far right didn't have Sibby's distinctive haircut, tattoos or piercings, but something about the restless way her body moved was just like my younger sister. As though she were so full of energy that her skin couldn't contain all she had to give.

My gaze landed at the one in the middle. A body I knew well. A body that had never moved like that.

But it had. One time. When she had been trying to entice a lover and had given in to a primal drumbeat that only she could hear. That seemed to come from within her to tempt him closer...

As though conjured from memory, said lover appeared. My lips parted as he moved toward the dancing woman, closed in behind her. His hands touched her flesh and molded to her as she swayed. He was completely in her thrall. Not in that zombie-like mindless way that happened when I enchanted people. It was as though she were all he could see. And he was desperate to hold what could never be contained.

The man was large and had shaggy dark hair. Kal. Somehow I *knew*. He was imprinted on my bone marrow as was the dance. The ritual.

Mother. Maiden. Crone.

Three words drifted to me. The voice wasn't the Mother Superior of Magic. It was older, wiser, and closer to the source of all I was. All I would ever be.

Mother. Maiden. Crone. The triple goddess. The three faces of woman, three distinct stages of life.

That sense of familiarity expanded as the universe expanded. The drumbeats that called to my inner self without words but were a summons all the same.

It was mine. This was mine. My memory. But not of the life I was living as Maeve Silver. Somehow, I *knew* this had happened long long ago.

Another life.

A quick glance told me my sisters had acquired their own dance partners. The golden-haired male that moved in time with Alys had to be Brock. I didn't call out to him because I was sure he wouldn't respond to that name even if he could hear me.

And as for Siobhan….

The man who moved in her orbit was all wrong. I couldn't say why. The other two couples moved like lovers, like those familiar with one another. This man seemed determined but he couldn't catch her. He had dark hair and features obscured by the firelight. Where Sibby's progenitor shone, he faded until he was no more than a shrubbery propped in the background.

Sibby's doppelgänger whirled her braid whipping, her

hips snapping hard as though fighting the beat of the drum. Then she froze. Her back to the fire, every muscle poised like a deer in a hunter's crosshairs.

I shifted so I could see what caught her attention. And gasped.

Glowing amethyst eyes watched her from the darkness. Eyes that yearned and promised and beckoned.

Sibby reached out a hand toward the owner of those eyes. I could feel her yearning. She wanted to cross the dark divide to the watcher. To lose herself in those eyes. That being.

It's forbidden.

I wanted to ask why, for my sister's sake. But I was only an observer.

Her rejected partner spied the eyes too. He made a hissing sort of sound and waved a hand. After one long look at Siobhan, the eyes shut and didn't reappear.

This isn't over.

It wasn't just instinct that made me so sure. My sister's stubborn streak was world-class. Tell Sibby she couldn't have a treat and she would snatch two out of spite. Tell her to stay away from the lurker in the woods and she would run into his arms.

The man who wanted to be her partner gripped her wrist. She yanked her arm free. He lunged for her again. She vanished before his eyes.

Movement in my peripheral vision made me turn. Sibby stood there, watching as the Maeve and Kal and Brock and Alys figures spiced up the dance. Hands grew bolder. What little clothing there had been was shed.

While she stood alone. And yearned for what they had.

"Don't, Sibby." My stomach knotted up as I tried to reach for her, tried to warn her. Something bad was about to happen. I looked to the other couples for support. Had they seen?

But they were too caught up in the ritual and one another to pay any heed.

Sibby stepped back and wiped at her eyes. Turned toward the woods.

"Sibby," I moaned again and the pain in my abdomen moved lower. Deeper into my womb as the world shifted out of focus.

❄

"*M*aeve wake the hell up!" A voice snapped in my ear.

I jerked and then groaned. The pain that had found me in the dream wasn't some psychic scar, but the very real feeling of menstrual cramping.

My period had started.

"Are you all right?" That was Sibby's voice.

"No," I groaned. "Why can't I see anything?"

"We're in a hole in the ground. About eight feet down." She moved closer and I could feel her fingers in my hair. "Did you hit your head? They dumped you in like a sack of potatoes. You've been moaning my name for over an hour. I thought you were brain damaged."

"Where are we?" The ground beneath me was cold and soggy. I was chilled to the bone and had a headache. "And who are they?"

"The zombies." Sibby blew out a breath. "They came for us while you and the snake were off in la-la land. I think this is their home base. Talk about a screwed-up revenge fantasy."

"Huh?" I was still half lost in the dream and couldn't follow the bouncing ball that was her train of thought.

"The dead left to walk above the ground and the living are buried underground? It must be in somebody's spank bank. Whatever gets you there, right?"

I had no clue what she was talking about. "Why didn't you teleport away?"

"And leave you to be carried off into the jungle by a bunch of dead guys?" She sounded pissed that I even suggested it. "You were completely helpless."

"Alys?" I was almost afraid to ask.

"I haven't seen her since she left the clearing." Her tone was too quiet as she added, "I don't think they captured her."

I bowed my head. My big sister wouldn't go down without one hell of a fight. She would rather be dead than captured.

She might be dead.

"Don't even think it," Sibby snapped. "She's probably mounting a rescue even now. Just you wait, any second a whole platoon of marines will come charging in here. With Alys barking orders at them all."

I laughed a little at the thought. "Can you get us out of this hole?"

"I've been trying. But something is blocking my magic."

I let out a sigh. "It's him. The Headhunter."

"Say what now?"

"The magic hunter that the Mother Superior warned me about. He can raise the dead. And since I can't enchant the dead guys, he's probably going to kill us all and take our magic so he can kill her." My head throbbed and the last thing I wanted to do was free bleed into the cold filth at the bottom of this pit. "You don't happen to have a tampon, do you?"

There was a pause. "You're kidding me."

Her dry tone got under my skin and I responded with pissy sarcasm. "Yes Sibby, I am kidding. No, my period did not really start while we are trapped in the rainforest by a magic hunter who can control the dead. It's just a big freaking joke!"

The fight went out of me and I sagged. "Like my life. One big cosmic joke."

"Oh stuff it, Maeve." Sibby snapped.

"What?"

"I'm so damn sick of your poor, pitiful me routine. You have an amazing life. You're a witch, an enchantress. You have two beautiful kids and a man who worships the ground you walk on. You're smart and have the best eye for design of anyone ever. Your skills are incredible. Your life is incredible."

"You think I don't know that?" I wished I could see her face. For some reason, my mind superimposed the image of Sibby from my dream, who looked at us with longing. I shook it off, instead focused on her words. "I thought you understood."

"I do. I understand that you are scared because this thing isn't going away. I understand that you're worried you will lose that awesome life. And you are. But not because of MS. You're making choices that are wrecking everything!"

I was about to respond when blinding daylight appeared above us. I recoiled from the sudden intrusion of brightness.

Sibby screamed. I shaded my eyes so I could see her. A rope had been lowered from above and wrapped around her torso. She struggled to free herself and I lunged for her, clasping her hand as above us, the zombies tugged.

Our eyes met. "If you have the chance to get out of here, go." I urged her.

She shook her head. The zombies yanked again. Our hands separated.

And then she was gone.

The stone rolled back over the mouth of the pit, leaving me alone, bleeding in the darkness.

❋

"*Annwyl*."

Helpless, Sebastian watched as the dead dragged Siobhan's naked body across the ground. She thrashed in their grip, still calling her sister's name. The rope they were using was made of hair from more of the Headhunters' victims. The death magic imbued in it would countermand Siobhan's abilities. Much as the cage of bones trapped him, she would be helpless while held within it.

He had barely paused in his digging and was close to tunneling beneath the reach of the bones. Only when he heard her voice as the dead carried her and one of her sisters into camp. Tossed them into the pit.

He gripped the bars as the dead brought her into the Headhunter's tent. Her shriek of outrage made him want to bellow her name. But he kept the impulse in check. Instead, he returned to digging.

He'd lost two nails in the endeavor but his efforts were beginning to pay off.

Once free, he would save Siobhan and then burn this place to the ground and piss on the ashes. Almost there....

Feet appeared outside of his cage. Living feet. He could see the pinkening that indicated actual blood that flowed from a beating heart.

He looked up into the unsmiling face of the Headhunter.

The man had painted jagged lines across his forehead with blood. His dark eyes held no definition between iris and pupil and seemed to suck at the tatters of Sebastian's soul.

Sebastian rose from his crouch and tried to affect a casual pose as though he hadn't been inches from freedom. "Are you here to kill me?"

The Headhunter didn't answer.

"No?" Sebastian raised an eyebrow in surprise. "Why not?"

The Headhunter pointed to the three-pronged brand that was tattooed into the flesh of his forearm. Then he pointed to where the same mark resided on Sebastian's bare shoulder. The brand of the magic hunters.

"Ah, the oath. But doesn't the oath also say that you aren't to entrap your own kind?"

This time the Headhunter smiled. It was a blood-curdling sight. When he spoke, his voice was low and smooth, and without any trace of an accent. "You're not really one of us anymore though, are you, dark fae?"

Sebastian worked to keep his breathing even. "I don't know what you mean."

"You've killed our kind to protect the unsanctioned witches. So while my oath keeps you alive, I must turn you over to the Council of Elders." Without warning, he lashed out his right foot. Out of reflex, Sebastian stumbled back. But he wasn't the target.

The Headhunter's kick knocked the cage back far enough that the hole Sebastian had been working on was three feet out of reach.

Sebastian looked to the tent, where the dead had taken Siobhan. She wasn't making any noise. "What are you going to do to her?"

That eerie smile returned. "I'm going to do what you should have done when you had the chance. Goodbye, Sebastian. Your jailers will be here by dawn to retrieve you. May your next life treat you better."

MAEVE

"Somebody help me!" I'd repeated the cry so many times that my throat ached. My heart pounded. It was useless. Hopeless. No one could hear. No one would be moved to set me free. To assist our escape.

Was Sibby even still alive? Was Alys?

"Help!" I shouted again. "Anybody, please!"

At this point, I didn't care if it was a big ass snake or a platoon of marines who came to our rescue. Just as long as somebody did.

"Help me out, here universe," I muttered as I sank against the wall of my prison. My head ached. My entire body ached. Besides the serious lack of feminine hygiene products, I hadn't been offered food or water either. Prisoners that were to be kept around awhile were given things to sustain themselves.

Sibby was right. This was my fault. All of it.

Who was my greatest enemy?

I looked up into the dark and saw her. Ms. Priss.

As I watched the vision the years melted away. The wrinkled skin smoothed, the pinched look vanished along with her cane. She was me. The crone version of me. Bitter and resentful.

I was my own worst enemy.

That was what the Mother Superior of Magic had meant. I pushed my body to the brink. And why? To avoid having a difficult conversation with my husband and children. To spare them from worry.

Except I hadn't even done that. They would worry when I didn't call to check in. When I didn't come home. I'd hung all of the relationships that mattered to me on the line. All for the hope for a miracle cure.

That hope would see me dead.

Would Kal ever find out what had happened to me? I hadn't left a note, a will. Nothing. I would be gone and he wouldn't know how or why. Who to call, what to do. He knew nothing about magic. He wouldn't be able to explain it to Bella or Philip. Would my children believe I'd abandoned them?

The sobs broke loose. Big, body-wracking spasms of pure misery. I curled over onto my side and cried while I cursed myself. I had done this. Me. Not my MS. I had made choice after choice to reclaim the woman I had been before. The one Kal had fallen for. His rescuer who had skied through a blustery winter night to help an injured stranger.

The maiden who'd been his hero.

But each step I took brought me farther away from him. From us. The woman he really loved. Not in an infatuated will they-won't they kind of way. But in a deeper closer way. Our beginning was just that. The beginning. But our bond had grown deeper over time. Like a plant allowed to dig its roots down deep into the soil at the same time it reached for the sun.

How ironic that if I had accepted the diagnosis, if I had brought Kal in, back in the beginning, I would be safe at home now. With my goddamned maxi pads. On the couch, watching, *The Princess Bride* with a corgi on either side, one child on my lap, the other on Kal's. Warm and safe and happy. Maybe I would have had to go to bed early. Maybe I would have tingling or numbness or constipation. But I would be where I belonged.

Instead, this was the final stop. I reflected bitterly on my surroundings. Alone, waiting for death, without any sort of dignity or love.

I had no one to blame but myself.

Something cold and hard brushed my knee. The onyx stone that Sibby had given me. I clutched it in my fist and let the tears fall.

"I'm sorry," I said to no one. To everyone. "I'm sorry I made these choices. It's not the MS. It's my fault. I wish I had the power to get us all out of this."

You do. That voice whispered. *You must embrace your enemy.*

Embrace my enemy? What the hell did that even mean?

But I knew. The answer was within me. I had been punishing myself since the diagnosis was confirmed. Hating the sick woman who was an object of pity. Who was so far misaligned with who I wanted to be that I didn't even recognize her.

Through tear-filled eyes, I saw Ms. Priss. Leaning on her cane. Bent and bowed from being so hated for so long.

I struggled upright. Took a step. And then another. She didn't strike out at me. Just watched and waited.

I pulled her into me and held on tight.

"I love you," I whispered. "Promise, I'll do better. For both of us. Even if Kal leaves, even if my sisters are gone. You've still got me. You're not alone."

There was a loud crack. My heart stopped as what had been so carefully contained deep within broke free.

CHAPTER TWENTY-FOUR

ALYS

"You've got to be kidding me," I muttered under my breath when recognition as to the identity of the man in the cage finally struck. I shifted behind the fallen log about six feet from where the rickety structure of bones held its prisoner. The thing looked as though a stiff breeze could blow it to bits. Why didn't the occupant bust free?

There had to be more going on. Even though the broad shoulders and naked back clearly belonged to a man—and therefore, not one of my sisters—I wanted more info on their captor. Like maybe who else the Headhunter had captured and how to turn him into an ally.

The enemy of my enemy can be useful.

But did I dare approach?

That was when the man turned and I caught sight of his profile. At first, my mind couldn't reconcile it. Sebastian Jones always appeared immaculately groomed and in control. Even the time Sibby had nailed him in the face with a door and he had blood gushing out of his nose, he'd maintained an air of dignity.

This man looked like a beggar from the Old Testament. His pants were barely more than rags. But that profile was distinctive.

Just to be sure I called out his name. "Sebastian?"

He turned and my eyes went wide when I saw the burning amethyst orbs which belonged to a very powerful being. A creature that had saved me. And had looked at my youngest sister with hunger.

"You," I breathed. "You're a wraith?"

He shook his head. "No, though I can usually leave my corporeal body. All of my kind can. You must hurry."

"Hurry?"

"The Headhunter has Siobhan in that tent." Sebastian jerked his head down toward the camp. "He plans to use her to lure you here."

"And Maeve?"

"There's a hole in the ground, covered by a boulder. The Headhunter won't go near Maeve while she lives. She was unconscious when they brought her here."

A scream ripped from the tent and I stiffened. Sibby.

Sebastian jerked as though he'd been stuck with a cattle prod. "Release me and I'll help you free her."

My teeth sank into my lower lip. If Sibby was being tortured as a way to lure me in, having someone else provide distraction made sense. I'd wanted that someone to be Maeve, but what if she was still unconscious?

As much as it galled me, Sebastian was my best hope.

"What is this thing?" I asked Sebastian as I approached.

"Don't touch the bones," he cautioned. "They will drain your magic and your soul."

No wonder he looked so fatigued. That also explained why he was sitting exactly in the center of the small confine. My earlier thought resurfaced and I asked, "What about if I use magic on them?"

"If you use magic, he'll feel it."

Another shriek from the tent. I stiffened. "It's a risk I'm willing to take."

Fear for my sister had my temper boiling. I summoned the winds. Overhead, the canopy rustled. I shut my eyes and focused the gusts on the cage. The winds swirled about and then lifted the bones high into the air. Sebastian crawled out from under it. I released my hold on the winds and they dispersed.

The cage fell to the ground. The bones smashed on impact.

Sebastian lay sprawled in the dirt, panting hard. He didn't look as though he could fight off a cold in his current condition.

"Get up," My attention focused on the tent. The flaps stirred, but there was no sign of the Headhunter.

The dead however were moving up the hill.

"Get Maeve," Sebastian pushed up to his hands and knees. "I'll deal with them."

I had serious doubts but wasn't about to stick around. If I set off an earthquake or a tornado, I'd risk my sisters. My magic wasn't exactly precise.

So I snuck back into the underbrush, intent on circling the camp to get to Maeve.

And tried to ignore the screams coming from that tent.

Sebastian felt the power seeping back into him as he waited for the dead to approach. It was a trickle compared to his usual river of magic, but it was more than enough to deal with the dead.

He summoned the curved blade of the fae from his personal vault. It glittered with a light all its own. The sword was more than just a weapon. It was a magical amplifier, imbibed with powers from the four elements.

As the first of the zombies approached him, he directed his intent into the weapon and swung. The blade ignited as it cut through the dead man, the decaying body caught fire.

Another strike and another foe burned before him. The dead had no fear though and they kept coming. But Sebastian was focused on his goal.

Siobhan.

He cut his way through the dead, his focus locked on the Headhunter's tent. The magic hunter would pay with his life for daring to hurt his female.

His. The rightness of that thought gave Sebastian more strength than he had ever known. He battled his way onward, uncaring how badly he was outnumbered. He would save her even if he died in the attempt.

MAEVE

"Maeve?"

Someone was calling my name. Late afternoon light turned my eyelids translucent and I knew if I dared to lift them, that the stone would have been moved away from the mouth of the pit. I groaned and flung an arm over my eyes.

Everything hurt. Every cell in my body thrummed with some sort of energy. It had nowhere to go and it was doubling back through my system. A crackling feedback loop of power.

"Maeve," More impatient this time. "Get up."

I would recognize that demanding whisper-hiss anywhere. "Alys?"

She sighed. "Are you okay?"

"My period started." It was a ridiculous thing to say, but easier to explain than everything else that had happened.

"Don't miss that," Alys said. "Come on, help me figure out a way to get you out of there."

"The dead guys had some sort of rope they used to lasso Sibby," I said.

Alys's face disappeared for a moment and then came

back. "No rope. Let me duck into the underbrush and see if I can find some vines or a tree branch or something I can lower down."

I waited for an endless moment, looking around for a way out. The pit was smooth, the walls made of just dirt. It actually amazed me that something dug so deeply in the rainforest hadn't filled with water.

Alys reappeared and made a face. "You're not going to like this."

"I promise I'll love it as long as it gets me out of here."

"Stand back."

I backed up and then screamed as the body of an anaconda unspooled over the side of the pit."

"You want me to climb up a snake?" I shrieked.

"It's dead," she said. "I hit it with a bolt of lightning."

Which explained while the body was still smoking. "Dear sweet dark chocolate," I breathed and reached for the snake. Touching the green and black scales made me feel wrong on every level. Its torso was as thick as my thigh but unlike my thigh, pure muscle. I reached up and, cringing a little, gripped the snake.

And hung there.

"Just shimmy up it like a rope in gym class," Alys advised.

The only problem with that, I had never been able to shimmy up the rope in gym class. Garbage upper body strength met plus-sized ass. No rope climbing for me. Damn it, I needed to get out of this pit.

The snake moved. "Alys, did you do something?"

She shook her head. "No."

"It's moving."

"That's impossible." My sister assured me.

I screamed as the coils of the snake wrapped around me.

"Maeve!" Alys's scream echoed mine.

"I thought you said it was dead!"

"It was. It is!" Three coils looped about my torso. The snake's gaze was sightless. I waited, sure it was about to start squeezing the breath out of me.

It didn't. Instead, the snake lifted me up and up and up out of the pit. My feet hit the ground of the world above and the coils unfurled.

The snake lay dead beside us. Its job was done.

"What. Was. That?" Alys looked like she was going to hyperventilate.

I shook from fear and adrenaline and relief. The dead creature had just come to life and fulfilled my wish.

"That was manifesting, Amazon-style," I said to my sister. "Where's Sibby?"

Alys eyed the snake once more and then turned and pointed. "This way. Come on."

SIOBHAN

Blood poured from the wound on my arm where the head-hunter had pierced my flesh with his bones. Four times he had hammered them in. Sharp as nails. He'd caught the blood in a bowl made out of a skull. He was chanting in a language I didn't recognize as he streaked my blood along his limbs. His eyes were flat and dead, like his zombies. Smoke filled the tent from the burning braziers.

I couldn't teleport. The rope the zombies had used to fetch me upheld my body in place. Horror had filled me when I realized that not only was the rope made out of human hair, there were still bits of flesh attached to some of the blond and black and brown and gray strands.

Tears continued to track down my face. "Please," I said again. My voice was hoarse from screaming. "Please. Why are you doing this? I've never done anything to you."

It didn't matter, though. I knew his kind. Evil. Selfish. Unable or unwilling to acknowledge the pain of others. I had something he wanted. And he was evil enough to take it. In fact, hurting me would bring him pleasure.

Too bad I couldn't entice him to fuck me. That would be

horrific but at least he would die directly after. What I'd said to Alys was true. My vag should come with a warning label. *Abandon all hope, ye who enter here.* Sex with me was a death sentence, served up within moments.

But the headhunter didn't seem to see me as a woman. Only as a source of power. His chanting grew louder, more fervent. Blood dripped onto the ground and tears filled my eyes.

Then it all stopped. The magic hunter paused. He turned. Something drew his attention. A moment later, a flaming sword ripped through the canvas tent.

My lips parted as I stared at the vision. Sebastian. Only not the Sebastian I knew.

This was…something else. His eyes glowed with an eerie amethyst color. His pants hung from him in strips and his chest was bare. That mark on his shoulder seemed to blaze with power. Others appeared as I watched. Raised markings that made one of the most beautifully horrific patterns I had ever beheld.

Our eyes locked. Something shifted within me. The flicker of a memory. I recognized him. It went deeper than visual memory. It came from the pit of my soul.

He broke eye contact as one of the dead threw itself at his back. Sebastian bent forward, sending the thing sprawling in the dirt. One of the incense torches tipped over. More fire, more smoke filled my lungs.

The Headhunter's nostrils flared as Sebastian strode forward. He put himself bodily between me and my torturer. "See what power you wield over death when yours is the corpse," Sebastian swung.

But the Headhunter only smiled as another zombie moved in the way of the strike. Sebastian cut the dead man clean in half. By the time the body fell to the ground, the Headhunter was gone.

"Are you all right?" Sebastian turned to me. He cursed when he saw the shards of bone, the bowl of blood. He yanked the bones out and then tugged the hair free. "Siobhan."

"My sisters," I rasped as I sagged against him.

Sebastian swung me up in his arms. "I'll take you to them."

"Your sword." I protested.

He turned and looked at it. A moment later, the blade vanished as though it had never been.

Sebastian emerged from the tent and we ran smack into Alys and Maeve.

"Sibby!" Alys cried. She tried to tug me free from Sebastian's grip.

"Can you transport yourself and your sisters from here?" Sebastian asked.

I shook my head and even though it galled me to admit it, I told him the truth. "Too weak."

"Then we'll have to fight them off until you regain enough strength. Come on. We need a better position."

"Who put you in charge?" Alys bitched. She did follow us out of the clearing.

I must have lost consciousness for a few minutes. When I came to we had stopped. Sebastian laid me down with my back pressed against a massive skull. "If you can gather the strength to leave, Siobhan, then take yourselves to safety."

I touched his face. "I won't leave you again."

His features softened. "I'll be all right, *Annwyl*."

Something rustled behind him and he turned. Somehow, that sword reappeared in his hand as he whirled around.

Maeve stood on his left and Alys to the left of her. They made a wall of life, blocking me from the army of the dead.

As one they moved forward.

And at the front line stood the Headhunter.

"Maeve?" Alys whispered. "Can you enchant him?"

Maeve frowned. "I'm trying but…"

The Headhunter laughed. "I've taken immunity from your bloodline."

He pointed to my arm and then to symbols he had written on his skin. "You cannot touch me now, enchantress. You and your sisters will die. When I strip your powers and grow strong enough, the Mother Superior of Magic will die. Death magic will rule. And as I rule death magic, I will rule all."

MAEVE

"Why do guys like you always want to rule everything?" I bitched as I stared at the Headhunter. "It's not like you do a decent job of it."

He sneered at me and then dismissed my remark. I knew that look. Had seen it from men all my life. I wasn't thin enough or pretty enough or young enough to pay attention to.

I wasn't really a threat. If they couldn't use me in some way, they shrugged me off.

But I was done being used. I'd spent so much of my life hating on my body. For not being the ideal. For being too fat, too slow, too old. Too sick.

Utter bullshit. Women who hated themselves were easier to market to. Easier to make money off of and convince to stay in their prescribed lane.

But I had seen the time before. A time when our female bodies had been celebrated and revered.

I was enough. Exactly how I was. Overweight, MS and all. I was plenty.

And I was angry. Standing with my back to my sister who

had been tortured by this lunatic, I wasn't afraid anymore. I was *pissed*.

The build-up of power within me was gaining in strength. It was like a song in my blood, one I couldn't quite remember the tune to. An itch I couldn't scratch and couldn't ignore. Pretty soon it would be at critical mass. Then, I was sure I would explode.

"In case you're thinking of draining them yourself, dark fae," the Headhunter said to Sebastian. "Know that their magic won't save you from the council's wrath."

"Dark fae," Sibby whispered. Out of the corner of my eye, I saw her stare up at Sebastian in confusion. "You're a magic hunter like him?"

"Not like him," Sebastian denied. "I am *nothing* like him."

"Oh no?" The Headhunter laughed and pointed to a mark on his arm. "He is one of our guild, though a traitor to our kind. His bounty is almost as high as the one on the three of you. A patient hunter who draws close to his targets and then sucks them dry when their magic has reached its full potency. Tell them how you healed the enchantress. Tell them how your raw energy could have killed her, but you chose to forge ahead without their permission."

Sibby made a broken sound. Like a sob that was being choked off. My heart went out to her and my anger grew. The Headhunter thought he held the winning hand.

But I looked up into the sky, where I knew the new moon was completely hidden behind the earth's shadow. The dark of the moon. Light and dark. Life and death.

And I let my power flow out.

The Headhunter was right. Whatever vile thing he'd done to Siobhan had made him immune to my magic.

But the dead weren't. Not with me whole in myself.

I invaded their minds with a single command. *"Destroy the Headhunter."*

As one they turned.

He frowned at them "What are you doing?"

They surged forward in an unending wave of death. He shouted and swung out with empty hands. Blue-black sparks emanated from his fingertips. It settled around them. Doing nothing. The dead reached for him. Their hands grasping pulling.

Rending flesh. Tearing him apart.

"Maeve?" Alys whispered.

"Yeah," I said, unable to watch the carnage. "It's me."

"How?" Sebastian asked.

I turned to face him. "Was he telling the truth?"

The dead stopped mutilating the body. They took a menacing step toward Sebastian. "Are you a magic hunter?"

"I was," he began.

Sibby made that horrible sound again as though she couldn't get air into her lungs.

"Give us one good reason why we shouldn't kill you too?" Alys said.

Sebastian's sword vanished and he held his hands up in supplication. "Siobhan."

"Don't." Sibby had struggled to her feet. "Don't say my name. Don't even think it."

"*Annwyl*, let me explain."

"Don't call me that!" Sibby cried. "You were waiting for us to grow strong enough. But you waited too long."

Her fingers wrapped around my arm, and a moment later the world tilted. I released the dead in the final moment.

And we stood at the threshold of our cottage.

The bite of winter wind sank into skin that had been perspiring in the jungle and we all scrambled for the door.

"How?" Alys asked with chattering teeth. "How did you manage to jump us this far?"

"Desire." Sibby's knees gave out and she sank to the floor,

naked and bloody. "I still want him. Even knowing what he is, I still want him."

Alys and I got to our knees and put our arms around her. There was nothing we could do but hold her together while her heart broke.

CHAPTER TWENTY-FIVE

MAEVE

"Could you give me a hand, Sibby?" I turned around to face my sister with lifted brows.

She hesitated then flashed me a grin that didn't reach her eyes. "You really have changed."

I shrugged and waited for her to pick her way over to my side.

Alys dug in her pocket and handed me something.

"What's this?"

"Disposable cell phone. Sibby's and my numbers are already programmed in. Just until you can get a replacement."

After Sibby had cried herself out, I'd only taken time enough to shower, eager to see my family again. Yet somehow in that short time, she had managed this. I hugged her. "How can you always be so on top of every little detail all the time? You amaze me."

Her lips parted but no sound came out.

"It'll be all right." I nodded and then an instant before Sibby opened the door added, "Keep an eye on her."

Alys rolled her eyes theatrically. "I always *try*."

"Is it just me," I said as we picked our way up the icy walkway to my front door. "Or does everything feel off?"

I'd taken my first shower in days. I hadn't lingered, hadn't wanted to waste any more time than a cursory cleanup so I didn't scare my family. But the running water, the artificial scent from the shampoo, the electric lights all of it felt foreign after my experience in the Amazon. The cottage was rustic, it hadn't even had electricity until earlier in the year. My house was going to be a circus by comparison.

"You've gone native now," Sibby said. Her voice was thick and she had been way too quiet since our return. "After living without the comforts of civilization, there's an adjustment. Everything feels chaotic for a while."

"So how do you get used to regular life again?" I asked her.

We had reached the front door and I turned to look at her.

She shrugged. "Embrace the chaos. Text me and let me know you're all good."

I touched her arm. "I'll be fine. I promise."

She leaned in and hugged me close. "Yeah, I think you will be."

I gripped her hand before she could escape. "You will be too."

Her face was a frozen mask and so un-Sibby-like in its uncertainty. "We'll talk tomorrow."

"Or maybe the day after," I whined as my cramps started up in full. "I feel like hell."

This time her laugh was genuine. "Own it, sister-witch."

I had my hand on the knob when the door flew open. "Mommy, mommy!"

I was attacked on two fronts. Bella took my left side and Philip was on my right. The corgis circled, bouncing and yipping and losing their minds. I hugged my children in the open doorway. They both wore their pajamas and smelled of lavender and sage and home.

Tears stung my eyes. "I'm so glad to see you guys. You don't even know."

They babbled questions and didn't wait for me to answer, instead launching into a rapid-fire catch-up of all I had missed. Philip had lost two teeth and had a gap that he proudly stuck his tongue through in demonstration. Bella had taught the corgis how to sit. I had to take her word on that one since Gimli and Grogu were racing back and forth to the living room bringing me tribute in the form of tennis balls and chew toys.

"Okay, guys, let mom come in and shut the door."

I looked up to see Kal's dark gaze as he watched our happy reunion.

My lips curved up at the familiar sight. "Hey."

He nodded and then focused on ushering the kids into the living room, shutting the door.

"Where's your luggage?" Kal asked as he helped me out of my coat.

"I lost it somewhere over the Amazon."

Kal blinked. "Did you find whatever it is you were looking for?"

"Yes and no." I'd lost more than my bags. My fear of enchanting him or our children was gone. The crescent moon talisman given to me by The Mother Superior of Magic gave me control over my gift.

I looked up into his eyes, those eyes that I missed so damn much because I had been too lost in self-pity to focus on what I still had. "Listen, I owe you an apology. And an explanation."

Kal's gaze was steady as he murmured. "Are you all the way back?"

I nodded and grinned. "As promised."

He gathered me into his arms. "That's enough for now. Let's get the kids to bed and then we'll talk about it."

So I let him lead me to the couch and then spent the next hour with my yammering offspring, delighting in every homey detail.

Eventually, the corgis fell asleep in their bed before the fire. Bella yawned and then Philip followed suit.

"Bedtime," I pronounced.

There was some half-hearted protesting but, I promised that I would spend the whole day just hanging out with them and they stumbled sleepily up the stairs.

Though I was tired, my heart pounded and I thought about getting up and getting a glass of wine or maybe a cup of herbal tea. But I stayed where I was. All the tea in the world wasn't going to do much to comfort the blow I was about to deal.

I heard his footsteps on the stairs and then he was before me. He didn't sit on the couch next to me. Instead, he knelt before me—on that faux bearskin rug that we'd pilfered from the A-frame so long ago—and waited.

I looked down at my blanket-covered lap. "I have MS." Then, feeling like a coward, I forced myself to meet his gaze. "Multiple Sclerosis. It's an auto-immune disease. Basically, my body is attacking itself a little bit at a time. It saps my energy, affects my eyesight, my motor control…a bunch of other things. And it's not going to get better. There's no cure."

Kal was silent for a long time. I had to force myself not to babble or demand he tell me what he was thinking. He had given me space for months to sort through my shit. Hadn't pushed for answers even though he was entitled to them. I could only give him the same space to process.

"How long have you known?" he asked quietly.

"The official diagnosis came a few weeks ago. Right after Thanksgiving."

His finger curled under my chin and he repeated the question, though his emphasis was on the final word. "How long have you *known?*"

This was the hardest part. "Over a year now. Since the doctors first mentioned it was a possibility."

There was so much emotion in his eyes. Confusion, sorrow, but most of all hurt. "Why?"

I understood what he was asking. It took great strength of will for me not to fidget or look away. "Because I didn't want to be sick. So not telling you let me pretend that I wasn't. It let me hold on to hope until it was confirmed. And then when it was...I freaked out."

I told him everything. The car accident, the coma, the midnight market. The trip to the Amazon, the dreams, and the Mother Superior of Magic. Realizing the ultimate truth.

"It was all my fault. I couldn't accept that this was how I was going to be forever so I fought it. I fought it so hard because I wanted to be the woman I was when we first met."

"You are," he said.

But I shook my head. "I'm not. That Evie, your Evie, she was brave."

One dark brow went up. "You just finished telling me how you fought zombies in the Amazon."

"Okay so maybe I'm still a little bit brave," I smiled but it faded fast. "Kal, I'm so sorry. I should have told you way back in the beginning when I just suspected there was something wrong. It was your right to know. And I've left you here holding down the fort, taking care of the kids while I went off and had a witchy mid-life crisis. If you want to leave me now, I get it."

"Leave you?" He looked genuinely confused.

"I'm sick," I said again. "My large motor skills come and go. I'm going to cut back to working part-time and even then, mostly from home. Sibby's going to take over at the office and on the job sites. I need to make some serious lifestyle changes. And that's just the tip of the iceberg. The stairs, the stupid icy walkway, the bathtub. I might have to move. I might need a home health aide or a walker. Or a wheelchair. The point is I don't know what direction this thing will take. This isn't what you signed on for. So please, don't stay out of some misplaced obligation or duty. It would ruin my memory of how things were with us before. I couldn't bear that."

Realization dawned. "Is that where all that crap about me having an affair came from? Have you been trying to push me away?"

I winced. "Yeah. I don't know. I glommed onto that idea, maybe because of what Alys went through or maybe because it would be easier to tell myself that you left because of someone else instead of you leaving me because I'm sick. Or staying because I'm sick. Because I can't leave this body. And I need to do better at taking care of it so I don't make myself worse."

"Jesus, Evie," Kal said and now he sounded genuinely upset. "Of course you don't know what the future holds. Just because you *know* things from time to time doesn't mean you have all the answers. We have been married for almost twenty years. We vowed in sickness and in health. If this is the sickness part, it's not so bad."

My jaw dropped. "Not so bad?"

"It's not terminal. Yes, there will be an adjustment period, hell probably more than one. But you're okay. God, I thought...." His eyes filled and he shook his head.

"What?" I gripped his hand and held him tight. "What did you think?"

"That you were dying. Or part of a cult. Or, I don't know, having an affair of your own because I can't…."

He looked away.

"Can't what?" I prompted.

He sighed. "I can't get an erection. At least not a useful one."

I blinked at him. "Since when?"

It was his turn to look uncomfortable. "The last six months or so. The doctor prescribed me medication but the side effects—"

I held up both hands. "You took medication?"

"On Halloween. Yeah."

My mind was utterly blown. "You, who wouldn't take even the mildest pain reliever for a busted leg, voluntarily took the little blue pill?"

His cheeks turned pink. "I didn't want to disappoint you. But then you stopped showing any interest and I just…I don't know. The doctor said maybe if I lost some weight the testosterone would rebound a bit."

And that explained his sudden interest in going to the gym. Not to get in shape for a new woman. Because he wanted to get his virility back to what it had been.

Sibby's words in the jungle came back to me. *They need to get a new line. Not everything is about numbers on a scale or BMI. Like women don't have enough shit to feel badly about as it is.*

But it wasn't just women, was it? Men had their own notions about what makes a man a man. And a raging hard-on was at the top of the list since the locker-room days.

Laughter bubbled out of me. It was a heartfelt sound full of relief and joy and the sheer absurdity of our situation.

Kal narrowed his eyes. "Are you really laughing at me?"

His question only made the tears stream faster.

"Glad to amuse you," he muttered.

I wiped my eyes on the sleeve of my borrowed sweatshirt

and then crawled off the couch until I was straddling my husband. "I was laughing at us. Because we're ridiculous. We've bought into this stupid idea of how life is supposed to be, who we're supposed to be. But all its done is make us so damn unhappy. All this angst and misery because we couldn't be honest with each other."

Kal pushed some hair away from my face. "Doesn't it bother you?"

"That we're not in our twenties anymore? Some days more than others." I ran my hand along the smoothness of his jaw. "But what bothers me more is that we gave up on ourselves and almost lost each other. No one else gets to tell us how to live, Kal."

"But what about sex?"

I shrugged. "What about it?"

He looked like a bear with his foot poised above an unseen trap. "Isn't it…important to you? All those books you read are full of sex."

Yeah, we really had done a number to each other. Society had made us this way. Being without it for a little while was the best thing I could have done because it let me see from the outside just how flawed and damaged the construct was.

How much time I had wasted buying into it. How it hurt people to not live up to magazine model appeal or romance novel cover standards.

How marketing and packaging were making us all fucking miserable.

"Those books I read are full of *intimacy*. That's what I want. The closeness, the connection. Do you still like touching me?"

His answer was immediate. "Of course."

"And do you still want me to touch you?"

He nodded.

"So okay then. We still have what we have. And sometimes it really is okay just to cuddle. Like when I am on day two of my cycle and feel as though there's a vice on my midsection."

Kal's lips twitched. "The dark of the moon."

"What?"

"Since the twins were born you always bleed with the new moon."

My lips parted. "You know that how?"

"I pay attention. I should have realized you were a witch just because of that."

I searched his face. "Are you really okay with all of this? All of my secrets? You're not staying out of some screwed up sense of guilt?"

He pretended to mull it over. "Nah. I'm staying because I'm dying to know what you'll say or do next."

"Thank you." I shoved at him playfully.

He narrowed his eyes on me. "That is all the secrets, right?"

I sighed and laid my head on his chest. "That's all of them. No more secrets between us. That's not what I want. That and to cancel that damned gym membership. Those places are cesspools of germs."

His lips twitched. "Done. I'll just have to find other ways to get some exercise."

He rose and then hauled me to my feet. "So, how does my lady witch wish to be pleasured tonight?"

I groaned. "I wish to crawl under the covers and sleep in your arms until our children and corgis demand attention. Or spring. Whichever comes first."

"That," Kal said as he led me up the stairs to our room. "I can do."

And that's what I wanted all along. Agency. That was the real power, the real magic. Control was an illusion, sick or healthy, old or young. Parts faded into the mists of time, and others were cloaked in mystery yet to be revealed. But we still had more living to do. More rooting and growing together.

Trust me. I *know*. I'm an enchantress with MS who bleeds at the dark of the moon. Power is in my blood.

Just ask my husband.

"One thing I don't get, Maeve." I took a sip from the mulled cider that Alys had brewed in the crockpot. It reeked of too many cloves but if we were going to be lunatics sitting outside at night in winter, any port in a storm.

"Only one?" Alys raised a brow and huddled deeper into her blanket.

"Who was the tart on your answering machine?"

"Harper?" Maeve poked a stick into the fire and smiled in a self-deprecating way. "She's Kal's brother's fiancée. She was calling to personally invite him to their wedding this summer. Since he hasn't been in touch with them in so long, no one had his cell number. I'm such an idiot."

She said this last with a good-natured smile. It heartened me to see my sister so at peace with herself. And her husband.

Kal had always been devoted to Maeve but in the weeks since we'd returned from the Amazon, the two were closer than ever. He had rearranged his work schedule so he could take her to all of her medical appointments. Together they

303

were laboriously researching treatments for MS and how best to manage symptoms. They had even talked about selling the house, though I was pretty sure Alys had cut that idea off when she offered to pay for any remodeling that might need to happen.

I had no idea what sort of kinky fuckery they got up to in their room at night but whatever it was, they were *loud*. Maeve was practically glowing with contentment and Kal had a spring in his step.

"So, is he going?" Alys asked. "After the disownment and all that awkwardness with his father it must be weird for him to think about it."

"He's not sure. I want him to go, but he's worried about leaving me and the kids. And probably a little worried about whatever his father might say or do." Maeve sighed.

"Is that what you wanted to talk to us about out here?" I shivered as the wind picked up. There was snow in the forecast and I would prefer to have any discussion indoors that could be had indoors.

Maeve shook her head and the light from the fire lit her eyes. "No. I had a vision when we were in the Amazon. A vision of the three of us. And our guys. Only it wasn't us."

"I don't understand," Alys leaned forward.

"I think…I think it was from a past life."

Her words chilled me more than the wind. "Are you sure it was us?"

She nodded. "I recognized our…energy. I know it sounds bizarre. And Brock was there with you, Alys. And Kal was with me. And Sibby was with someone else. Someone wrong."

My heart sped up. "Was it Sebastian?"

She shook her head. "No, and that's why I think the other man was wrong. He had a false face and presumed too much.

But you wanted to be with Sebastian. He was there. And he was watching you. You knew he was there and I could feel it."

"Feel what?" The words came out sounding breathless.

"Your connection." Maeve swallowed. "Sibby, I...I think the two of you might be soul mates."

I laughed and the sound held no humor. "It would serve him right."

Alys frowned at me. "Why would you say that?"

"Because any man I've ever slept with is doomed to die. I'm cursed. It was foretold to me."

"Foretold by who?" Alys barked.

"A seer I met in my travels." I didn't say anything more than that. There were some memories I just couldn't occupy and continue breathing.

Maeve went pale. "What? You never told us about this."

I stared into the fire. "It's not really something I like talking about."

"It's just coincidence," Alys said. "It has to be."

"That's what I thought at first too." I leaned back in my chair and closed my eyes. "The first six times. But when lucky number seven croaked, I just gave up. So maybe I should bed down with Sebastian. It would take care of one magic hunter at least."

And maybe kill off my libido for good.

My sisters were quiet for a long moment.

"We need to find out more," Alys said. "Maeve, is there any way you can return to that vision?"

"Maybe," Maeve paused. "I'll have to do some research."

I wanted to tell her not to bother. That a curse was a curse and there was nothing that we could do to fix it.

But Alys had come back from death. And Maeve had battled death and come out the victor. Maybe there was hope for me and my curse.

I looked up at the waxing moon and let myself dream of my own happily ever after.

She's single and killing it. Literally.

Siobhan's relationship status is...complicated. Any time she gives in to carnal temptation, her lover ends up dead. Forty, frustrated, and newly empowered as a witch, she and her sisters cast a spell to discover a way to reverse her curse.

Magic Hunter Sebastian never failed to collect a bounty. He was the stuff of legend until he met Siobhan. Now his magic is gone and he and the Silver sisters are the top targets for every supernatural bounty hunter in existence.

Can these two star-crossed lovers finally put the sins of their pasts to rest? Or will destiny crush their hope forever?

Witch Way is Up is the third book in the charming Silver Sisters paranormal women fiction series. If you like magical hijinks, true-to-life characters, and soul mates, don't miss Jennifer L. Hart's enchanting series.

Buy Witch Way is Up and summon your sister witches today!

GET A FREE SHORT STORY!

Sign up for my author newsletter and get Faery Wine, a Magical Midlife Misadventure FREE!

ITS NOT MY WORDS THAT COUNT, IT IS YOURS

Please consider leaving an honest review for this book. Reviews help readers determine if a book is right for them and help authors sell books to the right readers. What you love, someone else might want to avoid, so be honest. I found one of my favorite series based on a two-star review!

ABOUT THE AUTHOR

Are you sick of the teenagers saving the world? Do you want to see more women with a little life experience having adventures while dealing with real life, love and all the messy bits? Join a growing community of paranormal women's fiction fans, get behind the scenes access, advanced reader copies and read along as Jenn writes her next novel. Become a Patron of the Hart today!

Made in the USA
Las Vegas, NV
14 March 2022